Claire's love affair with Greece [...] cares to remember. Corfu w[...] teenager, and since then she h[...] the country, particularly the islands, and is even learning Greek, very slowly.

The sunshine, the culture, and the warmth of the Greek people, not to mention the food, inspired her to write this, her debut novel.

Claire is a long-time journalist and TV producer, who has worked in features, showbiz, and interiors. She is married with two grown-up children and lives in southwest London.

instagram.com/clairecarverauthor
facebook.com/clairecarverauthor

STILL GOT IT

CLAIRE CARVER

ONE MORE CHAPTER

One More Chapter
a division of HarperCollins*Publishers* Ltd
1 London Bridge Street
London SE1 9GF
www.harpercollins.co.uk
HarperCollins*Publishers*
Macken House, 39/40 Mayor Street Upper,
Dublin 1, D01 C9W8, Ireland

This paperback edition 2025
1
First published in Great Britain in ebook format
by HarperCollins*Publishers* 2025
Copyright © Claire Carver 2025
Claire Carver asserts the moral right to
be identified as the author of this work

A catalogue record of this book is available from the British Library
ISBN: 978-0-00-875466-2

This novel is entirely a work of fiction. The names, characters and incidents portrayed in it are the work of the author's imagination. Any resemblance to actual persons, living or dead, events or localities is entirely coincidental.

Printed and bound in the UK using 100% Renewable Electricity
by CPI Group (UK) Ltd

All rights reserved. No part of this publication may be reproduced, stored in a retrieval system, or transmitted, in any form or by any means, electronic, mechanical, photocopying, recording or otherwise, without the prior permission of the publishers.

Without limiting the author's and publisher's exclusive rights, any unauthorised use of this publication to train generative artificial intelligence (AI) technologies is expressly prohibited. HarperCollins also exercise their rights under Article 4(3) of the Digital Single Market Directive 2019/790 and expressly reserve this publication from the text and data mining exception.

To David, Scarlett, and Fergus for their support and love.

And also to my parents, Richard and Elizabeth, gone but not forgotten.

Chapter One

It was going to be extremely hot in Greece, and she'd need enough clothes for three whole months.

Grace Foreman went to bite the price tag off a floaty pink dress, before remembering her recent dental work and the five hundred pounds she'd had to pay for the crown now sitting atop one of her back molars.

A quick ferret in her makeup bag produced some nail scissors and she snipped off the tag without looking at it too closely. The items she'd chosen weren't expensive; it was all high street stuff, and in any case there was no one around to pass comment on what she'd bought. Phil had never questioned how much she spent on clothes when he was alive, which had been one of his many good points.

Behind her, the bed was covered with her purchases, the blue and white stripes of the duvet cover barely visible. Free accommodation was provided with the job she'd scored for herself at the language school on a little-known Greek island. But she had no idea about the washing facilities, or whether launderettes were even a thing there, so she'd need to cover all options. Or that's what she told herself.

She'd only gone for the job on the spur of the moment and had been surprised to even get an interview. Surely there couldn't be many other sixty-one-year-olds applying. That was borne out when she arrived at the company's London office to find herself in the middle of a sea of twentysomethings.

Confident that her experience, forty years as a teacher and tutor, couldn't be bettered, Grace had held her head high as she entered the interview room. She prided herself on being able to read people, and she'd been convinced that the initial reaction of the glamorous language school owner, Mrs Kokkinakis, to her had been relief, which was odd.

But the woman with the sad eyes had rung that same afternoon to say she'd got the job, so she wasn't going to waste any time worrying about it.

Salaries were lower in Greece, but the money wasn't such a big issue as she had her teaching pension to top things up. It was more important that she stopped herself going mad with boredom. The last thing she'd ever admit to in public was being lonely. She had friends, of course she did. Her days were filled with tutoring, the occasional lunch and plenty of walking and swimming. It was the evenings that killed her. Sitting alone in her Thameside cottage with an empty place at her side. She was so familiar with the output of the many TV streaming services that she could have been a critic.

Grace stared down at the bed. She'd possibly overdone it a little on the jewel-coloured shorts in blues, pinks and yellows, the leopard-print dresses in pastel tones, and the vests in every colour of the rainbow.

Strappy gold sandals and good old white pumps were also in the mix, and Grace turned to look at herself in the mirror one last time before she packed. She'd always been told she had good legs, hence the number of pairs of shorts.

She sucked in her stomach and pulled her top tight. Two pregnancies and two very big babies hadn't helped her stomach, or her stretch marks, but they were marks of love, or that's what she'd read in a soppy pregnancy book someone had given her many years ago. She'd bought a couple of tummy control swimsuits in navy and red to help things along, but at the last minute had thrown a leopard-print and a gold bikini into her basket. Bikinis hadn't featured in her swimwear for a while, but *you never know* was her new motto.

The hairdresser had been able to fit her in at short notice, and her blonde hair was newly highlighted, which covered most of the grey. As usual, the hairdresser had suggested she had her hair cut, especially as she'd be in Greece at the hottest time of the year, but Grace was determined to keep it long. Shoulder-length bob be damned! She could always tie it up. If it was good enough for Jerry Hall, it was good enough for her.

Her younger daughter was due to arrive any moment, so she needed to get a move on and stop parading herself in front of the mirror, as her old dad would have said. She tipped an imaginary hat to her father and got down on her knees to feel under the bed for the suitcase.

Her hand grasped the edge of the fabric, and she tugged hard, but it seemed stuck on something. Lying flat on the floor, Grace edged under the bed on her stomach, the fronds of her beloved pink sheepskin rug tickling her nose. The murky world underneath the bed was a revelation. There wasn't much light in the room at the best of times. It was north-facing, and she'd deliberately made it dark and womblike when she'd redecorated last year. The line of dust began where the boundary of how far she could get the vacuum cleaner under the wooden frame stopped.

A small collection of tissues, hairbands and a cheap pair of reading glasses rode above the dust like the curls of a wave. She'd never been what her mother would have called 'a good housekeeper', and she'd never wanted to be. Vaguely tidy and hygienic was more her style. Grace smiled, remembering her mother's wince each time she'd entered the kitchen and her soft voice saying, 'Do you mind if I give that oven a clean?' No, she most certainly had not. Both her parents were long gone, but not forgotten.

The bulky suitcase rose up from the oatmeal sisal carpet – in fashion at the time, but a nightmare to clean, especially if you had an ancient rescue cat who had trouble keeping his food down. She missed Clooney, but not his tendency to vomit regularly in his final days.

Grace stretched out her arm to grab the handle. As she pulled the case out from under the bed, she saw something small and dark that it had been snagged on, which lay just out of reach.

She took a deep breath and dived in, grabbed the offending item and held it up to the light.

It was a sock, a navy-blue sock with a Father Christmas motif on the ankle. Phil's sock, part of a pair he'd been given for his last Christmas, just a few months before his death. There certainly hadn't been any other men in her bedroom in the past three and a half years. Grace held it to her face and sniffed. Nothing, except a vague musty tang. No trace of Phil.

She sank to the floor, still clasping the sock.

Why were her hands suddenly wet?

Silent tears had crept up on her and the overflow was threatening to run all the way down to her elbows.

'Mum? Mum, where are you?'

Flo's voice floated up the stairs and Grace stood up carefully.

'Coming!'

Her voice sounded shaky, even to herself, but she couldn't let her daughter find her slumped on the carpet crying over a sock.

Flo and her wife, Jilly, were waiting in the kitchen, their own brightly coloured backpacks at their feet. Her daughter flew into her arms.

'It's so lovely to see you, Mum.'

She held Grace at arm's length and narrowed her eyes.

'Are you OK? You look like you've been crying.'

This wasn't how it was supposed to be, thought Grace. It was a bit early for the whole role reversal thing, where the children started being the responsible ones. She shook herself to get rid of the image of the sock lying alone and unloved under the bed.

'Don't be silly. It's just a bit of hay fever. We're into June now and you know how I am. Give me a proper hug. And you, Jilly.'

Grace pulled both women in, but not before she'd seen the look of concern pass between them.

'Sit down. Can I make you both a cup of tea?'

Her daughter's suspicious eyes were something to be avoided at all costs.

'Are you sure you're OK?'

'Yes. Earl Grey or builder's?'

'Builder's, please,' both women answered at once.

Bustling with the tea things gave Grace a chance to recover. She was really grateful to them for coming to stay while she was away, keeping an eye on the house. As lecturers at a prestigious northern university, they had a big block of time off over the summer, and when Grace rang to suggest a change of scene, her daughter had insisted they were thrilled with it.

'We'd love to look after the cottage, Mum. College life can be so claustrophobic, bumping into the same people all the time. And you know how much Jilly likes to kayak. We can spend our days on the water.'

'If you're sure…'

'What you're doing is so exciting, spending the summer in Greece on a crazy whim. You, who never goes anywhere.'

It wasn't that crazy, and she did get out occasionally, but she'd let it pass.

Grace put the tea things on the table, with a plate of cheese scones from the local bakery.

'Tuck in. They're your favourite.'

Her daughter's face creased into a smile, blonde hair flying everywhere, and Grace noted the answering smile on her daughter-in-law's face, dark cropped hair framing her beautiful angular features. These two would make anyone smile. Their love was so obvious that Grace wanted to reach out and touch it.

Would she ever feel even a tiny percentage of that sort of

love again? Did she even want someone new in her life? Someone who might become ill and die? Grace blocked out a vision of her husband lying in a hospital bed, surrounded by tubes. She honestly didn't know the answer to her own questions.

It hadn't been plain sailing for her younger daughter to find happiness. A string of unsatisfactory relationships with men had finally led Flo to see who was patiently waiting right under her nose. Jilly had played the long game and won her princess. Some of Grace's elderly relatives had been a bit funny about Flo and Jilly's relationship, and they'd been erased from Grace's contact list. She was just happy her daughter was happy. And at least Phil had lived to see it.

While Flo and Jilly went out on the river for a quick kayak now the rain had eased up, Grace took the opportunity to finally pack and change the sheets on her bed for her guests. The festive sock was carefully wrapped in a handkerchief and stored away in the back of a drawer.

Dinner was to be a Thai takeaway for the three of them, and once she'd put in the order, Grace placed her iPad in the middle of the table and called the others down.

'Let's see if your sister's up before our food arrives. I know it's late, but she's such a night owl, I'm sure she'll still be awake.'

Grace crossed her fingers under the table.

Lottie answered after just one ring, wide awake and sitting at her kitchen island in tiny white silk shorts pyjamas, her dark hair and eyes so like Phil's it always gave Grace a jolt.

'Mum! Sis! And Jilly! What a treat.'

A flurry of waving and air kisses gave Grace the chance to

put on her breezy not-bothered-that-you-live-nine-thousand-miles-away-and-I-never-see-you smile.

'Are you all ready for your Greek adventure then, Mum? Got the thong bikinis and the condoms packed?'

'Of course, sweetie. It's all that's in my suitcase.'

Grace wanted to reach in, grab her eldest daughter and pull her through the screen. She'd been gone for five years now, living in Perth, Australia, with a much younger blond diving instructor who'd swept her off her feet and persuaded her to return with him to his home city. They now ran a diving school together. Grace had got nothing against Brad personally, but the absence of her daughter from her life hurt so much more than she'd ever let on to anyone, except maybe her best friend, Sofia, and only after a vat of dry white wine.

If she'd lived abroad at that age, all her parents would have got was the occasional letter or a rushed call from a payphone, so she was lucky to be able to see and hear her daughter whenever she liked. Touch and smell she would have to do without. There was a bottle of her daughter's distinctive scent she'd left behind in the cottage, which Grace occasionally sprayed in the air when no one was about.

'What's the score with the language school? Do you get plenty of time off? Are there lots of cool bars on your island? When Brad and I visited Ios you couldn't move for bars, and Australians.'

Grace stopped trying to count the new freckles on her daughter's nose.

'As far as I can make out, it's nothing like that. There are tourists on my island, of course, but plenty of them are Greeks.

There's a thriving year-round community, and I think Australians are few and far between, thank goodness.'

Grace quickly rowed back as Lottie's boyfriend loomed behind her daughter, put his arms over her shoulders and kissed her on the top of the head.

'No offence, Brad.'

'None taken, Mrs F.'

'Call me Grace, please.'

Grace paused as her daughter angled her head back so Brad could move in for a full-on snog.

Flo put her hands over her eyes.

'Yuk. Make them stop, Mum!'

Everywhere she looked, the whole world seemed to be part of a couple, two people exchanging glances and more. She'd stopped accepting invites to dinner parties for that very reason. And if anyone said anything along the lines of 'John lost his wife last year. I know you'll have lots in common,' she could cheerfully strangle them.

Her married friends were obsessed with getting her coupled up again, but if she did accept an invitation as a solo guest, some of the women gave her a wide berth and acted as if she was desperate to cop off with their husbands.

The behaviour of the men who'd sidled up to her and made it clear that they'd be up for playing away from home was a shock as well. Thankfully none of her close friends' husbands, but she'd stopped going to the village greengrocer's after a rather too enthusiastic demonstration by the owner of how fresh his bananas were and plenty of winking, while his wife served a line of customers. Married men were definitely not her bag.

'Mum! Hello? You were saying?'

'Sorry, miles away. It's not a party place. It's a working island in the Cyclades with a lovely main town lined with marble streets. Anyway, I'm going to be grafting too hard to hang about in bars.'

Lottie blew her a kiss.

'You say that now. We've seen you in party animal mode, remember. Two wines and you'll be up on the table.'

Grace pursed her lips.

'But seriously, Mum, we want you to enjoy yourself as well. Ever since Dad…'

Grace grabbed for Flo and Jilly's hands as Lottie reached for Brad's.

'Died, you've been like a hermit. It's time to get out there again. You're a good-looking woman with plenty of life left in you.'

'Thank you, Oprah.' But Grace smiled to take the sting out of her words. 'I'm not looking for a man in Greece, sweetheart. Believe me, that's the last thing on my mind. Anyway, from the website it looks like the people I'm going to be working with are in their thirties at the most. I'm the oldest by a mile.'

Grace could see her daughter about to speak, and she wagged her finger at the screen.

'And before you say it, madam, I am absolutely not in the market for a toy boy.'

'Don't rule it out. It works for some of us.'

Lottie's adoring look at Brad had her sister miming sticking her fingers down her throat.

A ring on the doorbell was the sign Grace needed to shut down this particular conversation.

'Right, there's our takeaway. I'll ring when I'm settled. Love you.'

'Love you too.'

With the food despatched, Grace's eyelids began to droop. She decided to leave Flo and Jilly to it.

'Remember, we've got to leave at eight in the morning.'

Grace opened her eyes again in time to see Flo raise her eyebrows at Jilly.

'Yeah, we know. We're driving you. We've got it covered.'

Both women toasted her with the last of the sauvignon blanc, and her daughter stood on tiptoe to kiss her goodnight.

'Don't fret, Mother. You'll be leaving these grey skies far behind and basking in Greek sunshine this time tomorrow.'

Chapter Two

Twenty-four hours later and the world was a different place. Grace had waved goodbye to the unseasonably heavy rain in Oxfordshire without looking back. The moment she'd boarded the plane, she'd forced herself to stop worrying about climate change and what sort of planet her generation would be leaving behind for their children and grandchildren.

Swapping the big jet for a forty-seater island hopper at Athens, she stared down at the place that would become her home for the next three months as the tiny plane made its descent. Rocky land rose up from a turquoise sea, as the whitewashed houses came into focus, and the sun reflected off the many churches with their blue domed roofs.

Grace looked down at her hands, and before she could change her mind, carefully took off her plain gold band of a wedding ring and put it in the zipped compartment of her bag. Thirty-five years of marriage cancelled, just like that.

It was something she'd been daring herself to do for weeks. It would stop any awkward questions from people, and she needed to do it now, so she didn't leave a thin white line on her finger from removing the ring once she had a tan.

It was the perfect opportunity to say goodbye to old Grace, widow of the parish, and say hello to new Grace, international woman of mystery.

The plane came in low over the sea, and Grace could even make out the features of some of the people on the boats that thronged the port, though her tears made things a little blurry. The wind that the island was well known for playfully buffeted the plane as the runway loomed. Several of the locals did the sign of the cross as the plane came into land, and even Grace heaved a sigh of relief as the wheels touched down on the tarmac.

A blast of hot air hit her in the face as soon as she stepped off the plane, and she had to reach into her bag for her sunglasses to be able to see anything at all. Plus, she hoped they'd hide her puffy face. Crying always made her eyes look bright green, rather than the murky hazel they were most of the time, but she was fairly sure that the red rims and swelling that went with it spoilt the effect. After more or less dispensing with makeup since Phil died, she'd slipped a large bag of the stuff into her case, which she'd definitely need if Mrs Kokkinakis was any guide as to how much slap Greek women wore.

Her new boss was waiting for her in the arrivals hall. All around Grace were cries of recognition as it seemed that everyone on the plane was scooped up by a friend or relative and hugged half to death.

Mrs Kokkinakis satisfied herself with a handshake and a hello. Grace wasn't expected to know any Greek for her job, all the talking would be in English, but she'd learnt a few words and phrases to get her through the basics.

Nai for yes, *ochi* for no, and good morning, good afternoon and good night were *kalimera*, *kalispera* and *kalinichta*. Please and thank you, *parakalow* and *efcharisto*, were the two words she'd been taught to say properly by her Greek neighbour on the plane. The pronunciation of the word *efcharisto* made it sound like you were trying to get rid of excess phlegm from your throat, but she was sure she'd get used to it.

'*Kalispera*, Mrs Kokkinakis.'

The elegant brunette smiled her sad smile.

'Please, call me Elena, now that we're colleagues.'

'And I'm Grace.'

'OK, Grace, let's get you out of here.'

Grace followed her employer into the car park and watched her click the keys on an open-top Mercedes. The business was obviously doing well. Elena indicated for her to throw her suitcase into the back seat and revved the engine the moment Grace opened the door.

As soon as her bottom touched the seat, they were off down the hill from the airport and onto the main road into town, joining the other cars that seemed to Grace to be moving rather fast, their drivers overtaking each other every few moments and shouting out greetings to people they recognised, Elena included.

Grace lay back and let the wind take her hair and whip it up behind her. There was no point trying to talk over the noise of the engine.

Shops, cafés and restaurants painted white with their doors and windows highlighted in pastels whizzed past on her left, while the port opened up on her right. The odd superyacht with its nose nearly on the road lay side by side with the smaller boats, all swaying slightly in the breeze as the sunlight glinted on the water, scattering the sea into a thousand diamonds.

Everywhere she looked, people were sat outside, eating, and drinking in every possible location, from pavement cafés to boat decks, and the sound of laughter in the air and the smell of meat being grilled made her close her eyes for a moment and just take it all in.

She opened them again when Elena pulled the car into a violent left turn, and they ended up behind a large white four-storey building.

Elena grabbed Grace's case from the back seat and pointed upwards.

'We're here. There won't be many people around at the moment, as it's the quiet time, but come and meet my husband Giannis and I'll show you your room.'

Grace would have opted for a nice cup of tea and a lie-down if she'd been offered it, but she followed Elena into the school, going past a series of teaching rooms with their familiar plastic chairs and interactive whiteboards, until they came to a large office with the blinds down.

Standing in front of a huge desk was a good-looking man in his forties, wearing a navy polo shirt and white jeans that were just a little too tight.

'Welcome! You must be Grace. Our new recruit.'

Giannis was what her long-divorced friend Sofia would call 'a walking willy'. Catnip to most women. Not her type, he reminded her a bit of a Greek Danny Dyer, the actor whom a lot of women apparently wanted as their guilty pleasure.

'Yes, that's me. Pleased to meet you.'

Grace held out her hand and Giannis came towards her, took it and brought it up to his lips, but not until he'd given her a full top-to-toe once-over, lingering over her chest area a few seconds too long. She couldn't believe she'd be his type either, she was twenty if not thirty years too old, but he obviously just couldn't help himself.

'Enchanted.'

Grace hid a snort with her own hand. Definitely not to be trusted. She already felt protective towards Elena, who wasn't much older than her eldest daughter. Maybe it was all for show, and he was a devoted husband underneath, but she wasn't convinced.

Giannis lost interest almost immediately, which was fine with her, and ambled off into the corridor. Elena went to pick up Grace's case again.

'No, please let me carry it.'

She didn't want to give Elena the impression that she'd need help with anything.

Elena nodded and indicated a set of stairs. Four flights up, Grace wasn't so sure it had been one of her better ideas, and she had to hold onto the wall behind Elena's back to give herself a breather. She considered herself to be fit, but she wasn't used to the heat, and although only June, it was already in the low twenties. She prayed her room had air conditioning.

Elena opened the door with a flourish.

'You are the first of the new teachers to arrive, so I've given you the best room.'

'Thank you.'

The white walls and tiled floor were all fairly standard, but a pretty yellow throw on the bed and stunning framed shots of the Aegean dotted around the room helped no end, as did the large air-con unit.

Grace bobbed her head into the bathroom to show willing and murmured her appreciation. But it was the view beyond the French doors she was truly desperate to see. The bright blue shutters, the colour of the stripes in the Greek flag, were shut against the sun.

Grace pointed towards the port. 'Can we…'

'Of course.'

Elena opened the shutters and Grace watched how she did it very carefully, having once had an old shutter disintegrate on her as soon as she twisted the metal handle at a gite in Brittany. Phil had laughed and accused her of being cackhanded, and the 'Grace is clumsy' tag had become part of family legend. The thought that no more family legends would be created by their little gang of four made her stomach contract a little.

But the view outside was all she hoped for and more. A cute balcony with two white chairs and a table overlooked the port in all its glory. Grace stood for a moment and watched a big old ferry coming in, engines churning and port police in their smart navy uniforms blowing their whistles for all they were worth. She was going to enjoy spending time out here on her balcony, people watching.

Elena obviously had better things to do than watch the world go by as she was almost at the door.

'I'll leave you to it. We only have two major rules. The first is…'

'No boys after lights out?'

Grace wasn't sure why she'd said that. It took her back to a school trip to Paris aged eleven, when she and her friends had been caught with the deputy head's thirteen-year-old son hiding in their bathroom.

Elena frowned. 'What you do in your own time is your own business.'

Obviously, that hadn't translated well. She was probably overtired.

'The first is that it's not a good idea to drink the water from the tap. There's a small fridge here, with bottles of water that you can replenish anytime from the kitchen.'

'OK, thanks.'

'And…' Elena twitched her nose. 'I know this will be strange for you. But there is no paper allowed down the toilet. The plumbing on the island is'—Elena stumbled on the right word—'kaka … rubbish.'

Kaka indeed. Another Greek word she could put in her little book.

'There is a bin provided and the rooms are cleaned every day.'

Grace nodded. She needed to get away from the visual this conversation was creating, and she was sure Elena did too by the way she was looking at the ceiling.

'So, what will be a typical working pattern for me?'

'It's six hours a day on weekdays as discussed, and three on Saturday mornings. We start lessons at nine-thirty in the morning, there's a break from twelve-thirty until three when it's too hot to teach, and then lessons again from three until six.'

'Understood. Sounds good.'

'Obviously we're not expecting you to start teaching on travel day, so we'll see you down there in the morning.'

'Great. Looking forward to it.'

As soon as Elena left the room, Grace flopped face down on the bed, not even bothering to take off her shoes, and let out a huge sigh.

When she came to, it seemed like a minute had passed, but after scrabbling in her bag for her reading glasses, her phone told her she'd been asleep for an hour. Her hair was flat against her head with sweat.

She'd never seen the point of siestas before, but then she'd been on holiday whenever she stayed in a hot country. There'd always been so much to cram in that she hadn't wanted to miss a minute. Now she was fairly sure that she'd be taking advantage of her bed in the afternoons on a regular basis.

After a limp but welcome shower, she changed into shorts and a T-shirt, before drinking a small bottle of water. Hat and sunglasses in hand, it was time to explore.

Before she got to the door, Grace remembered sun cream and the dire warnings of her daughters. No, she most certainly did not want to turn into a leathery old crone with skin the colour of rolling tobacco, thank you. She picked up the factor fifty and nipped back into the bathroom to put on one of the new swimming costumes. There were beaches at the back of the town, only a ten-minute walk away, according to Elena, and a swim would be wonderful.

Grace crept down the stairs in case anyone was sleeping, but also because she wasn't overkeen to bump into Giannis again so soon. As she passed one of the classrooms on her way to the back door, she caught a flash of white jeans through a crack, and the sound of female laughter. She'd hadn't heard Elena laugh like that, but maybe she did when she was alone with her husband.

The door opened further, and Grace saw the bottom half of a young woman's long, tanned legs in very short shorts. It must be another of the new arrivals. Grace hurried towards the exit, and almost collided with a guy coming in.

As good-looking as Giannis, although a few inches shorter and several years older, the man smiled wide, showing perfect teeth. Was every male member of staff destined to look like a male model? At least he held out his hand in the usual way. Grace had washed her hands thoroughly after her earlier encounter with Giannis.

'Hi, I'm Thanassis. Director of Studies. You must be Grace.'

Grace returned the handshake.

'Welcome to our language school. I'm sure you'll be'—Thanassis left a long pause before continuing—'amazing, Grace.'

'Oh, I've never heard that one before.'

The smile dimmed a little, and confusion overtook his handsome face. Grace hadn't thought to research whether the Greeks had a sense of humour, but it looked like sarcasm was possibly off the menu.

'It's so lovely to be here, and I'm excited to start teaching tomorrow.'

She was gushing, but there was no point getting off on the wrong foot.

'And we are excited to have you. I won't keep you; we will go through everything in the morning before class starts. If you can meet me here at nine.'

Thanassis did a mock bow.

'Until then.'

Grace hotfooted it out of the door and breathed a sigh of relief as she left the car park. The shady backstreets were calling to her, and Grace wandered through the alleyways that led up and away from the town, where loops of pink and red bougainvillea grown across canopies gave café customers respite from the sun.

She sat down at one of the cafés and ordered herself an Aperol Spritz with ice. Eating or drinking alone in Britain was dismal in her experience. She'd only tried it once, and they'd shoved her on a table near the toilets. Here, it felt like it wasn't a problem, and many of the tables were occupied by a single woman or man. Grace stared into the orange liquid, bubbles of condensation dripping down her glass. Phil had hated the stuff, saying it tasted like cough mixture. She tried out the idea in her head that Phil's opinion didn't matter very much anymore, which made her both sad and a little bit excited at the same time. Grace took a long, luxurious slurp through her straw.

An hour later, she was desperate for that swim, and after walking to the top of the town, she glimpsed the beach in the distance, the water glistening invitingly. She made her way down the dusty slope, her body longing for immersion in the water with every step.

Ten minutes' walk seemed a bit of an understatement on Elena's part; she'd been going for at least fifteen already. Near the bottom, she was tempted to break into a run, or a gentle jog if she was being honest with herself. There seemed to be two paths to the beach, one winding and long, while the other cut through a garden with a wall.

Surely that would be fine? There was no one about. Grace climbed over the wall, and kept to the perimeter of the property, not looking up at the enormous house to her left. She was nearly there. A couple more steps and she'd be able to hop over and directly onto the beach.

'Hey!'

A male voice stopped her in her tracks.

'What the hell do you think you're doing?'

Grace turned to see a tall, tanned man, dressed all in black, bearing down on her. His brown eyes were full of fury.

He was now so near she could smell his lemony aftershave. He was obviously British by the accent. Grace couldn't miss the broad shoulders and the tensed muscles that bulged out of the sleeves of his polo shirt.

Up close he was even taller than she'd thought, long legs encased in black chinos, his close-shaven face looming at least half a foot above her.

Grace prepared to stand her ground. She wasn't going to give him the satisfaction of appearing frightened. They squared up to each other, just inches apart.

Chapter Three

The man, who Grace noticed had incredibly shiny shoes, spoke first.

'I repeat, what is it that you think you're doing?'

Grace decided to brazen it out.

'Going to the beach...' She pointed at her bag with the towel sticking out of the top. 'Obviously. Just what is your problem?'

'My problem is that this is private property that you're trespassing on. Did you not see the signs?'

He pointed into the distance where Grace could see something in red written on a white background fixed to the wall.

'That's miles away. How am I supposed to see that?'

'There are several on the outside of the wall too. Do you have problems with your vision?'

'No. Do you?'

The man was insufferably rude. He wasn't going to get away with it.

'I was told that all beaches in Greece were public. That they're not allowed to be private, which seems an incredibly sensible idea.'

'Yes, you've hit the nail on the head there. The beaches are public…' The man spoke the word 'beaches' very very slowly. What an arse.

'But the gardens of this villa are absolutely not public. I think most people would realise that.'

'Well, I'm not most people.'

'Clearly.'

Deep down Grace knew she was a teensy bit in the wrong. But he needn't be so nasty about it.

'The public path is quite obviously over there…' This time he emphasised the word 'public'.

'It's not that obvious to me.'

Grumpy man pointed back towards the house.

'I've been watching you for quite a while on the CCTV cameras inside the villa, from the moment you attempted to climb over that wall.'

'That must have been fun for you.'

Grace was wearing her shortest shorts over her swimming costume, and she didn't want to think about the picture of her bottom descending the wall, being watched on a screen by him and who knew how many more.

'I wouldn't describe it as fun exactly.'

The granite expression never altered. He was like a headmaster, with her as the naughty schoolgirl.

'Anyway, this time I'm going to let you off. But if I see you attempting to take this shortcut to the beach again, there will be consequences.'

'Oooh, I'm really scared.'

Grace found herself taking on the persona of a teenage girl. She never spoke like that, not to anyone. It was his fault. Arrogant idiot. He might be good-looking, but she hadn't disliked anyone so much for a very long time.

The man turned on his heel and made for the house. Grace ran for the wall. It was a bit trickier getting back onto the path than it had been getting into the garden. She threw her bag over first and tried to get a firm grip on the top of the wall but got stuck halfway over. She ended up straddling the brickwork, one bare leg either side, brushing up against the rough surface.

'Shit!'

In struggling to free herself, she'd scratched her left leg, and she could see a thin red line of blood emerging.

She turned to see him watching her, as she knew he would be, with his arms folded, up by the villa. He could go hang. With a huge effort, Grace lifted her leg up and over.

Just before she jumped off the wall, she raised the middle finger of her left hand in his direction.

With each step along the path, her irritation grew. She'd not been so angry with anyone since Phil had upped and died, leaving her to cope with everything alone. Just who did that guy think he was? The sweat was pouring off her, and her leg was sore. She needed to get into the water.

As soon as she reached the beach, Grace threw her bag down on the sand, stripped off her shorts and shirt, stepped out of her pumps and strode into the sea, tying her hair back with a band as she went, not stopping for a moment.

She waded in up to her chest, the warm water caressing her

skin like a fine silk scarf. The clear sea meant she could see her own legs and feet below, standing on the folds of sand. A tiny silver fish swam past her stomach, followed by another and then a whole shoal of them.

Grace waited until her heartrate was almost back to normal, took a deep breath and pushed herself off the bottom. She headed out past the separate groups of elderly men and women floating in the water in their sun hats, chatting animatedly, and on towards the horizon.

Once she was well clear of people, Grace let rip with a practised stroke. She'd gone back to the local pool specially to learn proper front crawl two years ago, one of the many activities she'd tried since Phil died, in a bid to stave off the reality of being on her own. Unlike French lessons and photography club, this was something she'd stuck at, joining a wild swimming group at a popular spot near her cottage. Although she had to admit this was a lot more pleasant. No little fronds of plant life waiting to make their way inside your costume, no muddy feet on the shoreline as you got out, and no manic rowers narrowly missing clouting you on the head.

As she ploughed up and down across the bay, Grace looked back at the beach, noticing the rows of sunbeds at one end that she'd missed earlier, so determined had she been to get into the water. They were all arranged in twos with an umbrella in between. She'd have to find out if she could just hire one. It was a bit pointless for today, but she'd think about it for tomorrow or more likely the next day. All she'd be fit for after her swim was food and an early night, boning up on the coursework.

Up bright and early the next morning, Grace made her way down to the main teaching room a few minutes before the appointed time. Thanassis was already there, laying out information packs on desks.

'Grace, welcome. You're the first. Would you like a coffee?'

'Oh, yes, please. Milk, no sugar.'

She'd only managed an orange so far this morning. It wasn't that she was nervous exactly, but she'd got so used to tutoring her rota of pupils that she could virtually do it with her eyes shut.

There hadn't been a whole lot of new experiences in her life recently. In her room was a bag of tricks she'd brought with her from Oxfordshire, props and lesson plans, tried and tested methods to engage students, which she hoped would work here as well.

Grace took the coffee from Thanassis and got a big grin back. He really did have a gorgeous smile.

'Lovely, thanks.'

She'd dressed in a smart pale blue linen shirt, and knee-length white shorts. It made her look a bit like an escapee from the entertainment crew at a holiday camp, but it was practical and would be reasonably cool. Grace sat down at the nearest desk.

While Thanassis was out of the room, a guy who looked as though he was in his early thirties came in and nodded in her direction.

Blond, and a bit on the short side, he exuded confidence.

More second-hand car salesman than language teacher, and he hadn't even spoken yet.

'Hey, I'm Charlie.'

'Grace. Pleased to meet you.'

'Hope you don't mind me saying, but you look a bit like my mum.'

That wasn't exactly the vibe she was hoping to project.

'That's funny. You don't look anything like my daughters.'

Charlie did a double take but rewarded her with a wink as he passed her desk and headed for one near the back.

Definitely a natural salesman.

Thanassis reappeared with a tray of cups and a pot of coffee.

'Ah, I see you two have already met. Please help yourself to coffee, Charlie.'

Three more people came in together, and Grace got the chance to observe them closely from behind her desk. Two women and a man, all in their early twenties by her reckoning. She recognised the first woman by her toned, tanned legs. She'd been the one in Giannis's office yesterday, giggling away.

Thanassis shouted to make himself heard.

'Now everyone's here, make sure you're coffeed up, find a desk please, and let's introduce ourselves. You five are our core teaching team, alongside me of course, and you all bring something different to the party. So, can each of you please give us a flavour of your teaching experience, plus one thing you like to do outside work.'

It was no surprise that confident Charlie volunteered to speak first.

'I'm Charlie. I mainly stick to teenagers, with the occasional adult thrown in. Okay, I knew that sounded weird the moment it came out of my mouth. Anyway, my dad's Greek and my mum's English, although they split a long time ago, and I was brought up between the two countries. I'm a full-time teacher at the school and I live here on the island with my girlfriend and my dog, Buster. Oh, and I'm a part-time DJ too.'

That figured. She could see him coming alive in front of a crowd. Deep down, so far down it was almost buried, it was something she'd always fantasised about having a go at herself.

The girl she'd spotted with Giannis was next.

'Hi, I'm Anna. I'm more early years, I draw the line at seven-year-olds.'

Charlie's hearty laugh seemed a bit over the top to Grace.

'Like Charlie, I'm also half-Greek, but it's my mum this time, and my parents have a place on the island too, although they're hardly ever here. I'm back for a while after being at uni in London … and I'm a pretty good tennis player.'

Grace noticed that Charlie and Thanassis hung on every word the woman said. She certainly was stunning, with her thick dark hair, olive skin and wide mouth painted red. She only hoped that Elena's husband Giannis wasn't the slavering wolf at the head of the pack.

There was a moment's silence, before Thanassis spoke again.

'Rose, can we hear from you next?'

Grace could barely hear what the girl was saying. She must remember to call her a woman. They were all women, not girls, as her daughters kept reminding her.

Thanassis raised his hands towards Rose.

'Speak up, please.'

Rose's voice, when Grace did get to hear it, was a soft Scottish burr, Edinburgh maybe. It fitted in with her glorious red hair and pale skin, but the woman would have to be very careful in the sun was all Grace could think.

'I'm Rose, and I'm taking a gap year following my degree and before I do a Masters in Education. I teach all ages but specialise in adults and ... I like to play board games.'

Grace caught Charlie and Anna exchanging glances and hiding smiles behind their hands.

'Thank you, Rose. And you, Daniel?'

'Hello. I'm Daniel, as you already know.'

The tall young man with the mousy hair had a kind face and a ready smile. Grace thought she detected a Welsh accent.

'I'm a secondary school geography teacher from Cardiff. I've taken a year out to travel and broaden my teaching experience. As you've probably guessed, I'm mainly teenagers too. And I'm a big film buff.'

Thanassis turned to face her.

'And last, but by no means least...'

'Hi, I'm Grace. I'm a former primary school deputy head and a tutor. Like Daniel, I also fancied a complete change. I'm comfortable with all ages, but love the seven- to eleven-year-olds. I've taught in a higher education college too, so adults don't scare me either. I love to dance when I get the chance.'

That was probably enough for now.

'Thank you, Grace. As you can see, we have a wide range of experiences and interests. You will stick mainly with one or two age groups, but you'll be expected to muck in if we have any gaps or illness on the staff. Any questions?'

Daniel put up his hand.

There was a snigger from Charlie.

'You don't have to put up your hand, Daniel.'

'Sorry, just a bit nervous.'

His honesty endeared him to Grace even more, and she could see Rose looking over at him and smiling. The two of them looked like something from a train company ad for a day out in the countryside. From the little she'd seen, they both seemed shy and a little awkward. But she wasn't here to matchmake for her colleagues, or, if she listened to Sofia, for herself. She was here to work.

Daniel cleared his throat.

'I was just wondering when we'll have the information about which classes and times?'

Grace zoned back in to what Thanassis was saying and dismissed a vision of Daniel and Rose walking hand in hand in a meadow. Sofia always accused her of being an old romantic at heart.

'You'll get given your timetables a week in advance, usually on a Friday. So please come and pick up your timetables for what's left of this week, and there'll be a new one tomorrow. Information packs on lessons are on the desks. Anything else?'

Rose raised her voice a notch.

'How much leeway will we have on the content of classes? I know we're all following the Cambridge curriculum, but do we have some space for personal expression?'

Without having to look, Grace could tell Charlie and Anna were raising their eyebrows at each other. They'd obviously labelled themselves the naughty kids. She turned to give them both a hard stare and they looked away too quickly to be completely innocent.

'That's a good question, Rose.'

Rose coloured as soon as Thanassis turned his gaze on her. Grace hoped that the woman didn't get Charlie's teenagers any time soon. They'd eat her for breakfast.

'You do have some leeway, as long as you stick to the set exercises. If you're planning anything really way out, then please check with me first.'

'Oh, no, nothing like that.'

Grace gave Rose an encouraging smile. In her opinion, young teachers relied too much on PowerPoint presentations and interactive whiteboards. They had their place, of course, but sometimes it was good to think outside the box. It looked like Rose would be her sort of teacher.

'If that's all, please pick up your timetables with the room numbers and familiarise yourself with the layout of the building. All the books you might need are in the room opposite this one. Introductory lessons start in half an hour! Good luck everyone.'

Rose and Daniel filed out with her to explore as instructed. As they headed for the upstairs classrooms, she glimpsed Anna and Charlie smoking outside the back door. Grace had already discovered that smoking was a lot more popular in Greece than it was in England. The Greeks didn't seem to have got the memo that it wasn't a great idea. Not that it was any of her business. Charlie blew out a series of smoke rings and gave her a cheery wave.

Chapter Four

I t had been a tiring but rewarding ten days. As the Greek
schools didn't break up for another week, Grace had
taught adults – businessmen and women from the town – in
the mornings and kids in the afternoons. The businesspeople
were eager to learn, and Grace had used several of the ideas in
her arsenal of tricks to push them.

She'd been determined that they weren't going to be sitting
there staring at a screen all morning. One of her most
successful lessons was when she'd handed out photocopies
with pictures and information on some of the country's top
tourist attractions, such as the Acropolis and the Panathenaic
Stadium in Athens, plus the ruins at Delphi, and asked them to
get into pairs.

One of the students got to be the tourist and the other a
tour guide. Grace asked the tour guide to explain in English
why the tourist should go to these places, how they could get
there, and why they were culturally significant. The tourist had

to ask lots of relevant questions. Then they had to swap over and do it the other way round.

It had seemed to go down well, if the buzz and noise was anything to go by. Thanassis had popped his head in for five minutes and given her an approving nod. She'd not seen anything of the bosses, Giannis and Elena, but she supposed they'd appear at some point.

Grace had taken full advantage of her downtime on the balcony and her lunchtime lie-downs every day, knowing that she had to teach children when she woke up. They were the easier of the two groups mentally, this was the age group she knew and loved, but it was physically demanding.

There was one eight-year-old boy, Stelios, who'd seemed slightly withdrawn, and hadn't improved as she'd hoped as the week went on, so she'd have to ask for a meeting with his parents. She'd much prefer to teach the children in the mornings when she had more energy. Thankfully she'd soon get her wish. The adults would be busier as the tourist season hotted up and would take their lessons in the late afternoons during siesta time, when all the shops and businesses were shut, before opening again around six in the evening.

Grace loved the idea of browsing around the shops of an evening. She'd barely had the chance so far; all she'd done this week was work, eat, go for a quick stroll and sleep a lot. But she'd survived, and now she could give herself permission to ease up a bit. Some outings were definitely on the cards in the coming weeks.

With the last child dismissed, her classroom tidied ready for the Saturday morning lessons, and the promise of easier times ahead, Grace was intent on getting down to the main beach again. She'd take the longer path this time; she didn't want to risk any more encounters with grumpy guy. He could guard his precious garden boundary all day long as far as she was concerned.

Her phone rang just as she'd stopped to take a shot of the beach below to send to the girls on their WhatsApp chat. It was OK for her to call them girls because they were her girls. Grace prepared to let it go to voicemail but changed her mind when she saw who it was.

'Sofia!'

'Grace, baby. How the devil are you?'

Her best friend from college, Sofia, was a force of nature. Phil hadn't been a fan and always considered her a bad influence. But he'd understood their deep bond well enough not to comment too much on his wife's nights out with her friend or time away together.

'I'm good. About-to-lie-on-the-beach-and-go-swimming good.'

'Oh, I'm sooo envious. I'm stuck in an office in rainy London.'

'It's been a tough first week. Believe me, I deserve it.'

'OK, I believe you! Don't get in a huff.'

Sofia had been fully briefed on Grace's three-month adventure and had mainly offered advice on attracting Greek men, which Grace had ignored. Sofia had truly international tastes when it came to the opposite sex. Her friend lowered her voice.

'Listen, I'm just about to go into a meeting, but I was wondering…'

As a successful divorce lawyer, Sofia was always just about

to go into a meeting, but the tone of her voice had Grace slightly worried. It was Sofia's 'I'm about to spring something on you' voice.

'Out with it.'

'I've got the week after next off, and I'm thinking of coming to your island for my break.'

'Thinking of coming? Or already booked a flight and about to descend on me?'

'Ah. I always said you were psychic. You know me so well.'

'I should do after more than forty years. Obviously, I'd love to see you, but you know I'm working full-time, right? You were listening carefully during that conversation? Mornings from nine-thirty and afternoons until six, with a break in between?'

'Yeah, no problem. There's no way I'm planning to see the hours before nine-thirty in the morning when I'm on holiday, as you well know.'

Grace could indeed recall a lot of waiting on balconies or early morning walks around foreign towns, waiting for her friend to get up, during their girls' weekends away.

'We can meet for lunch each day, go out and party in the evenings, and in between I can work on my tan, and check out the local talent.'

Grace couldn't suppress a laugh.

'You've got it all figured out, haven't you?'

'Yep. I'm flying into Athens a week today to stay with a friend.'

'Male, I presume?'

Rather than a sailor in every port, Sofia seemed to have a man in every capital city.

'Meow. Anyway, I'll get the little plane to your island the following morning. I've booked in at the Hotel Artemis, which I understand is walking distance to the language school. So, lunch on their rooftop terrace at one o'clock after you finish work, my treat.'

'Would I dare argue?'

Grace had fancied checking out the restaurant at the luxury hotel herself, but Sofia couldn't see the grin on her face.

The muffled voices in the background were getting louder and louder and Grace could hear her friend's name being called.

'Gotta go. See you next Saturday. Kisses.'

The phone went dead before Grace even had the chance to reply. She'd have to get her stamina up. As well as the full week of teaching ahead, the whirlwind that was Sofia would be in town. All the more reason for a lie-down on a sun lounger now.

The sun was still hot on her back, and there were people down on the beach, although it was past six-thirty in the evening. Many more passed her on the path coming the other way, carrying their parasols and cool boxes, making for home or the many hotels and apartments.

Grace headed straight for the sunbeds and chose a pair with a parasol on the almost empty front row. She stripped off to her costume and lay back for a moment, closed her eyes and let the sound of the sea wash over her. She came to with a young guy in a white T-shirt and a man bun standing over her with a smile. There were worse ways to wake up.

'Hi. I'm the sunbed guy.'

'Of course.'

Grace scrabbled for her purse.

'Listen, it's usually ten euros for the set, two beds and a parasol. But as it's so late in the day, I won't charge you for the bed, as long as you buy a drink.

'Perfect. I'll have a fresh orange juice please, with ice.'

She paid him, including a small tip, as she'd been advised that Greeks didn't really expect tips as such, just for you to pay the price as stated, which was a relief.

A fresh orange juice in Greece really was a different experience from anything you could buy in a British supermarket that marketed itself as fresh orange juice.

Grace smiled as the first sip hit her mouth and burst with flavour. Perhaps it was the sun that gave it that special ingredient.

She sat up a bit straighter and looked out to sea and then back along the beach. There were families with young children dotted around, and she smiled to see one young mum trying to take a spade away from a little girl intent on whacking her brother over the head with it.

Older teenagers in groups, who'd obviously come straight from after-school lessons, snacked on bakery treats wrapped in paper bags, their schoolbags abandoned on the sand. She hadn't really thought this one through. Hopefully there wouldn't be anyone who attended her language school among them.

Young couples, or groups of friends, sat on towels and drank after-work beers, while their more energetic counterparts took each other on at the beach volleyball court, or stood with their feet in the sea, playing bat ball, hitting the ball to each other and shrieking with laughter as an awkward missed shot made one or the other of them fall in the water.

One group in particular caught her attention. A blond guy was throwing a ball to a dog while a dark-haired woman in a white bikini and sunglasses lay on a towel on the sand. A couple of other men stood talking above her and glancing down surreptitiously every few moments.

The dawning realisation that Charlie and Anna were at the centre of the group made Grace reach for her sunglasses and hat, even though she was shielded from the sun by her parasol. Bumping into those two on the beach wasn't what she'd signed up for.

From behind her dark glasses, Grace was convinced that neither of them would spot her. She watched Charlie bend down to talk to a little boy who had come up to stroke the dog, Buster, if she'd remembered right. Buster was a Miniature Schnauzer; she knew that because her cousin had one. Her cousin's dog, Dora, was incredibly well behaved and easy tempered, allowed to go into work with her owner and sit beside her chair all day.

Charlie spent time showing the boy how to approach the dog and stroke him in the correct way, before allowing the youngster to feed Buster a treat.

Despite herself, Grace was impressed. Maybe she'd got him all wrong. She must try and stop making snap judgements. She'd surely been a lot more open-minded about people when she was younger. People could occasionally surprise you. At her age, not often, but you never knew.

An extra-long throw of the ball by Charlie had Buster racing her way across the sand. Grace watched in horror as the ball bounced and went straight under her sun lounger. Buster followed not long after, while Charlie was still way back on the beach. Grace tried to keep still as Buster snuffled around near her lounger, unaware that the ball was underneath. She loved dogs, almost as much as cats, but this one was going to bring its owner over too.

Grace reached under the bed to fish out the ball, which gave Buster the excuse to get his head into her beach holdall covered with green and blue starfish. She remembered a second too late that there was a slice of spanakopita in there that she'd bought at the bakery on the way for a snack tea on the beach. She was already a firm fan of the spinach and feta pies. Buster pulled his head out, with his teeth attached to the lump of pastry. She couldn't really blame the dog, the temptation was too much, and it wasn't as if she was going to eat it now anyway.

'Here, boy.'

Grace held out her hand, but Buster wasn't giving up his prize that easily.

She wasn't sure if dogs were supposed to eat pastry, and it was a bit late to Google it, as Buster had already demolished half.

By the time Charlie arrived, the slice was history.

Looking down at his dog and back at her, the pile of flakes and torn paper bag on the sand gave it away.

'Oh, God, I'm sorry. He's such a pig. He'll eat anything.'

Grace kept the brim of her hat down.

'No, it's fine. It was only some leftovers.'

That wasn't quite true, but she wanted him to go away.

'It's Grace under there, isn't it?'

So, her disguise wasn't worthy of the name. Rumbled. She took off her hat and sunglasses.

'Oh, it's you, Charlie.'

Grace bent down to stroke the dog and ruffle his spiky grey fur.

'He's a cutie, isn't he?'

'He's a menace, but he's my menace. Couldn't be without him.'

Grace handed him the ball she'd found under the sunbed and lay back down again.

'Here you go. This is what he was really looking for.'

Charlie threw the ball back in the direction of Anna and the guys.

'Thanks, Grace.'

'My pleasure.'

Charlie's eyes were now on her rather than the dog or his friends. She was suddenly aware she was lying flat out on a sun lounger in a high-cut swimming costume rather than the shirt and shorts combo she wore for teaching.

He raised a hand to wave and treated her to another one of his winks.

'Still got it, Grace.'

Cheeky boy. As he walked away, Grace thought she'd probably been right about him the first time.

Chapter Five

G race couldn't go back to the town beach. There were far too many hazards lurking there for total relaxation, current pupils and cocky young colleagues being the main ones. She deserved an afternoon of peace and quiet after her Saturday morning class of lively seven- and eight-year-olds, but she'd have to find somewhere else to go.

Striding past the path to the main beach, she upped her pace, and instead turned left and along the headland, enjoying the light breeze which regularly caressed the island. It meant that it never got anywhere near as hot as the Greek mainland, which would be a welcome relief as they approached July.

An impressive boat with its white sails flapping in the wind cut a path through the sea below her. Grace could see tiny figures rushing about onboard, and others lying flat out in bikinis on the shiny bonnet of the boat, or whatever the correct term was. Phil had been a keen sailor, dashing off in his waterproofs whenever he could to crew for mates with boats, usually based Portsmouth way. It was the trade-off for her spending time away with Sofia.

There were always trade-offs in marriage, but this one had worked for them. She'd been out on the boat with the crew once and felt her stomach lurch after the first five minutes. Never again.

Now there was no one she needed to consider or bargain with. The loss of her husband was a heavy price to pay for absolute freedom, but she owed it to him to enjoy the rest of her life as best she could. They'd had many a late-night chat in dim hospital rooms as the end approached, when he'd urged her to see more of the world and consider finding love again after he went, while she wept into her tissues.

In the immediate aftermath of his death, and for a good while longer, all she'd felt was numb, but like spring, little green shoots of hope were starting to sprout again, prompted by the soft caress of the Greek sunshine.

It was still too early for any thoughts of a new relationship, but reconnecting with her younger self, remembering what she'd liked and disliked before she became a wife and mother, was exhilarating. Not that she regretted a moment of their life together, but it was like the building blocks of who she was had been dismantled after Phil's death, and it was up to her to put them back together. All the same elements were in the mix, but the shape would change, and a different Grace Foreman would eventually emerge.

The boat sailed on past as the breeze whipped the ends of the waves into little white peaks, which reminded her of making meringues, not one of her favourite tasks, although Phil and the girls had always loved them. Her years of cooking big family meals were well and truly over, thank goodness, but cooking for one was especially unfulfilling.

Finding out that you could buy freshly cooked meals in town, or grandma's cooking as they called it here, was a delight. For around seven euros, she could pick up delicious dishes like gemista, green and red peppers stuffed with rice and herbs. There was also papoutsakia, the Greek for shoes, a hollowed-out aubergine stuffed with mince in a tomato sauce and topped with feta or, her favourite, briam, a huge variety of vegetables roasted in olive oil. You could even pick up the menu a week in advance, and plan what you were going to have.

Most Greek women spent quite a large proportion of each day cooking, as far as she could see, and it had been explained to her by Thanassis that the meals in the takeaway places were aimed mainly at working men, who needed a proper meal at lunchtime, poor things. But she wasn't going to let the men have all the fun. You had to arrive at the shop by one in the afternoon to get the best stuff, so she was always watching the clock at the end of a lesson to make sure she got there on time. But it really suited her to eat at lunchtime and have something light in the evenings.

Grace adjusted the position of the bag over her shoulder. She'd packed her essentials, including the fashion and interiors magazines that she hadn't had a chance to read on the plane when her mind had been whirling. She'd never get to wear the clothes, or live in the houses, but she liked to study the beautiful dresses and designer wallpapers to keep up with what was on trend. Some of it was laughable, and often just a direct copy of what she'd worn or decorated with back in the day.

The path widened slightly, and a cove below caught her attention. It was small, with just a few sun loungers and chairs on the pale sand, plus a little beach bar. Perfect. She'd been walking for about forty minutes, so she was unlikely to meet anyone she knew.

Grace made her way down to the beach and opted for a chair and parasol. The sun was strong, since it was the middle of the day, so she added her favourite white hat and more sun cream. The guy from the bar ambled over and introduced himself as Dimitris. He explained in perfect English that they never charged for the sunbeds as long as you spent a minimum of five euros on a drink.

After looking at the laminated menu he handed her, Grace's eyes strayed to the cocktails. She decided to treat herself to a Harvey Wallbanger. The brightly coloured drink had been a staple back in her wine bar days, along with pina coladas and the even more lethal B52s. There was obviously a retro revival going on.

Armed with a drink, she sat back and prepared to let the strain of the week seep out of her. She'd go for a swim later, but for now, she wanted to read about which couture gowns celebrities had poured themselves into and what paint colours were in fashion.

With the first magazine open on her knees, something made her glance up at the shoreline. A man was coming into view. Tall, dark-haired and dressed in shorts and a T-shirt, even from this far away he was fit. His long muscular legs covered the sand quickly as he came up the beach, head down, towards her.

When he got within a few feet, Grace almost dropped her drink in shock. It was Mr Grumpy from the villa garden. She let out an involuntary sigh, which made him look up. Their eyes met and recognition dawned on his face. He came and stood, legs planted in the sand, right in front of her. Close up, the tight T-shirt emphasised his broad chest and six-pack even more. A tiny glimpse of tattoo edged below the sleeve on his left arm. Grace lowered her sunglasses. What did he want? To give her another lecture on trespassing? She really wasn't in the mood.

'I was hoping to bump into you again.'

I was hoping not to bump into you were the words on the tip of her tongue. Just what was it about him that made her revert to her fifteen-year-old self?

Grace waited.

'Seriously, I wanted to apologise for my behaviour the other day. I was a little … rough on you. I overreacted, and I'm sorry.'

Wow, a proper apology. Not what she'd been expecting at all. But it didn't make the way he'd treated her acceptable.

'Thank you for apologising, and yes, you were more than a little rough with me.'

She'd meant to say 'on me'. Grace blinked hard to get rid of a vision of him pushing her up against a wall. What was the matter with her?

Something she'd said seemed to be amusing him. But he wasn't off the hook by a long chalk.

'Was there any reason for your … behaviour?'

'We'd had a couple of dodgy characters hanging around the villa the previous day. I was a bit on edge.'

'And you thought that I might be with them? Part of a gang maybe?'

She was going to keep this going a little longer.

'Not at all. You don't look anything like a gang member.'

'That's nice to know.'

He held out his hand.

'Anyway, I'm Will.'

'And I'm … Grace.'

Their eyes met, and she couldn't help breaking into a big smile, which was mirrored in his eyes. Anyone under thirty-five wouldn't have a clue what they were smiling about.

She held out her hand too and found it enveloped and shaken by his much larger one. He spoke first.

'What are the chances, eh? *Will and Grace*. One of the best sitcoms ever made.'

'Agreed. It was right up there.'

Grace could have appeared on *Mastermind* with the TV sitcom as her specialist subject. The story of New York interior designer Grace, and her flatmate and best friend, a gay lawyer called Will, was a must-watch in the late nineties. The romantic ups and downs of the lead characters had hooked Grace as a busy mum of two, back in the days when you had to wait for a new episode each week, rather than binge-watch a whole series in one weekend.

Will nodded his agreement.

'Never missed it. Fabulous characters, and so funny. Groundbreaking stuff at the time. But wasn't as keen on the revival.'

'No, me neither.'

They actually had something in common. A week ago, Grace would have bet money that that was never going to happen. Maybe there was more to him than met the eye.

Will took a step back.

'Good to chat. I don't want to disturb you further. Enjoy your afternoon. Fabulous earrings by the way. But I'd take them out if you're going swimming.'

Grace's hands went up to her ears. Damn. She'd forgotten to remove her sparkly gold drop numbers after lessons finished.

'See you around sometime.'

Not if I see you first was what Grace wanted to say. There was still something about him she didn't quite trust. He always seemed to be on the brink of laughing at her.

'Yes, maybe.'

Will, whose name she could now never forget, strode off up the beach and onto the path to the houses above the beach, the individual muscles in his back moving in unison.

Grace touched her hand to her head.

Of course. Will was gay. Not that she was bothered either way. But it all fitted together. He was far too attractive to be straight, for one thing. Plus, he loved *Will and Grace* and had called it groundbreaking. Phil couldn't bear the show and she'd usually watched it while he was at the pub and the girls were in bed.

Plus, Will had noticed her earrings. No straight man she knew cared about earrings. If you blindfolded them, they wouldn't be able to tell you the style or colour of the ones you'd had on all day. And he smelt wonderful. It wasn't conclusive evidence, but how many more clues did she need?

Chapter Six

Stelios's little face still had Grace worried. The boy's solemn dark eyes seemed huge in his head, and he hadn't put up his hand once during the lesson. When she'd pushed him to answer a direct question, his reply was vague. Even when she'd allowed the others to let off steam with a five-minute race around outside, he'd just sat on a bench and watched everyone else.

During her long career in primary education, she'd seen everything from children losing their parents before they were ten to pupils having to cope when a father went to prison, and, in a couple of cases, full-on abuse. She really didn't think any of these scenarios applied here, but she knew what an unhappy child looked like.

The bell rang for the end of the class and Grace waited in the playground and ticked off her list as each child went home with a parent or trusted carer. When Stelios's mother, a smartly dressed but harassed-looking young woman, arrived, she took her opportunity.

'Can I have a quick word with you in the classroom, please.'

The woman frowned but nodded.

'Can you take Stelios, and I'll be in in a minute.'

Grace was unsure how much Stelios could understand, so she didn't want to take any chances. She settled him with a book in the corridor outside and ushered his mother in.

'Please call me Grace.'

'And I am Konstantina. Pleased to meet you.'

Thankfully the woman's English seemed adequate for the conversation ahead.

'I won't keep you, but I'm a little concerned about how quiet Stelios is in class. I don't want to pry, and be assured that everything that is said here is strictly confidential, but is there anything going on at home that I should know about?'

Konstantina's eyes immediately filled with tears, and Grace was compelled to put her hand on the woman's arm.

'His pappoús, or grandfather … my father'—the woman sat back for a moment—'is dying. We are very near the end now, and although we haven't told Stelios everything, I know he feels it.'

Grace's heart went out to her.

'They adore each other. Stelios is an only child, and you know how close Greek families are. My husband and I own a couple of restaurants in town, and we work long hours, so his pappoús has been a big figure in his life. He taught him how to swim, how to fish…'

The woman's tears were streaming down her face now.

Grace got up and put a box of tissues at her side. Konstantina had a good blow before she spoke again.

'I'm so sorry to be like this. Most of the time, I'm fine. I can keep it together at work, but the thought that it's affecting my little boy…'

'Don't worry about it. It's only natural for both of you to be sad. I understand what you're going through.'

Grace was taken right back to having to tell the girls that Phil wasn't going to make it. That all the treatments, the hospital stays, the special diets and the exercise programmes had been in vain. But this wasn't about her. She needed to focus.

The woman's eyes were on her, and Grace saw the compassion in them.

'Yes, I really do think you understand.'

Stelios's appearance in the doorway stopped the conversation in its tracks.

'*Esai etimi, Mama*?'

Grace didn't need to speak Greek to know that the boy was bored and wanted to go home.

His mother was already up and out of her chair.

'Yes, I'm ready, little one.'

Grace spoke under her breath.

'So, I will come up with some ideas to help Stelios, and we'll speak again. I wish you the very best.'

'Thank you. I'm so pleased you are his teacher.'

An idea came to Grace as Stelios put his hand in his mother's and they walked out together. She rushed upstairs to the shared kitchen. Great, Charlie was still there.

She had to admit his ready smile had a certain charm.

'Grace. What can I do you for?'

When she explained what the boy was going through, and what he could do to help, Charlie didn't hesitate.

'Of course, no problem. I was close to my grandad too. He was the one constant in my life, especially after my parents split up.'

Charlie was no longer smiling. There was certainly more to him than Grace had first thought.

'So, if I OK it with Thanassis, you're up for coming in towards the end of the lesson tomorrow?'

'Sure thing.'

———————

The whole class cheered when Charlie came in with Buster just before lunchtime. After explaining all about dogs and how to look after them, Charlie got the children to point out and name all Buster's body parts in English.

A long, slow look around the classroom followed.

'And now I need an assistant to help me with some tricks…'

Every single hand went up.

Charlie pretended to look from child to child before alighting on Stelios. He gave Grace a quick glance, and she dipped her head to confirm.

'How about you? Do you like dogs?'

Stelios nodded and looked more animated than Grace had seen him since lessons began.

'Would you like to help me?'

The nodding got more frantic.

'OK, what's your name?'

'Stelios.'

'Come and sit on the floor by me, Stelios.'

The boy did as he was told, eyes wide with wonder.

'Children, you must always ask the owner if it's OK to stroke their dog, because sometimes dogs just aren't in the mood, just like you. They may be tired, hungry or not like being touched.'

Charlie repeated his words in Greek, which wasn't usually encouraged for the bilingual teachers; it was English-only in the classroom. But the message was important enough to make sure every word was understood.

'Luckily, Buster loves strokes, so say hello to him, Stelios.'

The boy put out his hand, gingerly at first, but as soon as the dog yelped and danced around, there was no stopping him. Stelios hugged and held onto Buster for dear life.

'And now'—Charlie left a dramatic pause—'I'm going to whisper in Stelios's ear, and he's going to get Buster to do some tricks.'

The boy listened with intense concentration before speaking in a strong voice that Grace had never heard before. He was usually so quiet.

'Buster, sit!'

After Buster had placed his bottom on the classroom floor several times, it was time for a new trick.

'Buster, beg!'

The classmates shrieked with laughter as the dog went up on his hind legs and waited for a treat from Stelios.

'Buster, shake hands!'

There were plenty of *awwww*s as the dog lifted his paw and Stelios reached out to grasp it.

Charlie whispered one last time in Stelios's ear, and the boy made a gun with his hand.

'Bang bang!'

Buster rolled over and the class went wild. Grace wasn't too sure about bringing that sort of imagery into the classroom, but Stelios's shining eyes wiped away her uncertainty.

Charlie's eyes were shining too. She'd certainly been wrong about him. A more natural teacher she couldn't hope to find.

It was like she had time and space on the island to delve deeper and not just take the people she encountered at face value. Her circle of friends had slowly diminished over the past few years as divorce, death and retirement had narrowed it down and people had moved away. She needed to widen it again. Will's face flashed into her mind. Perhaps he was worth further investigation. Just as a friend, of course.

She mouthed 'thank you' at Charlie as he left with Buster. He mouthed back, 'See you tonight.' It was the introductory meal for the teachers, hosted and paid for by Elena and Giannis. She didn't really want to go, but it looked like that wasn't an option.

There were still fifteen minutes until the end of the lesson, and she needed the class to calm down after the excitement of the dog's visit.

'Who wants to draw a picture of Buster?'

It was a resounding yes.

She'd try and speak to Stelios's mother this week about getting the boy a dog. Although it was a big commitment, it might help him over the worst, and as an only child, he would have the dog as a companion for years to come. Her girls had always had each other to rely on. Konstantina had driven off in a new BMW, so she didn't think she was putting any financial pressure on her. If only all problems could potentially be solved so easily.

Grace was the first to arrive at the restaurant, which was a couple of streets back from the port. It looked like something out of a tourist brochure. Grey painted tables and chairs were laid out in rows on the cobbled street, each setting adorned with a red placemat, an upturned glass and a bowl, and on each table a caddy with olive oil, vinegar and serviettes. A narrow throughway for pedestrians separated one row of tables from another.

The cream plastered walls of the restaurant were broken up with red painted doorways and window frames, and a huge bougainvillea had been trained up and across the street, its strings of bright pink flowers hanging at different heights above their heads.

There were a few tables inside when she peeked in, cosy against the thick stone walls, but who would want to be trapped inside when they could eat out in the street on a warm evening?

She'd worn white linen tonight, a new dress with a deep V neck, and broderie anglaise detailing on the sleeves and hem, and teamed it with a necklace of beads in different colours and some big gold earrings.

White had always suited her, and she'd got a few glances from older Greek men as she made her way down to the port from the language school. But maybe she was kidding herself.

She hoped she wasn't mutton dressed as lamb. It was one of the phrases her daughters found hilarious and accused her of making up. There was a whole raft of sayings that seemed to have just vanished within a generation. She supposed she'd learnt them mainly from her mother. Things like 'in for a penny, in for a pound' or 'the early bird gets the worm' had her daughters rolling around.

She and her friends still used them occasionally, but she'd have to remember not to utter any at the meal, as she'd be the oldest guest by far, and she didn't really want to point it out.

Daniel and Rose arrived together, and sprang apart when they saw her, which made Grace smile. She'd seen them secreted together in corners, and hoped it was going well.

By the time all the teachers had arrived, it was half an hour past the agreed time. Grace had noticed that time seemed to be a bit of an elastic concept for Greeks, particularly in relation to social events.

Giannis and Elena turned up a fashionable forty minutes late and sat at either end of the table. The atmosphere cooled a few degrees as they glared at each other. Giannis positioned himself next to Anna, who was wearing a skintight black dress, which, Grace had to admit, looked stunning.

Grace took the seat next to Elena. She'd wanted to grab her anyway, to find out more about the one-to-one lessons she'd been asked to provide for her and Giannis's children when the language school was officially closed during August. Nearer the time, they'd all get a list of private clients who wanted to be taught in their homes, but she'd been singled out to go to the house of the bosses for some reason.

Thanassis sat down opposite her, looking very dapper in a white linen shirt. Out of the classroom, he scrubbed up well.

'Look, Grace, we are matching. You mustn't tell everyone we got dressed together.'

'You're hilarious.'

Charlie was on her right, and after she'd thanked him again for his help with Stelios, they got into a conversation about his DJing. Grace was fascinated to learn more, but their chat was cut short by Giannis standing up.

'I hope everyone has wine. Let's raise our glasses to a successful summer term. *Yamas!*'

'*Yamas!*'

Grace knocked back some more of the taverna rosé that was dotted down the table in jugs. It wasn't at all bad. She'd had a glass earlier while waiting for the language school owners. And some of the yummy homemade bread with maidanosalata, a delicious creamy parsley dip.

'This restaurant, run by a local family, has been here for over a hundred years,' said Giannis, raising his glass in the direction of the waiters. 'All the food is wonderful, especially the stuffed squid which they are famous for. I hope you don't mind that we have pre-ordered a series of dishes that we will all share together, which is the Greek way. So, please, enjoy the food and wine.'

It was the signal for the waiters to file out with a plethora of ceramic dishes, red like the woodwork, all held high over their heads. Grace's mouth watered. She'd held back on her usual snack tea, and the smells that floated through the air were amazing.

Many mouthfuls later, of everything from moussaka to

squid stuffed with feta and chopped peppers and drizzled in a sharp lemon butter sauce, Grace was stuffed. She'd also drunk her own bodyweight in wine and needed the loo.

She stepped inside but pulled back at the sight of Giannis and Anna, heads bowed, in the corner by the fireplace. She couldn't hear any of the conversation, which was in Greek anyway. Anna was moving her hands around a lot and Giannis's face was strained. The bonhomie of his earlier toast had vanished with the daylight.

Luckily the sign for the toilets pointed upstairs, and Grace rushed up the sweeping staircase in the hope she hadn't been seen.

When she came down, they were still at it, talking in fierce undertones. Grace returned to her seat just as Elena got up. It wasn't clear exactly what was going on inside, but it was certainly something Elena didn't need to see, in Grace's opinion.

'Elena. I wanted to catch you. Can we have a quick chat?'

The younger woman sat down again with a barely audible sigh. Tonight's outfit was a glorious mix of cappuccino and caramel linen separates, paired with fabulous gold jewellery, but the sadness in her eyes made Grace want to scoop her up for a hug. She was sure her boss wouldn't want her interfering in her life, or gently helping things along, as she liked to call it. Her daughters would probably have a different description.

'Yes, of course.'

'I just wondered if we could go through what I'll be teaching your children when we start the private lessons.'

'Oh, I see.' Elena's slightly horrified look told Grace that it wasn't quite the done thing to discuss anything business-oriented at the works dinner. But she was stalling for time. She hadn't seen Giannis or Anna come out of the restaurant yet. Elena's perfectly manicured hand, complete with unchipped coffee-coloured nail varnish and several gold rings, one with a sparkling stone the size of a pea, landed on her arm.

'I will invite you to the house for coffee in a couple of weeks' time, and we will go through it all then.'

'That would be lovely. I look forward to meeting your children.'

Out of the corner of her eye, Grace saw Anna take her seat again.

'Good.' Elena stood up. 'And now, if you'll excuse me.'

At least her husband would be on his own inside the restaurant. Grace let out the breath she'd been holding and wondered if she'd make a good deep-sea diver.

Chapter Seven

The clock clearly said twenty past one. Sofia was late, as usual. Her friend would fit in well with the Greek mentality. Several women in their friendship group had taken to lying to Sofia and telling her the time for any rendezvous was half an hour earlier than it really was, in the hope of her being vaguely punctual, but Grace never bothered; she knew it was hopeless. At work, Sofia had a team of people around her making sure she was at the right place at the right time, but her social life was a different matter.

Grace mostly took it in her stride, otherwise she'd be permanently irritated with her friend. After a lifetime of timetables and lesson plans, she was hardwired to be there on the dot, or usually ten minutes before.

Seated at a table for two on the rooftop terrace of the best hotel on the island, Grace had ordered herself a coffee and waited, which was no hardship. It was a superior coffee, served in a bone china cup, with a gorgeous mini pastry on the side, a disc with a sort of chocolate and hazelnut soft centre.

Grace gazed out at the view as she sipped her coffee and nibbled her delicious morsel. She'd read in a guidebook that the hotel was one of a handful converted from the grand houses built by the shipping magnates of the island's main town almost two hundred years ago.

The houses were arranged over many floors, with stunning views over the bay, but their massive proportions and crippling upkeep meant that very few were still private residences, and some had sadly fallen into disrepair. Elena and Giannis owned one, though, as she'd discovered when she'd checked out the address Elena had given her, and Grace was desperate to have a good look inside when she went for her chat.

History, especially when it dealt with old buildings and the people who'd lived in them, had always interested her, and she'd never been able to mooch around the interiors as much as she'd wanted to when they were on family holidays. There'd always been someone moaning about wanting an ice-cream, needing the loo or asking to go swimming.

Even when it had just been her and Phil, he was usually more interested in keeping up with the football and cricket scores on his phone than finding out about the inhabitants of a historic house. She'd have to draw up a list of places to visit on the island and really indulge herself with long, lazy visits, examining every inch and getting a real sense of how the owners had lived.

The terrace was filling up, and more and more of the metal chairs with their green and blue striped cushions and matching parasols were occupied. It was still early for the Greeks to have lunch – three in the afternoon was more their speed – and

Grace could tell from the voices and the clothes that most of those eating were tourists. The diners were discreetly screened from each other by large plants in pots that matched the aged stone floor.

Sofia eventually appeared from behind a large piece of greenery, followed by a waiter with a couple of menus and an adoring look.

Grace embraced her friend warmly and they exchanged cheek kisses.

'Darling, you're here already!'

'Incredible, isn't it? Where else would you expect me to be at'—Grace broke off to look at her phone—'one-thirty?'

Sofia took the menus off the young man, who seemed glued to the spot. Grace had observed the Sofia effect many times before.

'Don't be grumpy. I just had to have a proper shower and do my hair after the rather scary plane journey.'

'Of course, dear. Can't have you out in public looking anything other than exquisite.'

Sofia stuck out her tongue and Grace grinned.

'I'm just thrilled you've arrived.'

It really was lovely to see her friend, whose freshly washed dark locks tumbled over her shoulders like a shampoo advert.

They'd bonded in their first year at university in Scotland, both freezing cold and far from home. Sofia's worried Spanish mother had sent regular care packages including lots of pairs of cashmere socks, and jars of special chilli-infused hot chocolate, which Sofia had been happy to share.

With Grace being tall and blonde and Sofia brunette and tiny, they'd been dubbed The Light and The Dark by a college wag, and the name had stuck for the duration. At sixty-two, Sofia still turned heads, as a few of the men on the terrace could testify.

'So…' Her friend leant in towards her. 'How's it going? Met any hot guys yet?'

'You know that's not what I'm here for. It's mainly work, work, work so far.'

'Boring.'

'But necessary.'

'Anyone you work with that's cute?'

'Well, I have to admit that Thanassis, the Director of Studies, is good-looking… But it's against the rules to have work relationships.'

'Bah! Rules are made to be broken. Married? Single?'

'We really haven't got that far. We've been focusing on the lessons, incredibly.'

'He sounds promising.'

'Is that all you ever think about?'

'When it comes to you, yes. It's been three years now since Phil went. You need someone to show you a good time. It's going to seal itself up down there, like one of those Egyptian tombs.'

'Sofia! Honestly. That's disgusting.'

Grace looked round to check that no one was listening to their conversation. But Sofia was in full swing.

'You need a Harrison Ford type to come sweeping in and pull away that boulder to get at the treasure inside.'

'Right, that's enough.'

But Grace turned away so Sofia couldn't see her smile.

'I know you're laughing. Don't try and pretend you don't

like sex, little Miss Innocent. I know everything about you, remember.'

When you'd been friends for forty years, there was nowhere to hide. Neither of them had had any trouble attracting men at university and both had done their fair share of experimenting. Grace had met Phil on her postgraduate teacher training course, and quit the experimenting for good, while Sofia had carried on regardless.

Sex really was the last thing on Grace's mind these days, or so she kept telling herself. The intimacy of sharing a bed was something she would admit to missing, if pressed, and since she'd arrived in Greece some of her dreams had been a bit on the raunchy side, but that didn't mean she wanted to go out and grab hold of any man who might wander past. The dreams she put down to the hot weather and too much goat's cheese.

Their attentive waiter was back.

'Have you decided what you'd like, ladies?'

Sofia flapped her hands.

'No, sorry, too busy chatting. Can you give us a few minutes, please.'

The guy looked at Sofia like he'd agree to chop off a finger if that's what she wanted. Her friend inspired slavish devotion in men, and it hadn't changed over the years. After an early marriage to a much older lawyer, Sofia had escaped with a mews house in Chelsea and a taste for younger guys. Sofia put down the menu.

'I'm not really very hungry, so I'm going to have the salad with pear and Roquefort. What about you?'

Grace was starving after a morning's teaching and missing

her lunchtime dose of grandma's cooking, which she'd have been tucking into by now.

'I'm going to have the seafood kritharoto.'

'What's that when it's at home?'

'A type of pasta that looks like rice with lots of prawns, squid and mussels. It's delicious.'

'OK, I might try a bit.'

Sofia also had a habit of digging into anything you chose and assuming all meals were to be shared. So, Greece was the perfect place for her. Phil had considered it incredibly annoying. He'd found Sofia a bit much at the best of times and had gone out of his way to avoid her. If he ordered a dish in a restaurant, he expected it to be all his. Grace had always had the feeling that her friend found Phil a bit boring. But that was one place they'd never gone.

Her friend was perusing the menu again with intense concentration.

'What about drinks?'

'Shouldn't we stick to soft drinks if we're going out tonight?'

Grace had never been a fan of day drinking. It always made her want to go to sleep.

'Rubbish, it's the first day of my holiday. A little carafe of white wine won't hurt.'

'Fine.'

At least she didn't have to work the next day.

'And after a long lunch we can hit the shops.'

'Remember they'll be closed during the afternoon.'

'OK, we'll eat slowly.'

Watching Sofia flex her credit card was truly an experience. Her friend flitted from shop to shop, trying on everything from trousers to shirts to dresses. Grace found the clothes in Greece a lot more expensive than England, and a bit too bling for her liking. And because she was tall, a lot of them weren't made for her.

But Sofia lapped up the metallic touches and soft fabrics, and since she was five foot two and a perfect size ten, everything fitted. Initially people thought she was Greek, with her Mediterranean colouring, something that never happened to Grace. But as soon as Grace used even the most rudimentary Greek words, people just answered in English.

And once the shopkeepers realised Sofia was serious about spending money, nothing was too much trouble. They were offered seats, coffees and several phone numbers if the shop owners happened to be male.

Her friend had halted outside an upmarket shoe shop.

Grace was reaching the end of her shopping stamina, and it would get dark soon. In the main tourist season, a lot of the shops stayed open until midnight, but they weren't quite there yet, and shutters were being drawn down all around them.

'Can we stop now and get a drink, pretty please?'

'OK, let's just nip in here, then we'll stop, I promise. Have you seen anything you like in the window?'

A pair of pale pink suede espadrilles with pink velvet ties caught her eye, but the price tag of a hundred and twenty euros instantly put her off. She'd never paid that much for a pair of shoes in her life.

Sofia wasn't taking no for an answer.

'Come on, let's both go and try something on. I love those lime green wedges. Then I promise we can go and party.'

That wasn't exactly what Grace had said, but she let it go.

The pink espadrilles fitted perfectly, as she'd feared they would.

Sofia the shopping devil was on her shoulder.

'They are fab. You've got to get them. What are you working so hard for otherwise? Go on, treat yourself.'

Her friend did have a point.

The shop owner was thrilled to have two big sales just as she was closing, and Sofia ended up buying the wedges in electric blue as well as lime green.

After dropping off Sofia's bags with reception, they made their way up the many steps to the old town. Grace was keen to show her friend the sunset from a little bar she'd discovered. It looked fairly ordinary downstairs, serving drinks and a selection of tapas plates, but up the rickety stairs was a rooftop bar with a panoramic view.

Grace kept the backdrop a secret until her friend reached the top of the stairs, and they both stood and took in the stunning one-hundred-and-eighty-degree views which encompassed the port, the many churches below, the ships out at sea and the islands beyond.

'Wow!' was all that Sofia could say.

They were alone on the rooftop, and they made for the

prime spot, the table right at the front. A waitress followed them up.

'Anything I can get you?'

Sofia didn't hesitate.

'Two espresso martinis, please.'

Another two more each, and the sunset over, Grace was feeling the effects. The way back down the staircase was far more hazardous. She stumbled on the last step.

'I really think we should eat something.'

Sofia, who Grace knew could drink most blokes under the table, took her arm as they exited onto the street.

'How about this place? It looks nice.'

A restaurant with white distressed tables and chairs and padded patchwork cushions in muted reds and blues was only a couple of steps away, and Grace was happy to sink into the comfy embrace of a large bench seat.

The owner rushed out to greet them, and pointed at the specials board, written in Greek. Grace always thought it was a good sign if the restaurant didn't have everything written out in English.

'We have lovely rabbit stifado tonight, stuffed peppers and drunken pork with wine and peppers.'

Grace knew stifado was a type of stew. She wasn't too sure about rabbit, but she didn't get the chance to ask about alternatives before Sofia piled in.

'Sounds great, we'll have one of each please, with a Greek salad. Plus a carafe of white wine and some water.'

Grace closed her eyes for a moment. Sofia wasn't the one who'd been teaching all morning.

'Hey, wakey wakey. The night is still young.'

Grace poured out a glass of wine and one of water for both of them, knowing the food would take a while. The Greeks believed a meal should be a relaxed experience, and service was never quick.

They sat back on the bench and watched the passersby while they waited, commenting on their clothes and guessing at their ages.

A tall man appeared at the bottom of the street, walking their way.

Grace put her head behind the nearest plant.

'Quick, hide.'

'What? Why?'

Sofia stayed where she was and stared into the street.

'Woah. He's hot. A definite ten.'

'Keep your voice down.'

Will had almost reached them, but Grace saw with relief through a bunch of leaves that he was talking animatedly to a male companion and not looking their way.

'Who's that? Do you know him?'

'Yeah. Sort of. It's complicated. He's called Will, but that's about all I do know.'

Sofia stared at the two men all the way up the road until they disappeared out of sight.

'But still… Can you introduce us?'

'Believe me, it wouldn't help you. He bats for the other side.'

Sofia mimed swinging a cricket bat and both women got the giggles. When she could breathe again, Grace took a slug of wine.

'My kids would kill me for saying that. It's another of those phrases we're supposed to forget we ever knew. Will is gay, I should say.'

'Shame. The good ones often are. You have to admit he's a hottie.'

'I will admit that he's cute, as there's no possibility of it ever happening, for either of us.'

Sofia drained the rest of her wine.

'Well, that's progress, you admitting you fancy someone.'

'I never said that!'

'OK, keep your hair on. But I do want to talk to you seriously about dating. Don't give up on men just yet.'

'Why are we talking about men again?'

'You're a gorgeous, vibrant woman, and you have been hiding yourself away for too long.'

'You sound like my daughters.'

'Well, they're right. Look, I'm not talking about marriage, or even love, I'm just talking about a good old-fashioned earth-shattering bonk.'

Grace nodded and smiled at two elderly Greek ladies in black passing by at that very moment. Hopefully they didn't speak English.

'I'm not convinced the girls want me to go off and have meaningless sex.'

'I'm sure they wouldn't be against it. You've made a good start leaving behind your cosy little life and coming to Greece, but you need to take the next step.'

'I don't like you using the word little about my life. It's a perfectly good life.'

'Sorry. For a nun, maybe.'

As usual, Sofia's bossiness was increasing in direct relation to the amount of alcohol she'd consumed.

'I know it's not the sort of life you'd want, but it doesn't mean there's anything wrong with my "cosy little life" as you call it. I'm quite happy on my own. And I've still got the girls to think about. I know you never wanted children, but mine still need me.'

'Do they, really? They're both in their thirties and settled with their partners. It's time you started putting yourself first.'

Grace had been thinking along those lines herself. Just being in Greece for a few short weeks had shown her how little she was needed by her grown-up children. It was tough to think she'd been overemphasising her importance in their lives since Phil went. It didn't mean they didn't love her, but love and need were two very different things. Not that she'd admit that to Sofia. She couldn't let her be right all the time.

'Look, I had a long and happy marriage, and it ended through no fault of my own. I'm not sure I could ever consider anyone else, even for meaningless sex.'

Grace hadn't noticed the waiter arrive at their table.

Sofia's eyes sparkled.

'You should give it a go, believe me.'

The guy topped up their glasses with a shaking hand. Grace reached for the water. This was only the first night of her friend's visit, and she'd already drunk more in a day than she had since she'd arrived.

Sofia ignored the water and turned to look at her over the rim of the wine glass.

'What I did envy was your friendship with Phil, the fact

that you were a team. He had your back against the world, whatever happened. I've never had that.'

Sofia stared into her drink. Grace had never heard her voice these thoughts before in all the years she'd known her. Like most people, cool, confident Sofia was much more complex that she first appeared. Grace knew most of her friend's likes and dislikes, but this was new.

'But I always thought you thought Phil was boring.'

'No, not really.'

'I think the addition of not really isn't hugely convincing.'

'Look, Phil was a lovely guy, not my cup of tea personally if you want me to be completely honest, which is a good thing, believe me – you don't want to lust after your friend's husband. Way too complicated.'

Grace wasn't sure how she felt about that statement, but Sofia was obviously speaking from experience.

'But I loved how much he adored you. I was jealous of your relationship, which was why I tended to avoid being alone with the two of you.'

So, Sofia was avoiding Phil, while he avoided her, both of them coveting her as their prize, like two dogs with a bone. It was like the plot of a bad sitcom.

Bubbles of laughter were forming in Grace's stomach.

'And I envied you your freedom, your ability to drop everything and fly off at a moment's notice, while I was stuck with nappies and sick.'

'Lovely.'

'And if I'm being completely honest too, having the chance to try out a new man whenever you felt like it.'

'See, you're not as buttoned up as you make out, lady.'

Grace let the laughter rip out of her and Sofia joined in with gusto. They were teenagers again, drunk on cider in the uni bar, comparing the terrible chat-up lines they'd been subjected to.

Sofia grabbed for her hand.

'But I do believe you're built to be with someone, my lovely friend. There's at least one more chapter to come in your love life, maybe more. You've just got to get some proper practice in.'

Chapter Eight

The heat of the sun on her face woke Grace from a fitful doze. She felt for her hat, which was thankfully still in place on her head, along with her sunglasses. She'd gone out onto the balcony for a five-minute sit-down after a long morning teaching the little ones. They were cute, but exhausting. She didn't usually get given the five- to seven-year-olds, but Anna was off sick with a stomach bug, so it had been Grace's turn to get stuck in. Singing nursery rhymes and playing shops might be improving their English, but Grace thought she'd scream if she heard 'Ring a Ring o' Roses' again anytime soon.

Sofia had finally left the previous morning, after a week of eating, drinking and shopping together. They'd had a lovely time, but a week was long enough when one person was working and the other one was on holiday.

They'd had lunch every day on the hotel terrace, and Grace had noticed the smouldering glances between her friend and the head waiter. His name was Adonis, and it was an apt description of the man. Tall, golden and definitely this side of forty.

On day three, a beaming Sofia had admitted that Adonis was her go-to entertainment after Grace had gone home for the night. At least it meant the evenings had ended early enough for Grace to get enough sleep to function at work.

A glance at her phone told her she'd been sleeping for an hour, and it was now mid-afternoon. There were only a few minutes left until her weekly call with Lottie in Australia. It was Lottie on Saturdays and Flo on Sundays.

It was strange to see her younger daughter sitting at the kitchen table in the cottage back in Oxfordshire. It was even stranger that she didn't miss anything about it. Everything looked tiny and the view outside the window was nothing compared to the wide-open vistas all around her on the island.

Grace went back into the room and let her eyes adjust to the dark interior before she poured herself a glass of cold water from a bottle in the fridge and settled down at her desk in front of the computer.

The familiar ping told her that Lottie was online, and as soon as she clicked on the picture and saw her daughter's beaming face and Brad standing proudly behind her, she had a pretty good idea what was coming.

'Mum! You'll never guess!'

Grace readied her face.

'I'm pregnant! We're having a baby. You're going to be a grannie!'

Grace let out a squeal.

'That's wonderful, darling. And you, of course, Brad. I'm so excited.'

Lottie's hands moved down to her stomach.

'I've wanted to tell you for ages'—her daughter looked up at her boyfriend—'but Brad insisted we wait until the three-month scan. As you know, his sister Suzie's a nurse at the hospital here, and she explained that lots can go wrong in the early stages, and we didn't want to get everyone's hopes up.'

'Very sensible.'

Lottie held up a picture.

'But here it is. The magical three-month scan. We've made it this far.'

The bean-shaped blob on the screen caused Grace's heart to hammer in her chest. In front of her was an image of the grandchild that Phil would never meet. The first new baby in their little family. How he would have loved to live long enough to hold a grandson or granddaughter in his arms.

But she mustn't let her sadness show. This was Lottie's day.

Grace clapped her hands and got as close to the screen as she could.

'I couldn't be happier for you both. How have you been feeling, love? Any sickness?'

Lottie smiled up at Brad.

'Yeah, quite a bit at first, but it's calmed down now.'

'Good. I was sick as a dog for the first few months with both of you. And I had a weird craving for tuna and gherkin sandwiches at all times of the day and night.'

'Yuk. For me, it's burgers. Really greasy burgers, dripping with mayonnaise and mustard.' Lottie grasped her boyfriend's hand. 'But Brad's been so good. He's happy to go to the drive-thru any time to satisfy my every whim.'

'Yes, your father got so that he could whip up a tuna and

gherkin sandwich in seconds. And you know what a terrible cook he was…'

Grace stopped speaking as her daughter's face crumbled. Phil had become the elephant in the room. She hadn't meant to mention him; it had just slipped out. She'd been thinking about her husband less since she'd arrived in Greece and there had been whole days when she hadn't thought about him at all. But with something as monumental as this, their first grandchild, she couldn't stop herself.

Her daughter's imminent tears were about to set off her own. Grace fought to be the calm one. She couldn't lose it. Her daughter needed her to be strong.

'Oh, Mum, I can't stop thinking about how thrilled Dad would have been.'

Grace blew her daughter a kiss to give herself a moment.

'He would, darling, he would have been over the moon. But please don't upset yourself, it's not good for the baby.'

Protecting her daughters from all the things they'd lost with Phil's death was second nature to her now, but sometimes she wondered, who was going to protect her? Those plans for the future had gone up in smoke for all of them, not just the girls. Most of the time she managed to keep a lid on it, but when it was staring her in the face, like today, it hurt.

A tear made its way down her daughter's tanned cheek.

'It's bloody unfair that Dad will never know my child.'

Brad's arms went round her daughter, and she laid her head against his chest while he stroked her hair. Grace experienced a pang of envy that she quickly dismissed. It should be her comforting her daughter. But she'd passed that baton on a long time ago.

'Sweetheart, please don't cry. Your father will know about the baby, somehow, somewhere, I really believe that.'

'I'm glad you do, Mum, because I absolutely don't believe in any of that stuff. Dad's gone and he's never coming back.'

Her daughter's voice was muffled and the dark tearstain on Brad's T-shirt was spreading rapidly as Lottie kept her head against his chest. A change of subject was needed urgently.

'Have you told your sister, and Jilly, about the baby?'

Lottie turned back to the camera, and Brad passed her a tissue. Grace waited for the answer while her daughter blew her nose several times.

'Not yet. It was you first. After Brad's family of course. As Suzie pulled a few strings to be in charge of our maternity care, she's known from the start.'

Lottie ruffled Brad's hair.

'And we didn't think it was fair that she'd have to lie to her own parents about what was going on, so we told them too, a couple of weeks ago.'

'No, of course.'

So, Grace wasn't quite first, but she wouldn't let it matter.

'So, do you have a plan?'

A plan was always a plus for Grace.

'As long as everything progresses as it's supposed to…'

Both Lottie and Brad crossed their fingers at the camera and met for a kiss.

'I'll keep working at the dive centre for as long as I'm able. I can take over a lot more of the admin as I get bigger, and we'll look for temporary staff to cover me on the diving side.'

Grace was glad her daughter wasn't planning to throw herself around underwater while heavily pregnant.

'That all sounds well thought out.'

'And in just under eight weeks' time, it's the twenty-week scan. To give ourselves something to look forward to, and because there's still so long to go, we're going to have a gender reveal party!'

Her daughter had never been big on patience, but at least there was some animation in her voice.

'It's so exciting. You have a scan, they give you a piece of paper with the sex written on it in an envelope, and you give it to a close friend or relative without opening it, which will be Brad's sister for us. They bake a cake or get a confetti cannon, something with the inside in the right colour, blue or pink, and then you invite friends and family to watch you cut it open or pull the string and you all find out together!'

'Yes, I've seen them on Instagram.'

Privately, Grace thought the whole thing was a bit naff. What was wrong with waiting until the baby came out, and finding out then? What was the rush to know so early? She and Phil had been more than happy not to know beforehand.

'And you're sure you don't want to wait until your baby is born?'

'Mum, don't be so old-fashioned! Everyone's doing it. We can plan beforehand, buy the right clothes, decorate the nursery, and focus on imagining what our child will look like.'

'Obviously it's up to you, darling. If that's what you both want.'

'It is. And we'll set up a link so you can watch too.'

'Great.'

Grace tried to make her smile look genuine. It was weird constantly looking at yourself as you spoke. It was wonderful to be able to see her daughter in person, but it also meant she had to monitor her facial expressions pretty closely. It was a whole layer you didn't need to worry about on the phone.

'There's something else as well...'

Lottie took a long look at her boyfriend, who nodded, and they both stared into the screen.

'One thing we really, really, want is to have you out here, Mum, for the birth, and the weeks before and after the baby arrives. We've already paid for an open ticket for you. We're hoping you can come for a month.'

Grace swallowed.

'Oh, that's too far too generous. You should be saving your money. Babies are expensive.'

'Don't be silly. You're my family. You, Flo and Jilly. We're hoping that they can get some time off to come over too, as hopefully it will coincide with their Christmas break. We're a small but mighty team. I couldn't do it without you all.'

'Then it's a lovely gesture, thank you.'

In truth, Grace wasn't sure she'd want to spend a whole month out there, and she still had her pupils back in England to worry about, but the details could wait. The fact that they wanted her to be involved was paramount.

The ring of a doorbell in Australia paused their chat.

'That'll be Brad's aunt and uncle, Di and Josh.' Her daughter's eyes were bright. 'We've asked them over for a meal, and we're going to put the scan picture on Di's plate. They've got no idea. They don't have kids, so they'll be like honorary grandparents too.'

The list of people who would be intimately involved with

this baby seemed to be growing by the minute. But it would be lovely for Lottie to have lots of people around.

'I won't keep you then. Congratulations and love to both of you, and we'll speak next week.'

'Yeah, love you lots.'

'Love you too.'

As soon as the screen went blank, Grace crawled onto her bed and shut her eyes. The most important thing was that this child arrived safely. Her daughter was knocking on for thirty-eight, so it was time she got on with it. But would Grace ever get to know her grandchild properly if he or she was living on the other side of the world?

It wouldn't be like bringing up the girls, seeing them change and grow, day by day. She'd be lucky if she saw this child a couple of times a year.

She was desperately sad to think that Phil would never get to know his grandchild, but was she going to fare much better? Obviously, these were horrible, selfish thoughts, not to be voiced out loud, but Grace couldn't help but think about how different her vision of being a grandparent had been. She'd imagined her and Phil taking the kids for a weekend to give their parents a break, pushing them on the swings as they screamed to go higher, eating ice-creams together and putting blobs of it on each other's noses, and finally snuggling on the sofa with them in matching pyjamas at the end of a busy day. But conjuring up pictures in her mind was pointless. She had to stop torturing herself.

The tears, when they came, racked her whole body, and Grace gave in to them in a way she hadn't done since the terrible months following Phil's death.

Chapter Nine

When she woke, her mouth was like sandpaper and her eyes so sore she could barely open them. A glance at her phone and the light pouring through the open shutters told her it was six o'clock on a sunny Saturday evening in Greece. She should be celebrating the fact that her daughter was pregnant, not worrying about how much involvement she'd have with her grandchild. A cold shower should help.

Grace dressed carefully in one of her leopard-print dresses, choosing the pink and grey version to go with the new suede espadrilles she'd bought with Sofia. A little eyeliner and mascara helped to make her eyes look less piggy, and the sun cream she wore anytime she was outside smoothed out her skin a little where it had been patterned by the cushion she'd laid against.

A generous spray of perfume and she was ready to go for a walk in the town and maybe a bite to eat. She'd got used to being on her own most of the time – she'd had to – and going out alone didn't hold any fear.

In the lobby, she was surprised to bump into Thanassis, who emerged from a room across the hall as she reached the bottom of the stairs. Lessons had finished hours ago, so he must have been doing some planning work. His usual cheery persona seemed to be having a day off too if first impressions were anything to go by; even his navy linen shirt was crumpled.

'Grace, hello.'

Grace inclined her head.

'Thanassis.'

'You are looking very festive. Have you got somewhere nice to go?'

'Not really, but I need to go out and get some fresh air.'

She wasn't about to divulge the contents of her phone call to him. She'd made sure none of the staff knew very much about her. If anyone asked her a direct question, she wouldn't lie, but jumping straight in wasn't her style. She'd already discovered that most Greeks loved a good gossip, including the men, and while she wasn't averse to it herself sometimes, she didn't want to be the subject.

Thanassis sighed heavily.

'I know what you mean. It's been a tough day. I need to go out too.'

Grace smiled politely as Thanassis took a step towards her.

'How would you feel about us going out together? For a drink?'

Her face must have given away her shock as he put up both hands in a gesture of surrender.

'Just as colleagues, of course. We never have time to talk when we're teaching.'

Her first instinct was to come up with an excuse, but Grace stopped herself in time. He'd made it clear that it was only a friendly chat, almost a work commitment if you thought of it like that. It wasn't a hardship to go for an innocent drink with an attractive man. Sofia had begged her to take more chances. And the poor guy really did look like he had the weight of the world on his shoulders. As Phil used to say, she'd always been a sucker for a sob story.

'Yes, why not.'

Thanassis's blue eyes brightened up considerably, and creased into lines as he smiled.

'*Kataplictiko.*'

From her limited, but gradually expanding knowledge of Greek, Grace knew the word meant amazing. She hoped she wouldn't regret it.

'I know a place right at the top of the town with fantastic views all round the island. It's a bit of a walk though, are you up for that?'

Her espadrilles had a wedge heel which Grace deemed solid enough for walking.

'Sounds fun.'

After twenty minutes of climbing up and away from the town, during which time they'd chatted mainly about the pupils and their progress, Grace was finally sat in a tiny bar with bright blue metal tables and chairs.

The bar itself was inside a ruined stone tower, open to the elements and strewn with strings of fairy lights across the missing roof, jazz playing softly somewhere in the background. It did indeed boast fantastic views on all sides.

The calm turquoise sea was in front of her, but to her right she could see all the way up into the hills, where goats scampered over rocky ground far away. It wasn't anywhere near dark yet, and there were very few people around. Grace could actually hear the tinkling of the animals' bells as they followed the goatherd luring them back to base with the promise of food.

It was an incredibly peaceful spot. Her colleague had chosen well, and her initial glass of Mythos, the dry Greek beer she was fast getting a taste for, was almost empty.

Thanassis lit his second cigarette of the evening and leant back in his chair. The man hadn't said very much at all since they'd reached the bar; he seemed lost in his own thoughts, which suited Grace. But it looked like he was about to change that.

'Is the language school what you imagined when you joined up?'

Grace drank the last mouthful of beer before replying.

'It's better than I hoped, to be honest. I love the variety of ages that we get to teach, the weather's fabulous, and everyone has been so friendly.'

'Good, I'm glad.' Thanassis put up his hand for the waiter and pointed at her glass. 'Another of those?'

'Unless there's something else you think I should try?'

'Have you had ouzo yet?'

Grace shook her head.

'You can't be in Greece and not drink ouzo.'

All she knew was that it was a spirit flavoured with aniseed, and she usually steered well clear of spirits, but what the hell.

'Ouzo it is then.'

Two long thin glasses containing a measure of colourless liquid arrived at their table, plus a jug of water and ice.

Thanassis picked up several ice cubes with the tongs and put them into her glass, topping the whole thing up with water. His hand brushed against hers as he did it.

'Watch the magic!'

Grace smiled as the liquid inside the glasses turned cloudy.

Thanassis clinked his glass to hers.

'*Yamas!*'

'*Yamas!*'

Grace knocked back a mouthful but had to stop drinking as a coughing fit took over. It was strong stuff.

Thanassis was up and patting her on the back in a flash.

'Sorry, I should have warned you.'

His hand lingered on her back for a little longer than was strictly necessary, but the mini massage wasn't unpleasant.

'No, it's delicious.'

Grace drank a little more to prove she wasn't a wimp and saw that Thanassis had moved his chair a little nearer. He really did have the most gorgeous eyes, dark blue flecked with gold.

'Is there someone waiting for you back home in England?'

His question caught her off guard. Her fingers went to touch the familiar ring. But of course it wasn't there. She'd taken it off on the plane.

'No, no one, I'm free as a bird.'

'A bird?'

So, Thanassis might technically be fluent in English, but he wasn't such an expert on expressions.

'Sorry, yes, I'm single.'

'I am surprised. An attractive woman like you.'

Grace waved off his compliment. It was the first time she'd referred to herself as single, rather than widowed. It felt strange, but good.

'And what about you?'

Thanassis put his head in his hands.

'Ah, it's a long and sad story…'

Grace waited. The Greeks she'd met had a tendency to be a trifle dramatic. At first, she'd assumed that shouting and gesticulating meant anger and rows, but she'd come to learn it could just be innocent conversation. What would pass for a disturbance in Oxfordshire was friendly banter here. Grace smiled as her younger daughter's face flashed into her mind. Flo hated her using the word 'banter' and always put her hands over her ears and yelled, 'Stop it!' She seemed convinced it was only for the young.

Thanassis had stalled mid-sentence.

'Come on, you can tell me. What's said in the bar stays in the bar.'

Why was she putting on a sinister Italian accent?

Thanassis waved the waiter over and ordered more ouzo.

'My wife and I are … separated. It's all over between us. There's no going back.'

'Oh, I'm so sorry.'

'It is her decision…' Thanassis filled up her glass again. 'And I have come to accept it. So, yes, like you, I am officially single too.'

Grace wasn't sure you could call it official unless you were divorced, but Thanassis seemed convinced.

'I have been living at the language school recently. They keep a spare room for me there, in case I have to work late.'

'That must feel a bit lonely after what you're used to.'

'You're right, Grace. I am lonely. Which is why it is so lovely to be out with you tonight.'

The bedraggled puppy look was growing on her. They were just a couple out for an evening drink in a beautiful setting. He may be a few years younger than her, but age was just a number.

Several drinks later, Grace had lost count exactly how many, she knew all about Thanassis's parents and brother back in Athens, his university days and his love of teaching. The content of some of the conversation was hard to recall, but she was mesmerised by her companion's mouth. His lips looked like they'd be soft to kiss. She let Thanassis talk on as she imagined reaching over and putting her mouth to his.

He'd moved even closer so that their shoulders were virtually touching, and the spicy smell coming off his body was aftershave overlaid with a tinge of sweat. Male sweat was something she hadn't smelt for a while. It wasn't that she craved it, that would be weird, but it was something that had disappeared out of her life when Phil went.

Thanassis topped up her drink with the large bottle of ouzo that had been left on their table by the waiter, now busy with other customers. Thanassis's hand was resting on top of her fingers on the table, causing her heart to flutter wildly. She wasn't so out of touch that she didn't know when a man wanted her.

Maybe she should just throw caution to the wind, as Sofia

advised, and sleep with him. It would be a gentle introduction back into the world of sex. There was no danger of her falling in love with him, but they could definitely have some fun. He had his own room to go back to, and they could make a pact not to let anyone else at the language school know what they'd been up to. Did that make her sound like some calculating floozy? Did she even care what anyone thought? It was her body and her life.

She turned to face Thanassis, their hands still entwined. But before she could think about kissing him, a figure loomed up behind her companion, tall and bulky. Grace recognised that crooked smile immediately. No! Not him, not now.

Chapter Ten

'Hey, Thanassis!'

Grace watched Will embrace her drinking companion in the Greek way, with a half hug and a pat on the back, before turning his attention to her.

'And … Grace, isn't it?'

He knew damn well it was. She gave Will what she hoped was a wintry smile.

'What are you two doing out so late?'

Grace followed his glance down to the table and the empty ouzo bottle. Maybe someone else had joined them and she'd forgotten, which was unlike her.

She remembered the beginning of the evening well and being introduced to the delights of the drink. She'd wanted to see the magic happen again and again. It was delicious as well, nothing like alcohol, more like tasty medicine. After the first few, things had got a little hazy.

The pleasantly woozy feeling she had now couldn't be

anything to do with the ouzo, surely, more to do with staying on her balcony in the sun for too long this afternoon. There were several plates with flakes of pastry on too, which was proof there had been snacks at some point, little bits of sausage and spinach pie as she recalled, but that did seem a very long time ago.

Why was Will questioning what she and Thanassis were doing? It was none of his bloody business. He was like some overbearing big brother. If she wanted to stay out all night, he couldn't stop her.

Will leant down so close to Thanassis that wafts of his lemon aftershave blew her way too. His voice was low, but Grace heard every word.

'Isn't it time you got back to Maria and the kids, mate?'

She jerked her head back at the words.

Thanassis had told her he was separated. That it was well and truly over with his wife. The bastard! To think she'd been considering giving him the honour of being the first man she slept with since Phil died. Three whole years of being celibate. And quite some time before that if she was being honest. Phil's illness had made anything other than a kiss and cuddle impossible.

Grace put her hand on Thanassis's arm and forced him to look at her.

'So, you're not really separated?'

Thanassis stared at the ground and mumbled something.

'Speak up!'

Grace found it hard to modulate her voice. The one that came out of her mouth was the one she used in the classroom with the naughtiest of children.

A shamefaced Thanassis finally met her eyes.

'We had a huge argument. I moved out a few days ago. I really thought it was over. And it's true I've been staying at the language school. It's broken my heart. Hence … this.' Thanassis moved his arm across the table, managing to knock off one of the glasses. He caught it just before it hit the floor and placed it back on the table.

Will was still hovering like the spectre at the feast. She wanted nothing more than for both of them to disappear in a puff of smoke.

Thanassis picked up his phone and cigarettes from the table.

'I'm sorry, Grace.'

She had to play this down. Giving away any hint that she'd considered sleeping with him could ruin things at work, let alone embarrass them both. And there was nosy Will to think about too. She didn't want his pity.

'You have nothing to apologise to me for, honestly. We're just colleagues who've enjoyed a fun night out. No harm done.'

Even to herself her words sounded stilted but, having had the rug pulled out from under her, she had to regain the advantage somehow.

'Thank you, Grace.'

'No problem.'

She fixed her eyes on Thanassis with some difficulty.

'But will you promise me something? That you'll try and make it work with your wife if there's something worth fighting for. For her sake and the sake of your children.'

Grace's voice caught in her throat, and she willed her eyes

not to well up. She wanted to shake the man and tell him to grab his chance while he still could.

Thanassis did the sign of the cross on his chest.

'I promise.'

He seemed sincere, but Grace barely knew him. She barely knew either of the men standing in front of her. She wished Thanassis well, but she had to face her own truth. It looked like she wasn't cut out for casual sex. She wasn't like her wonderful friend Sofia, taking her pleasure where she could, without a backward glance. Grace Foreman needed to get to know someone well before she offered up her body. She admired Sofia for going for it, and it would be nice to have a man's arms around her again, but not at the price of someone else's marriage.

Will's dark eyes were boring into her. Why was he still hanging around?

Thanassis got to his feet and held out his hand.

'Let me take you back to the language school. I will stay there in my room tonight, and I promise I will talk to Maria tomorrow.'

Grace tried to stand, but there was something wrong with her legs. They appeared to belong to someone else.

It was Will who caught her arm as she stumbled on the stone floor.

'Don't worry, mate, I can take Grace home.'

Grace looked back and forth between the two of them. The dawn was starting to come up behind the sea, and she needed her bed. She made her decision. As a gay man, Will was hardly likely to try anything on. Grace turned towards him.

'OK.'

'OK, what?'

'Yes, you can take me home.'

'It will be my pleasure.'

Will's smirk could have earnt him a slap. She had to remember that he was doing her a favour.

A deep frown appeared on Thanassis's forehead.

'Are you sure, Grace? Do you know him well?'

'Well enough.' Grace spoke to Thanassis behind her hand in what she hoped was a whisper. 'And I'm going to be safe with him, aren't I?'

The frown was replaced by a confused smile.

'If you say so. *Kalinichta*…' Thanassis indicated at the lightening sky, 'or should I say *kalimera* as we now have a brand-new day.'

'*Kalimera!*'

Grace raised her hand to wave at him as he ambled off down the hill, which made her lean on the table rather heavily.

Will's eagle eyes were on her again.

'I think we should go for a coffee before I take you home. The bars in the port will still be open and it's on the way anyway.'

'Yes, oh leader!'

Grace's salute had Will turning his back. He was laughing at her – she could see his shoulders shaking – but she couldn't prove it. He held out his arm.

'Do you think you can manage the steps? There are quite a few of them on the way down.'

'Of course, what do you think I am? Some sozzled old hag who can't put one foot in front of the other?'

Will's raised eyebrow made her want to upgrade that slap

to a punch. But she did need to get back to her room, and she had no real idea of where she was. A sense of direction wasn't a highpoint of her skill set.

She vowed not to speak to him again until they'd got down to the port, hoping that silence would help her concentration. She reluctantly took his arm, which felt solid and surprisingly warm.

They made slow progress on the age-worn stone steps, and after she'd slipped for the third time, Will's heavy breathing told her that he was more than a little fed up. He let go of her arm and turned to face her.

'Fasten your seat belt, honey. It's going to be a bumpy ride.'

Before she could complain about the awful American accent, Grace was hoisted up into a fireman's lift and over Will's shoulder.

'Aaaaah.'

'Don't scream. You'll wake all those people who are having a well-deserved Sunday lie-in.'

'Put me down at once.' Grace was speaking into Will's T-shirt with her face up against the hard wall of his back.

'Really? You're happy to take several hours to get home, are you?'

Grace kept quiet.

'This way, it will take us a couple of minutes. I've carried people weighing a lot more than you over my shoulder, believe me.'

Grace wasn't sure it was a compliment. She beat her fists lightly on his back for a moment but decided to give in gracefully. The upside-down view was surprisingly interesting.

There were lights coming on in the tall painted houses on either side of the narrow steps, more and more of them the nearer they got to the water. Grace wondered what was going on in all those rooms. Pictures of breastfeeding mothers, small children jumping on beds, and couples sharing an early morning kiss and maybe more rushed into her head, although she shut that thought down immediately. She hadn't stayed out all night for years. It would be Brownie points from her daughters when she told them about her adventures. Well, not about almost sleeping with a married man, obviously. Aside from the embarrassment, no grown-up child ever wanted to hear about their parents' sex lives.

The shudder that ran through Will's body to hers on every step was having a weird effect on her heart rhythm, which sped up by the second. Just as she got used to it, it stopped abruptly, and she found herself on her feet again and facing the sea. Being torn away from all that warmth was a shock and she shivered in the cool air. She'd dressed for a hot June evening in a flimsy dress, and now she wished she'd added a cardigan. Not quite as chic, but a lot more useful.

Will indicated the nearest table.

'I'll go in and order. What do you want?'

'Erm, cappuccino, please.'

Another shiver overtook her.

'Are you cold?'

Grace bit back a reply. Without speaking, Will took off the jumper slung round his neck, passed it to her and made for the bar.

The jumper slipped easily over her head. The sleeves came

down way past her fingers, but she pushed them back up to her elbows. The fine black wool smelt of lemons and wood, obviously some expensive aftershave. It was a bit of a cliché that all gay men smelt good and wore freshly laundered clothes, but one she was happy to go with.

It was clear the night was far from over for some people, if the noise inside the bar was anything to go by. Raucous singing in Greek was followed by shouts and cheers. Grace was happy to sit facing the port and just lose herself in the orange sky.

The sound of a tray being put down on the table was loud, too loud. Will was back.

'Were you asleep?'

'Of course not.'

'You had your eyes closed…'

'Just thinking.'

'Hmmm. Get this down you. It will keep you awake.'

Grace picked up the foaming coffee and took a long sip as Will took the seat beside her.

'Thank you. How much do I owe you?'

That smirk was back.

'I think I can afford to stand you a coffee.'

'I prefer to pay my way.'

'You can get the next one then.'

Will took a finger-shaped piece of pastry dusted with icing sugar from a plate on the tray.

'Here, try one of these. They're called bougatsa. Freshly baked next door.'

He pointed at the bakery, where all the lights were already on.

'It's a traditional Greek breakfast, filo pastry filled with a type of custard.'

For a moment, Grace thought he was going to reach over and put one in her mouth, but he left it on her saucer. She was tempted to refuse, but her growling stomach told her otherwise.

Will helped himself to one too and they bit into them at the same time. Gooey, sweet custard filled her mouth and Grace couldn't help letting out a moan.

'Fabulous, aren't they?'

Grace nodded and sat back in her chair, watching the sun rise in the sky as it turned from orange to pale pink and blue. A fishing boat was coming into port with its catch, the men shouting to each other in the cool morning air.

They sat in silence sipping their coffees and helping themselves to a couple more bougatsas each, allowing the peace of the new day to wash over them. It was a relief not to have to speak, and just be, for a few moments. There'd been precious little just being in Grace's life since Phil died. Filling the day and not thinking about missing her husband had been an art in itself at the beginning.

She was almost ashamed to admit that it had got easier in the last few months, and even easier in the weeks since she'd arrived in Greece. That in turn made her worry she was being disloyal to his memory. There weren't many people of either sex that she could sit in complete silence with and not feel the need to speak. She wouldn't have had Will down as one of them ... until tonight.

The man in question finished off his last bougatsa and turned to her.

'What did you mean when you said to Thanassis that you were going to be safe with me?'

Grace took a deep breath. He obviously had the hearing of a bat.

'Well, you know, with you being a gay man…'

The roar of laughter that greeted her words even had some of the fishermen looking their way.

It was a few moments before Will could even speak.

'Sorry. But what the hell gave you that idea?'

Grace licked the icing sugar off her fingers before speaking.

'When we talked on the beach, and discovered that we both loved *Will and Grace*, you know, the career woman and her gay best friend, you seemed so into it, that I just assumed…'

Will leant back with an amused look on his face.

'Always dangerous to assume.'

'Plus, you're so'—Grace almost said 'good-looking', but stopped herself in time—'neat and tidy all the time. Well turned out. And you smell nice. And clean.'

'Ah. You'll have to blame my years in the army for that. The self-discipline and routine stay with you. A clean body leads to a clear mind. And all the other clichés, which are actually pretty accurate as it goes.'

Grace had to look down at her empty coffee cup at his use of the words 'clean body'. She didn't want visuals of Will in the shower now she knew the truth. She'd been picked up and thrown over the shoulder of what she thought was a gay man. Her bottom had been just inches from his face and his arms had clamped her thighs to his chest. It hadn't been unpleasant, quite the opposite now she thought about it. She willed herself not to go red.

Will's brown eyes were on her again.

'Your evidence seems a little flimsy, M'Lud.'

Grace rolled her eyes.

'Can I ask, would you have had a problem with me being gay?'

'God no, don't be ridiculous. My youngest daughter's gay. Nothing like that, believe me.'

She had much more of a problem with the idea of him being straight, but she could hardly say that.

'Good. Otherwise, we couldn't be friends.'

Why was he automatically assuming she'd want to be friends with him? Admittedly, it was something that had crossed her mind too, but he'd driven her up the wall on the three occasions they'd met. She'd seen his temper at close quarters too. OK, he wasn't gay, but he could be married with six kids for all she knew. She certainly wasn't going to ask.

'But I can assure you that I am one hundred per cent, well ninety-nine per cent, heterosexual.'

'Right. Thanks for letting me know.'

Grace really had had enough of this conversation. All in all, it had been a surprising but draining twenty-four hours, and she'd been awake for nearly all of it. The walk and the coffee had sobered her up in super-quick time. She sipped the dregs of her cappuccino. It was time to go.

'Are you feeling better?'

Will's face was the picture of innocence.

'I feel fine. Thank you again for the coffee. I can make my own way from here. It's a two-minute walk.'

'Nonsense, I insist on taking you right to your door.'

Grace sighed but knew enough about the man now to know that he was serious.

'How come you're out at this ungodly hour anyway?'

'I'm a terrible sleeper. Can't help waking with the dawn. And then I like to walk. You see lots of interesting sights at that time of the morning.'

He was irritating her again. Everything he said seemed to have an edge to it.

'And how do you know Thanassis?'

'He's married to Maria, our housekeeper at the villa. Lovely woman.'

Grace's neck got even hotter. He couldn't prove she'd thought about sleeping with Thanassis, but it was like he'd read her mind.

'As you'll know, after only being here a few weeks, island life is different. Everyone knows everyone or is related in some way. It can be a bit much sometimes.'

Grace did know. What had she been thinking, contemplating sleeping with someone she worked with?

'Do you think their marriage has a chance?'

Will smiled.

'Those two are always on-off, on-off. They fight like cat and dog, and he's a terrible flirt…'

Will met her eye.

'But she always takes him back.'

Great, so she'd almost gone for it with a known womaniser. She really needed to get out of there.

Lightheaded, but surefooted, Grace made her way back to the language school with her escort in silence. She made sure her key was in the door as quickly as possible and kept her goodbye to a minimum. An extravagant bow from Will only irked her further. She'd had quite enough of him for one day, several weeks in fact.

Once in her room, Grace lay face down on the bed. Something tickled her nose, and a burst of lemon went up her nostrils. Damn, she still had his jumper on. Now he'd think she'd done it on purpose.

Chapter Eleven

Mortified wasn't the word. Horrifically embarrassed, totally ashamed and completely furious with herself were nearer the mark. Grace turned over in bed and attempted to open her eyes. Even the sliver of light coming in through the shutters was too much. She closed her eyes again and lay on her back. Her stomach was doing somersaults and her head pounded. The events of the previous evening came back to her in glorious Technicolor.

She'd virtually thrown herself at a colleague, been rescued by a smirking Will and, to top it all, informed him he was gay, when he clearly wasn't. Things couldn't get much worse. Her mind snagged on the words. It was a silly expression because she knew from personal experience that they could. Way worse. No one had died. She had to stop feeling sorry for herself.

That ouzo had a lot to answer for. Even the thought of it turned her stomach, and she was sure if she as much as smelt it again, she'd be sick on the spot. She'd had a similar experience as a teenager with Pernod, and after snogging a neighbour's son, she'd passed out in their garage, been escorted home by her unsmiling father and vowed never to touch the stuff again. The aniseed thing was obviously a theme.

But there was a big difference between being a naïve teenager and being a sixty-one-year-old woman who'd drunk herself stupid.

A long glass of water and a couple of painkillers helped her feel slightly more human. Sunday was her longed-for day off, and her mother's voice told her that she couldn't waste it lying around in bed. It was already gone two.

The town beach was still too risky, so she'd head back to the cove for an afternoon of relaxing on the beach and plenty of rehydration. The man's jumper lying crumpled on the bed took her aback for a moment. Where had that come from? Had she been a whole lot drunker than she realised? She remembered with a sigh of relief that Will had given it to her at the port. She'd taken it off sometime after dawn because it was far too hot.

She'd head for the cove. Surely Will wouldn't be there again? It was one tiny spot among thousands. At the last moment, Grace shoved the jumper into the bottom of her bag in case she saw him on her travels. She wanted to get rid of it as soon as possible.

Seated in the same chair on the beach at the cove, with a fresh orange juice in her hand, Grace was still fighting the queasy swell in her stomach. She gazed out at a passing tourist boat in the distance, ferrying people to the lesser-known beaches that were inaccessible on foot. The thought of being out on the water wasn't a pleasant one in her condition.

Instead, she focused on the swimmers much closer to shore. One man's powerful arms moved through the water in a perfect crawl. Grace was impressed with his technique, or that's what she told herself. Back and forth he went, until he changed direction and swam towards the beach.

Grace continued to watch as the man stood and walked out of the sea, navy swim shorts tight against his thighs. Her afternoon had just got a whole lot worse. The swimmer was Will. Of course, it was. She looked away, but she could tell he'd spotted her. Droplets of water on her bare legs moments later forced her to look up. He stood inches away from her, bare-chested and shaking himself like a wet dog.

'Hey, Grace.'

'Will.'

'How are you feeling this morning, or should I say afternoon?'

His hands raked though his thick dark hair as he said it, slicking it back to his head. He was at it again, making sarcastic remarks at her expense.

'I'm fine. Bit surprised to see you here though.'

'You shouldn't be. I live just up there.'

Will pointed in the direction of a row of little white cubed houses with bright blue paintwork in the traditional Cycladic style.

'Oh, I see.' He'd wrongfooted her yet again. This was his home turf, not hers. She was desperate to get into the cool sea. The temperature on the beach had rocketed all of a sudden. She stood up in the hope that he'd get the message and carry on walking.

'I'm just off for a swim.'

'Great idea. That'll wake you up.'

She was acutely aware that they were facing each other wearing just a few bits of flimsy material over their naked bodies. He didn't seem to be moving off any time soon.

Her stomach suddenly growled loud enough for the whole beach to hear.

Will smiled.

'Are you hungry?'

Her treacherous body played into his hands and gave another big growl.

Grace remembered a few mouthfuls of spinach pie around eighteen hours ago.

'I haven't eaten for a while. Why?'

Was he going to give her lecture about healthy eating?

'It's just that I've got a couple of fresh fish up at the house that I was about to grill. Do you fancy joining me after your swim?'

Grace was lost for words. This man confused her at every turn.

'I can whip up a simple salad to go with it. But if you're busy…'

'No … it's not that. I just wasn't expecting an invitation to lunch.'

'It's nothing fancy. Just a simple meal.'

'Then, thank you.'

'Take your time with your swim.'

Will pointed up at the row of houses, and Grace could see the whole of his tattoo for the first time. It was a star, with a name in the middle. But she wasn't quite close enough to see it clearly.

'It's the second house on the left. Just come up whenever you're ready.'

'Will do. Thanks again.'

'Don't get too excited. I'm OK with the basics, but that's about it.'

It was more than Phil had ever managed, but maybe she could take the rest of the day off from thinking about her husband.

———

The swim had cleared most of her headache and she rinsed the salt off in the open-air cold-water shower before changing in one of the cute metal-doored huts that also seemed to be provided on most Greek beaches, usually painted green or white. Back in her white denim shorts and pink spotted linen shirt, she was prepared, more prepared than she'd felt in a swimming costume. She had no idea what she'd find at Will's.

It was unlikely he was married, given he'd been wandering the streets of the town on his own at dawn mere hours ago, but after her experience with Thanassis, you never knew.

Will was stood on his terrace, alone and, she was relieved to see, covered up again in navy shorts and a white short-sleeved shirt. He waved as she walked up the path.

'Welcome to my humble abode.'

'Thank you for inviting me.'

The terrace was big enough for a table and chairs, plus a couple of sun loungers in a smart blue and white stripe and an enormous barbecue with a domed lid.

'Make yourself comfortable.' Will indicated the table. 'Sit

back and enjoy the spectacular view. We're all set to go. The fish is done to perfection. I'll just fetch the salad.'

Will certainly seemed to have picked up the Greek habit of bigging up the food and the views. The Greeks were justifiably proud of both, but it took a bit of getting used to. Grace much preferred it to British diffidence.

The table was set for two, and she took a seat that faced the cove and the sea beyond. It was indeed stunning. You could see for miles but were protected from both the sun and, she assumed, very rare rain by a white bamboo pergola.

Will set the traditional Greek salad, which she now knew was called horiatiki, on the table, along with a jug of some sort of sauce, and a large bottle of water.

'I'm presuming you don't want alcohol?' There was the smirk. 'I think I've got a bottle of ouzo inside somewhere.'

He had to spoil it, didn't he?

'Water's fine for me, thanks.'

Will lifted the lid of the barbecue, and the most divine smell coated the air, which caused her stomach to growl for the third time. At this stage, although she wasn't a big meat eater, the proverbial horse would be in trouble if it was anywhere nearby.

'Let's eat.'

The freshness of the fish teamed with the lemon and butter sauce was a revelation and they ate in a companionable silence as they watched people going about their business below on the beach. For the second time in twenty-four hours, Grace didn't feel the need to fill the space with words. Usually, she hated silence.

Will offered coffee and suggested they move to the sun loungers, which Grace happily agreed to.

'Thank you for a truly gorgeous meal.'

'My pleasure.'

He'd brought out a small plate of baklava for each of them, another Greek staple which Grace had become a big fan of.

'Thanks. Can I ask, do you own this place, or are you just renting?'

'I bought it ten years ago when prices were low. I came here on holiday and fell in love with the island. I needed a base of my own after years of living in rental properties or getting free accommodation with the job.' Will took a sip of his coffee. 'My wife kept the house in Britain after our divorce.'

'I see. I'm sorry your marriage didn't work out.'

'No, it's fine, honestly. It was years ago. We've been apart longer than we were together. And my marriage had been over for a long time before that. Having to leave at a moment's notice, sometimes for months on end, and not be able to say where you're going is hard on any relationship.'

She knew he'd served, and she wasn't an expert, but it all sounded a lot more full-on than the regular army.

'But don't they have married quarters?'

'Yes, for when you're based in the UK, but the type of places I was being sent to weren't anywhere you'd want your nearest and dearest to be, believe me.'

Grace's mind was whirring.

'Were you Special Forces by any chance?'

Will's eyes clouded over, and he looked up and out to sea.

Grace put up her hands. She hadn't meant to say it out loud.

'Sorry, I know you're not allowed to talk about it. It's just me being nosy.' She could only imagine the things Will had seen and taken part in over the years. 'Please carry on.'

'As I was saying, my wife was happy when we lived up in Yorkshire, close to her family. But as soon as our son Jack was born, everything changed. We were so young, and she wanted to stay where she had guaranteed support. So, we bought a house near her parents, and tried, in vain, to make it work.'

It was the most she'd ever heard him speak about himself. Grace had no real idea of his age; she thought he was a bit younger than her, maybe mid-fifties, but it was so hard to tell. A tan always helped, and he was obviously fit. Interesting that he had a grown-up son.

'But that's enough about me. What about you? What are you doing over here?'

'I've taken a summer job at the language school in town, teaching English.'

'Ah, I thought you might be a teacher when I saw you with Thanassis.'

Grace bit into her baklava rather too fiercely, causing honey and nuts to ooze out of the sides. She didn't want to be reminded of last night. Will's eyes were on her as she licked the honey from her fingers.

'And have you left anyone behind at home in Britain?'

'Just two grown-up daughters. Well, one lives in Australia.'

'You don't look old enough to have grown-up daughters.'

'Well, I started early too…'

What was she saying? Although it was true, she was making herself sound like a child bride.

'So, you're divorced, like me?'

'Not exactly.' Grace took a deep breath. There'd been enough misunderstandings. 'I'm a widow.'

'Ah, sorry to hear that. How long?'

'Nearly three years. It was prostate cancer, caught too late…'

Grace's voice broke and she bit her lip to stop herself from crying. He was the first person she'd told since she arrived. They desperately needed a change of conversation. She didn't want to break down in front of a virtual stranger. A good-looking stranger who could cook, but a stranger nevertheless.

Most new people she told the truth to stopped talking immediately or made some excuse to get away from her as soon as possible. Only those who'd been through it themselves were willing to go further, and she really had no desire to sit in a room full of widows talking about their dead husbands for hours on end. She was sure it was useful for some people, but it wouldn't work for her.

Will eased back into his sun lounger.

'Did you know that next month is the fifty-fifth anniversary of the moon landing – July the twentieth, nineteen sixty-nine?'

Thank goodness he'd got the hint. A bit random, but it would do.

'It's a very special date for me because it's also my birthday.'

'Do you mean it's the day you were born?'

That would make him almost fifty-five.

'No, I was already a very excited five-year-old. I had a party and then my parents let me stay up to watch the main event the next evening as it was a Sunday. I can remember Neil Armstrong stepping out onto the moon surface, clear as day.'

So, he was about to be sixty. Only a little younger than her then.

'It was in black and white, of course. We had a tiny television, and there were five us crowding round, me, my two older brothers, my mum and, unusually, my dad, who was home on leave, which made it even more special. I didn't get to see a lot of my dad. It was one of the best days of my life so far.'

'It's the most watched television event of all time, isn't it?'

'I believe so. You're obviously far too young to have caught it?'

His question wasn't as innocent it seemed.

'Is that a roundabout way of asking me how old I am?'

Will smiled. 'Busted.'

Grace debated a moment. In the past she'd just kept vague about her age, thinking it was no one's business but hers. If you told some people that you were over sixty, especially if you weren't meeting them in person, they immediately formed an image of you in their minds. Age was just a number, but the preconceptions had a lot to do with how the previous generation had behaved or been treated.

She remembered a party for her own father's fortieth birthday, which was full of jokes about getting old. One of his presents was a bottle of the iron supplement Phyllosan, with guests singing the accompanying jingle, 'Phyllosan fortifies the over-forties.' It had made her worry that her father wasn't going to last long.

These days, thankfully, forty was still considered young. And sixty-plus wasn't old either. It was perfectly possible to be fit and current. She was irritated by some of her friends, or more accurately acquaintances, who seemed determined to throw themselves headlong into old age. No meeting up in the evenings, lunchtimes only, no driving at night, hair chopped into a uniform bob. And if anyone sent her another grey-haired-old-lady emoji to explain away something they'd forgotten to do, she'd scream. Her real friends still had jobs and full social lives, and, if they were retired, were off travelling the world.

When she opened her eyes, Will was staring at her. She'd told him she was a widow, so she might as well go the whole way. What did it matter?

'No, I didn't stay up to watch it, as my parents were two of the few people in the world who weren't that interested. But I will admit that I was six at the time, which as I'm sure you can work out, makes me sixty-one.'

Will let out a low whistle.

'I really wasn't expecting that. I thought you were early fifties at most.'

'You wouldn't if you'd seen me when I woke up this morning. Makeup everywhere and hair sticking up like a bog brush.'

Why was she giving him mental images of her in bed and bringing toilets into it?

'Okaay. If you say so.'

'And I'd really appreciate it if you didn't mention my age or the fact that I'm a widow to anyone else. Particularly Thanassis, as I don't want it getting back to the other teachers. I'm not keen on people knowing too much about me.'

'I'm with you there.'

'Which reminds me.' Grace reached for her bag. 'I've got

your jumper in here.' She handed it over. 'I could wash it if you like. There is a washing machine at the language school, but there's limited drying space. It looks quite expensive; it probably needs hand washing.'

'No, it's fine. Another thing I learnt in the army. How to wash my own clothes. And I'm sure it's not so dirty that it needs washing after being next to your skin for just a couple of hours.'

Why was he talking about her skin?

Will put the jumper under his sunlounger with a smile.

'Were you hoping to bump into me again? Is that why you had it in your bag?'

Arrogant git.

'No, not at all. I just shoved it in there on the off chance.'

'Well, thank you for returning it.'

'No problem.'

Grace gathered her things together.

'I'd better be getting back. I have a weekly chat with my youngest daughter every Sunday evening at the same time, and she doesn't like it if I miss it.' She turned to Will. 'Do you speak to your son often?'

His eyes clouded over again, and Grace wished she could take the words back. There was a fine line between nosiness and genuine interest, and she'd been known to fall off the balance beam a few times.

'Not really.'

'OK, sorry to bring it up.'

Will sighed.

'No, you've been honest with me. We have a difficult relationship. His mother blamed me for us splitting up, and she poured all her anger and frustration into Jack. It's got better as time's gone on, once he understood that there's more than one side to every story. My wife got together with a guy from the village after we split, and they went on to have two little girls. I stayed out of the picture completely. I thought it was best to let them get on with it at the time.'

'That's so sad, for you and for Jack.'

Grace couldn't imagine Phil not having been involved with the girls on a day-to-day basis as they grew up. With both of them being teachers, they'd spent the long summer holidays travelling across Europe in a battered Volkswagen camper van, stopping wherever the fancy took them, swimming in rivers and lakes, before eventually making it to the coast of whatever Mediterranean country they'd chosen and parking right on the beach. She was grateful for those memories now. There wouldn't be any more.

'Don't get me wrong. I'm not saying I was blameless. I did make mistakes, but letting my ex-wife effectively isolate me from my son is probably my biggest. We're working on it, but we've still got a way to go.'

'I really hope you work it out.'

Will shrugged.

'So do I. But at our age, we've all got a bit of baggage, haven't we?'

She'd opened the wound, so she might as well ask one more question before she tried to stitch it closed it again.

'And did you never meet anyone else?'

Will raised his eyebrows.

'Well, I'm not pretending I've been a monk since my divorce. That would make me a little odd.'

The look in his eyes could have melted snow.

She wasn't asking for a list of his sexual conquests, if that's what he was thinking.

'I've had my moments, and one or two long-term relationships. But I've not met anyone I could live with, or even fall properly in love with, since. I'm probably too used to being on my own.'

'Yes, probably.'

Grace got up from the sun lounger and stretched her legs.

'Lovely as this has been, I really do need to go.'

'Understood.'

'Thank you again.'

'No problem. It got a bit deep there, didn't it?'

She wasn't quite sure which bit of the conversation he was referring to, but she'd opened up to Will more than to any of her new colleagues. It helped that they were a similar age and had shared memories of world events. She often wondered what Sofia and her toyboys talked about, but talking was probably at the bottom of the list.

Just as she got to the path, she heard him shout something.

'Sorry?'

Grace retraced her steps.

'Do you like films?'

Was that why he'd stopped her from leaving? Who didn't like films?

'Err, yes, why?'

'There's a fantastic open-air cinema in the town. Serves snacks and everything. Would you be up for going sometime?'

She'd seen it advertised online. It looked a lot more interesting than your local Odeon.

Now she'd been here a month, and the work side of things was under control, she'd started to feel a little lonely in the evenings. She wasn't looking for a romantic relationship, and neither, it appeared, was Will, so the pressure was off.

'Yeah, why not.'

'OK, let's swap numbers, and see if we can agree on a film.'

That would probably be a trial in itself. She hoped he wasn't into high octane action films featuring his army buddy types, or, even worse, horror movies.

'Have you got your phone handy?'

Will lifted it into the air.

'I'll read my number out, and you WhatsApp me later, so I've got yours.'

'Yes, madam.'

When she finally got back to her room, Grace fell asleep as soon as she'd chatted with Flo.

She tried to keep herself awake, as she knew she wouldn't get through a whole night if she slept now. It reminded her of when the girls were toddlers and she'd been desperate to keep them going during the afternoons, so they wouldn't be up half the night.

But after all that swimming, eating and walking, her eyelids kept closing. She stopped fighting it.

When she woke, it was just after five in the morning, and she could see a faint glow in the sky. There was no going back to sleep now. She didn't want to wake the others by wrenching open the shutters. The teachers' rooms were next to each other in a line, with hers at one end, Rose and Daniel's in the middle and Anna's at the far end, next to the stairs. Charlie lived at the back of the town somewhere with his girlfriend. They all had work in the morning, and they deserved to sleep on.

She could slip out and go for a walk, or down to the port for a coffee, to the place she'd been with Will. Grace dressed quickly and opened her door very carefully. A figure at the end of the corridor was doing the same thing. Instinctively, Grace pulled her door almost closed again. She strained her eyes in the gloom, closed them in astonishment and looked again. There was no mistake. It was her boss, Giannis, giving Anna a lingering kiss goodbye in the doorway before he crept down the stairs.

Chapter Twelve

G race stood on the doorstep of a grand house with the most amazing views out over the bay. To the left of the port and up the hill, it was in the middle of a terrace of similar beauties, painted in rusts, blues and creams. Nothing below but rocks and sea. It was a hard climb, and Grace took a moment to catch her breath before she reached for the impressive brass knocker in the shape of a fish.

She'd tried hard to banish the vision of Giannis coming out of Anna's room. Combined with what she'd seen at the restaurant, she had no doubt that they were having an affair. She was always surprised when people blamed the woman in these circumstances. Anna was young and single, and maybe behaving unwisely, but it was Giannis who needed to shoulder the burden of responsibility. He was the one who was married with a family. He should know better. She'd been barely able to look at him since finding out, although luckily he'd been away for most of the week, and she hadn't had to. He definitely hadn't spotted her the other morning, that was one thing she was sure of.

The situation explained the pain that Grace saw in Elena's eyes whenever she caught a glimpse of her coming out of her office or driving around town in her open-top Mercedes. Today Grace was having coffee with the woman to talk about teaching her children. A noise behind the door told her that someone was coming. It probably took hours to get to the front door, the house was so big.

The door creaked open to reveal a middle-aged woman in a smart black dress.

'Mrs Foreman?'

'Yes.'

'Mrs Kokkinakis is waiting for you downstairs on the terrace. Can I show you the way?'

So, Elena didn't even open her own front door. Grace found it hard to believe that language schools made this much money.

She looked about her in wonder as she followed the woman down two flights of stairs. The house was definitely magazine-worthy. The walls were plastered in a pale terracotta, with ornate mirrors and chandeliers every few feet, and soft wool runners in jewelled colours underfoot.

Most of the doors they passed were closed, but one was partly open, and Grace glimpsed an enormous marble fireplace with a spectacular gold mirror above, dark blue walls and deep green velvet sofas and chairs arranged in a semi-circle. What looked like antique furniture, gleaming occasional tables and a bureau were arranged against the wall either side of the fireplace. Presumably she'd hit on the living room, or sitting room as it would be called in more refined circles.

At last they came to the biggest kitchen Grace had ever seen, boasting pale blue wooden units with brass handles, and marble worktops veined in gold. She had to stop herself from stroking the stone as she went past. It must have taken an army to even get it down here, or maybe it came in by sea.

To one side was a dining table, in the same veined marble as the worktop, which could easily seat twelve, and chairs in the same shade as the units. Grace wondered if the children were ever allowed to eat there. It all looked pristine.

Beyond the kitchen was a partly covered terrace at sea level, a vast stone stage littered with more sofas and chairs in pastel linens, as well as small tables with umbrellas and metal chairs in the sun. And beyond that, just the blue of the sea, stretching as far as the horizon.

From the covered part of the terrace, Elena rose from one of the sofas to greet her.

'Grace, welcome.'

'It's a pleasure to be here. What a truly stunning home you have.'

Elena indicated for her to sit down out of the sun.

'Thank you. It has been in my family since it was built and passed down the generations.'

Ah, so Grace had her answer. Family money.

'I was born here. And apart from my time at university in Athens, I have always lived here. When I married Giannis, we did a big renovation, but kept all the original features.'

Grace couldn't help but compare it to Will's much more modest house above the cove. She hadn't got as far as looking inside, but it was a lot more manageable. In this house, you'd be frightened of breaking something. She had a couple of wealthy friends, and some with virtually no money, but she preferred being somewhere in the middle.

The housekeeper was still hovering behind her mistress, waiting for instructions.

'Grace, would you like coffee?'

'Yes, please. Is some sort of cappuccino possible?'

'Yes, of course. We have everything you could want. Just an espresso for me, Anastasia.'

'Yes, madam.'

Anastasia bustled off, and Grace couldn't help but take another look at the view.

Elena got up and walked towards the edge of the terrace.

'Come and see.'

Grace dutifully followed.

'We have our own swimming platform here, with metal ladders leading down into the water, as well as a mooring for our boat. Giannis is out on the boat today, entertaining clients, which is why I thought it would be a good time to talk about the children.'

Grace nodded and inspected the mooring as instructed. With lessons over for the day, she could only hope that he wasn't entertaining Anna as well.

Beneath the expert heavy makeup, Grace could still spot the dark circles under Elena's eyes. This woman wasn't sleeping. Plus, she'd lost weight since their in-person interview back in the spring in London. Grace remembered thinking it slightly strange at the time that Elena's first reaction to her had been relief.

Grace had deliberately dressed down on that day in a severe navy suit and flat shoes, with her hair tied back and minimal makeup. It had been her first interview for a very long time, and she'd thought that dour traffic-warden vibes were the way to go.

But it was all starting to make sense. It looked like Giannis had form, and Elena knew she'd be safe with Grace. But she was loving the job, and her time in Greece, so why her rather than someone else still didn't matter. She couldn't believe that Elena had agreed to employ a bombshell like Anna though, if that was the way the wind was blowing, but maybe it hadn't been her choice.

Anastasia returned with a tray of coffee and a plate piled high with mini pastries.

'Shall I pour, madam?'

Elena waved a hand in the housekeeper's direction.

'No, we're fine, thank you.'

Her boss's hand shook as she passed the cup to Grace.

'Please … help yourself.' Elena indicated the pastries. 'They're all homemade.'

Not by you, I'll bet, thought Grace, before choosing a bougatsa and what she hoped was a mini chocolate croissant.

She'd learnt that to refuse food from a Greek was tantamount to offending them. It was an expression of being welcome in their home, and even a simple coffee had to be accompanied by a little something.

Grace noticed that Elena didn't eat anything herself. It was more important that you, the guest, ate. It wasn't great for the waistline. She'd have to think about upping her exercise regime.

129

Coffee over, Elena buzzed some sort of intercom connected to the terrace.

'Anastasia, could you bring the children in now, please.'

'Of course, madam,' was easily audible.

'I wanted you to meet them before you started the lessons,' said Elena. 'They go to a private school in the town in term time, and they have a tutor here in the afternoons. Obviously, they couldn't attend our own language school, as it would be awkward for everyone, pupils and teachers alike.'

Her boss was probably right. Grace and her husband had avoided working at any of the schools their girls attended, and her long stint as a deputy head had been at a school in the next town. Plus, you never wanted to bump into parents when you'd had a few down the local pub. Not that she could imagine that was a problem Elena would ever have.

'But in August, although the school is shut, we'll be staying put and enjoying the island this year, so I'd like the children to take lessons from you to keep improving their English – in the mornings, as discussed.'

'Of course.'

The light came back into Elena's eyes as three immaculately dressed, dark-haired children, two girls and a boy, filed into the room one by one, in height order, like something from *The Sound of Music*.

'Say hello, children.'

'Pleased to meet you, Mrs Foreman.'

'And it's lovely to meet you. Please tell me, in English, your names, your ages and what you most like doing.'

The tallest girl stepped forward.

'I'm Athena. I'm ten years old. I love maths, painting and drawing.'

The boy was pushed forward by his big sister.

'I'm Vasilis. I'm seven and I like fighting.'

'Vasilis! What a thing to say.' But there was still a smile on Elena's face. Grace had heard a lot about Greek mothers and sons. They certainly seemed to get away with a bit more than their sisters.

A scared face peeped round her sister's legs.

'Go on, Katty, your turn.' Elena took her youngest daughter by the hand and brought her over to Grace.

The little girl reminded Grace a lot of Flo when she was young. Obviously shy, she spoke in a near whisper.

'I'm Katerina, I'm six, and I like … butterflies and flowers.'

'Well, Katerina, I like butterflies and flowers too.'

Grace was rewarded with a smile.

'I'm so excited about coming to spend time with you all. We're going to have a lot of fun.'

Meeting the children made her even angrier with Giannis. It was none of her business really, not that that always stopped her. But how dare he risk their futures for a silly fling?

'OK, children, say goodbye to Mrs Foreman.'

'Bye, Mrs Foreman.'

'Goodbye. I'll see you soon.'

Elena stood up and Grace noticed Anastasia waiting in the gloom of the kitchen.

'If you get into your swimming costumes, I'll take you down to the beach.'

'Yay!'

'And Anastasia, could you please show Mrs Foreman out.'

Is that all the woman did all day, show people in and out of the house and make coffee?

'I'll see you back at the language school, Grace.'

'Of course.'

Out of the house and back on the pavement, Grace took a couple of deep breaths. Having tons of money wasn't all it was cracked up to be sometimes. It certainly wasn't making Elena Kokkinakis happy.

She switched her phone back on and saw there'd been a message from Will.

> Film tonight? New programme. Psychological thriller. Mixed reviews.

He certainly wasn't a big texter.

> Why not?

> That a yes?

> Yes, ok.

> Don't get too excited. I'll get tickets and you buy the gyros. Meet me at Tony's, directly opposite the cinema at 8?

> Deal.

Grace debated whether to add a kiss as she usually did at the end of her messages but decided to leave it.

Grace arrived in the square with five minutes to go, but Will was already waiting. He pointed at a spare table under a tree.

'Quick, grab it. Tables here are like gold dust. I'll go and order at the bar.'

Grace raised a hand.

'Hello usually works for me.'

'Amusing.'

She did as she was told and sat down at the table just a couple of seconds before another couple, who tutted and carried on walking. It was then she realised that he hadn't actually asked her what she wanted. She hated men who did that, ordered for a woman. And what was so special about this place anyway? There were tons of gyros bars on the island.

Will sat down with a glistening bottle of Mythos beer in each hand and put one in front of her with a glass.

'I presume you like Mythos.'

'And what if I don't?'

Will smiled.

'I'll drink both of them.'

'As it happens, I do.' Grace poured herself a glass and took a long draught. 'But you never asked me what I wanted.'

'Sorry, no time. Anyway, you can't come to Tony's and not have the pork gyros with all the trimmings. It's what they're famous for.'

'And what's so special about this kebab?'

'Wash your mouth out, young lady. Don't let the Greeks hear you say kebab. That's a Turkish word, or more accurately an Arabic word, and you know how the Greeks feel about the Turks.'

Grace had noticed some animosity from even the most

level-headed Greeks towards the Turks. It seemed that every country needed another country to pick on.

'The Greek word gyros comes from gyro, which means turn or revolution, a reference to the way the meat is cooked on a spit and sliced off.'

'Yes, just like a kebab.'

She hadn't come here for a linguistics lesson; she'd had enough of teaching for one day. Will could come across as a bit of a know-it-all at times.

He raised his glass to hers.

'*Yamas!* Settle in because there'll be a bit of a wait.'

'*Yamas!* This had better be worth it.'

Will shot her a wink.

'You'll see.'

Grace sat back with her beer, but the situation with Giannis and Elena wouldn't let her relax. She might as well do some research.

'So, what are your employers like?'

Will put down his beer.

'Where's that come from?'

'Just interested. And because I've got a problem with mine.'

'Mine are great. A Greek–American family that I've been with for ten years, ever since I stopped being a personal bodyguard.'

Visions of Kevin Costner carrying Whitney Houston in his arms to safety raced through her mind. She'd have to find out a bit more about that later, but it wouldn't help her with her current problem.

'I'm now head of security at their villa, in charge of a small team. Of course, you've been there, or the gardens at any rate, haven't you?'

Grace ignored the dig.

'It sounds like a good place to work. No problems between them as a couple?'

'Err, no. They get on well with each other and don't mistreat their kids. What is this about?'

'Can I ask your advice?'

'Sure.'

'If you knew something about one of them that would hurt the other one, but you felt it was something they ought to know, would you tell?'

Will raised both hands.

'Things are never black and white, but if you want my opinion, leave well alone. No one will thank you for it. Don't shoot the messenger and all that.'

She could have betted that's what he'd say. It was what Phil would have said if he was alive. It was the male answer to most things. Don't get involved.

'And if they're wealthy, I'd be even more careful. The rich play by their own rules. You don't want to get caught in the crossfire.'

'Oh, look, I think our food is coming.'

Two plates with parcels wrapped in brown paper and a separate bowl of fries arrived on the table. Will grabbed one of the chips and put it in his mouth.

'Fantastic! The fries are hand-cooked, you know, using their own potatoes that they grow here on the island.'

Was she going to be allowed to have an opinion? Did they

make their own paper by hand round the back to wrap the gyros in as well?

Grace bit through a layer of toasted pitta bread and took a mouthful of the soft pork, along with some tzatziki – yoghurt shot through with cucumber and herbs – as well as onion and fresh tomato. The combination exploded in her mouth. Will might be a know-it-all, but he certainly knew where to get a decent gyro. Grace added some chips to the next mouthful and the taste was even better.

'I have to admit, this is sensational. That's one-nil to you.'

He needn't look quite so smug.

Settled with more beers and some popcorn in the outdoor cinema, Grace looked around her. It certainly was one step up from a typical British cinema, where you were crammed indoors together with giggling teenagers and elderly people unwrapping sweets.

The huge screen was set against a backdrop of old buildings several storeys high, with lights coming on and off in some of the windows. Black metal chairs were laid out in rows in a walled garden where climbing plants produced flashes of red and pink. On either side of the rows of chairs was a series of brick-built nooks meant for couples, with just enough room for two to squeeze in together.

She and Will had swerved those and opted for two chairs in a row halfway down. The air was warm, and the sound of people talking and laughing on the other side of the walls made it feel cosy. Twenty minutes in, she knew the film wasn't for her. Although it featured a big Hollywood actor that she'd been quite keen on years ago, he hadn't aged well, and the script was tortuous. The dialogue was so stilted it was hard to empathise with any of the characters.

Each time Hollywood Guy felt moody, he'd go down to the beach and play the flute, badly, for some reason. She presumed it replaced the need for actual acting. The first time he did it, she just found it bizarre, but the second and third times made her want to giggle. The fourth sight of him gazing out to sea while trying to hold a tune had her pinching her hand to stop herself from laughing.

She stole a glance at Will. It wasn't completely dark; the exit signs gave enough light to see that his shoulders were shaking. That started her off too, and she had to cover a snort with a cough.

Will pointed with his thumb towards the exit and she nodded. Crouching low, they made their way out of the cinema and down the steps to the square, before they both let rip, letting the laughter pour out. Grace had tears running down her face as she held onto her knees.

'God, that was truly terrible, wasn't it?'

Will was still bent double.

'Stop it. I can't breathe. I haven't laughed like that in years.'

'It's certainly one-all now after that. You won't be allowed to choose another film, that's for sure.'

Will saluted from his new position, before managing to stand up straight.

'Agreed.'

He took another deep breath.

'Quick drink?'

'No more alcohol, thanks. I've got work in the morning.'

'Me too, let's make it a coffee in the port and then I can escort you home.'

'There's really no need. I can look after myself.'

'I don't doubt it. But I arranged the worst cinema outing ever, so it's only fair I see you back.'

'OK, you win.'

They set off towards the port, passing through the marble-lined streets at a lick. Grace matched him stride for stride despite their difference in height. Will seemed surprised. But she supposed she couldn't blame him. The last time they'd walked down to the port together, she'd been over his shoulder like a sack of potatoes. She didn't want to be reminded of that night, so she upped her pace even more. Will was the one who stopped for a breather first.

'Slow down a sec. Are you a hiker by any chance?'

'I am. I walk everywhere at home in Oxfordshire, and I love to go for a good old yomp at the weekends.'

Will smiled. 'Yomp's a great word, isn't it?'

Was he taking the mickey?

'But seriously, hiking's a great way to see the bones of a country.'

'If I recall, you like to roam the island at weird times of the day and night, don't you?'

He'd made a few references to that night, and her near disaster with Thanassis, so let's see how he liked it.

'I don't start at dawn every day, honest. That's only for special occasions. But I do like to get going early.' Will paused a moment. 'Do you fancy hiking up into the hills with me on

Sunday? Usually I go alone, but it would be fun to do it with someone else.'

He made it sound like she could be anyone he happened to fall over in the street. But she'd wanted to see what was beyond the old town, right out on the tip of the island, for a while. She was well over halfway through her contract at the language school already and it would be a shame to leave without seeing every inch of the place that she currently called home.

'Yes, I'm in.'

'OK, we need to leave early, as we're moving into the hottest part of summer. It's too far to walk all the way, if we're going to get to the best views. So I'll pick you up at eight, and we'll take it from there. I'll bring a packed lunch, to make up for the film.'

Grace couldn't recall there being a car parked anywhere near his house, but maybe he had a spot round the back.

'You're on.'

At least she'd stopped thinking about Giannis and Elena for a couple of hours.

Chapter Thirteen

Another week of teaching was coming to a close. Grace had just waved goodbye to the eight- and nine-year-olds she'd been with all morning. A talk on the weather had led to questions about where rainbows came from, which had got a bit technical for her liking. But an exercise to write a sentence using one of the colours of the rainbow had proved a big success and quietened everyone down.

Stelios's mother, Konstantina, had brought his new dog, Mikey, a Maltese crossbreed, to meet her son from class, which had sent everyone crazy.

While they were fussing over the white ball of fluff, Grace had managed to ask about the boy's grandfather. She couldn't really ask Stelios anything in class. She didn't want to make him cry in front of the others, and he seemed to be making such progress, joining in regularly and venturing his own opinions.

'My father died at the weekend...' The woman was obviously doing her best to hold it together. Grace didn't want to push her, but she needed to know the basics for her pupil's sake in case it impacted on anything the kids were learning.

'I'm so sorry to hear that.'

Plus, she'd grown quite fond of the little boy. Boys were in short supply in her family. She had one sister, Angela, who also had two daughters, like her. They were all up in Scotland, and she didn't see anything like as much of them as she wanted to.

She squeezed Konstantina's hand as the woman tried to say more.

'And the funeral was on Wednesday. We like to bury our dead quickly here. He had a good life, and he was ready to go.'

Grace thought it was a much better system than letting people lie around in cold storage for weeks. She hadn't wanted to see Phil's body again after he died. As soon as the light had gone out of his eyes, he wasn't Phil anymore for her. Like Konstantina's father, he'd had a good life, as far as it went, but it had gone far too soon, and he hadn't been at all ready to go. Fifty-eight was no age. She wasn't religious as such, but she did believe that Phil's spirit had gone off somewhere else. Hopefully somewhere lovely.

Konstantina was waiting for her to say something.

'It's still hard, isn't it, however old they are?'

The woman nodded in agreement.

'In forty days, we will have his memorial, where we gather together and celebrate his life.'

'That sounds like a lovely idea.'

Grace reached forward and hugged the woman hard.

When Phil had died, she'd wanted people to acknowledge what had happened. One neighbour had crossed the road to avoid her rather than have to talk about Phil's death. For her, physical touch was an important part of showing you cared, and the Greeks were big huggers. She was sure her hug wouldn't offend Konstantina.

They embraced for a few moments, and when they parted, the younger woman's eyes were full of tears again.

'Thank you.'

Konstantina pointed at Mikey.

'That dog has brought a lot of love into our lives, particularly Stelios's. We wouldn't be without him now. So, thank you again.'

'No problem. Look after yourselves.'

Charlie appeared in the hallway just as Grace was locking up her classroom.

'All right, Grace? You look a bit mizzy.'

'Just tired, Charlie.'

The conversation with Konstantina had shaken her. The third anniversary of Phil's death was coming up in a few weeks. It was only a date, but, as Grace knew, however much you told yourself that, it still had the power to wound deeply. You couldn't stop the memories coming.

'Well, don't overdo it. I'm off home for lunch with Sarah. You're welcome to join us.'

'Not today, but thanks anyway.'

Sarah was Charlie's girlfriend, a model, who featured in the promotional material for the language school, which was how they'd met several years ago. If people thought all the teachers were that attractive, they'd be in for a bit of a shock. Sarah occasionally came to the building to pick her boyfriend up. Though she was outwardly scary, Grace had discovered that Sarah was a pussycat, who suited Charlie down to the ground.

Grace had taken to going for long coffees and the occasional lunch with Charlie once a week to talk teaching methods. He'd asked her to give him tips on how to make the lessons more fun for all age groups. He really wanted to expand his knowledge and possibly open his own school at some point in the future. She had a lot of time for the man.

He'd reciprocated by insisting that for fifteen minutes at the end of each session, as a thank-you, he taught her the basics of DJing, after she'd expressed such an interest in his part-time job.

Grace could now speak with authority on beatmatching, mixing, phrasing and scratching, something she wouldn't have believed possible a couple of months ago. She'd even been round to his flat a couple of times and had a little go herself on his decks.

Most of his gigs were at eighties nights, and they'd managed to put together a set of Grace's favourite soul music from the decade. When she was ready, he was planning to let her have a turn live on stage, a prospect that made her feel sick. They'd kept it a secret from everyone except Sarah. Her daughters would be flabbergasted, not that they'd use that word, but it was the astonishment on Will's face she'd enjoy seeing the most.

Charlie broke into a grin at the beep of a car horn.

'Don't forget we've got a session tomorrow. It won't be long now before you're up there on stage.'

'Mmmm. Maybe. See you later.'

Grace began the long walk up the stairs to her room, and the Greek salad she'd got in the fridge.

On the turn of the first stair, a sound stopped her in her tracks. It was unmistakably a woman crying.

As far as she knew, everyone had left the building. She'd seen the other teachers walk out together. They'd been informed that Giannis would be away all week on business. She glanced out of the window on the stairwell. Elena's Mercedes was still in the car park.

Her gentle knock on the door was answered with a muffled 'Come in'.

Elena's dark head was bent over the desk.

'Is everything OK?'

Her red-rimmed eyes told Grace that this was very much not the case.

Will's warning about not getting involved ran through her head, but Grace wasn't just going to leave the poor woman there alone.

'Can I take you out for a coffee? Maybe down by the port where it's quiet. We don't have to talk about anything if you don't want to. We can just watch the boats.'

Elena hesitated before nodding agreement.

Taking her by the arm as if she was an invalid, Grace steered Elena to a café at the end of the port wall. There was no one sitting outside, so she grabbed a table with an umbrella.

'Espresso, right?'

Elena nodded.

'And I'm guessing you haven't eaten this morning?'

Elena shook her head.

'OK.'

Grace went inside the café to order, so the waiter wouldn't keep coming out and disturbing them. A row of croque-monsieurs behind the glass counter caught her eye. They'd only need heating up. Plenty of stodge and cheese would be good for Elena, and Grace hadn't had lunch herself.

After a couple of mouthfuls of the toasted sandwich and half a cup of coffee, Elena looked a tiny bit less pale.

'Is that helping?'

'Yes, thank you, Grace. I'm sorry. This is so unprofessional of me.'

Grace stroked the younger woman's arm.

'Don't worry. Just try and eat.'

A few mouthfuls more, and Elena was finished. Grace had long since demolished hers, but Elena pushed the plate away as if horrified with herself for eating such rubbish.

'Thank you.'

Grace waited for Elena to make the first move.

'Can I speak to you in confidence? I've got to talk to someone, or I will go crazy.'

'Of course.'

'Do you promise not to say anything to anyone?'

'I promise.'

Elena's tears were falling again, and Grace passed her a paper serviette. Whatever her boss had to say had to be said. It was like lancing a boil. A horrible image, but accurate.

'I think my husband is having an affair.'

So, she'd been right. This is what it was all about. She needed to tread carefully.

'Why do you think that?'

'All the little things that a wife notices. Mysterious absences, keeping his phone close to him at all times, not being affectionate, and, once, the smell of a perfume that I know is not mine.'

'Are you sure about this?'

Elena looked down at the table.

'It has happened before… Only once, but it nearly broke me. It's the same thing all over again. I don't think I can cope this time.'

'Have you tried to speak to him about it?'

The despair in her eyes tore at Grace's heart.

'He says that I am mad, paranoid, crazy…'

Does he now? 'Bloody liar' were the words that came into Grace's mind.

'He says that because he made a mistake once, I am unfairly accusing him. He has mended his ways and he would never do it to me again.'

Grace's anger was growing with every word Elena uttered.

'I cannot sleep, I cannot eat… He has got me wondering if I am indeed mad.'

'You're not mad, Elena. You're as sane as the next person. You are stressed and sleep-deprived, but there's nothing crazy about you.'

A tiny smile was Grace's reward.

'If he was, and I say was, having an affair, do you have any idea who it might be with?'

Elena sat back in her chair.

'I'm not certain, but if I had to pick someone, I would say Anna is his type.'

Now she looked at Elena carefully, Grace could see the similarities between the two women. Elena was stunning, but Anna had twenty years on her boss, and, more importantly, wasn't weighed down with the responsibilities of children and a business to run.

So, Giannis had found himself a carefree lookalike with plenty of free time instead.

Grace had to force herself not to speak. She was so close to blurting out the truth.

Elena stopped her silent weeping and wiped her eyes.

'Nobody knows this, not even Giannis, but I am pregnant, with a child that we have longed for. I had a miscarriage last year, and we've been trying ever since for a fourth baby. Now I have to keep such a secret from my husband, as I do not know what the future is for my unborn child, or myself.'

'Oh, Elena. How awful for you.'

'I keep worrying that the stress of trying for a baby has driven him over the edge. But maybe he is right … and it's me who's been driven over the edge.'

The red mist descended, and Grace knew she couldn't stop what was about to happen. Giannis was a selfish pig who deserved everything he got if he was prepared to treat his wife like this.

She grabbed Elena's hands.

'Listen to me, Elena. You are most definitely not going mad. I know for a fact that Giannis is having an affair with Anna, as I caught him coming out of her bedroom this week in the early hours of the morning.'

Chapter Fourteen

The words hung in the air between them. She'd done it now; there was no going back. Elena's hands dropped from Grace's and back onto the table as if she'd touched fire. The frozen expression on her face scared Grace. This woman had a life growing inside her that she needed to look after, as well as three children who depended on her.

'I'm so sorry to be the one to tell you. But I thought that you should know. It's not right that you should be made to think that you're going mad.'

Elena seemed incapable of speech.

Grace got her phone out of her bag.

'This is a lot to take in at once. Let me order a taxi to take you home. Anastasia is there? Yes?'

After a few moments' delay Elena nodded.

'I'll come with you and explain that you're ill. You can leave your car at the school and collect it later. But I think you need an afternoon in bed.'

The plan to get Elena home was easy. What came afterwards was going to be far more complicated.

While they waited for the taxi, Grace coaxed Elena to drink a glass of water from the carafe on the table.

'You don't need to make any decisions in a hurry. Just focus on yourself and your health for the time being. You're a strong, capable woman, and you will do what is best for you and your children.'

Grace wasn't sure exactly what that would be, but she'd probably done enough suggesting for now. She'd opened this can of worms, or helped Elena to face the facts, as she liked to see it.

Elena was independently wealthy, and she could easily start over again without Giannis. Separating the business was more of an issue. Grace stopped herself racing ahead. That really wasn't anything to do with her.

The taxi drew up, and Grace helped Elena in, putting gentle pressure on her head to get her to sit down, and then reached over to do up her seatbelt, like a child.

On the short journey back to the house, Elena remained silent. Grace paid the driver and helped the younger woman up the stairs.

Anastasia opened the door before she had a chance to knock. She'd obviously been peering out of the window.

Grace handed her charge over.

'Mrs Kokkinakis doesn't feel well. I think it may be a migraine.'

The housekeeper helped her employer inside and shut the door in Grace's face. She was very obviously surplus to requirements.

After a restless night and very little sleep, Grace was looking forward to a peaceful afternoon on her balcony and maybe a stroll through town. She'd woken several times before dawn and couldn't help wondering what was happening at the house up the hill. She hoped that Elena had got some rest, at least. As far as she knew, Giannis wasn't back until the following day, so hopefully Elena had the opportunity to do some serious thinking before she had to face her husband. Grace knew exactly what she herself would be doing – kicking his sorry arse into touch – but it wasn't her decision to make.

Before she could even think about grabbing some downtime, she had her Saturday morning class to deal with. The kids were in a lively mood, and she'd had to split them into small groups to get any work done. There were only two weeks to go before the August shutdown, and there was a demob-happy scent in the air. She'd planned a lesson on holidays which would lead naturally into talking about other countries and their languages.

She'd already had to tell off two ten-year-old boys for flicking rolled-up balls of paper at one of the girls, and the girl in question for screaming. She was glad when the lesson came to an end.

All the parents were familiar faces to her by now and one by one they started to leave the playground with their children. Grace became aware of someone standing behind her. She glanced round to see Giannis, no longer looking like an affable Danny Dyer, more like a furious Phil Mitchell.

He spoke under his breath, so quietly that only she could hear.

'How dare you interfere in my life? My office, nine sharp on Monday.'

He strode past her to Elena's car, abandoned there the afternoon before, smiling and waving at parents as he went.

Grace shivered in the hot sun.

Upstairs in her room, she lay on the bed and let the thoughts whirl around her head like flies round a rotting carcass.

Was she about to be sacked? She'd never been sacked from a job in her life. Could he even sack her? It was a temporary job in a foreign country, so he very possibly could. But he and Elena owned the language school together. Surely she'd stand up for her. Was Elena going to leave her cheating husband? Should she have given her the evidence? It was too late now to change that anyway. Will's disapproving face came into her mind. Why had he popped up out of nowhere?

The sun streamed in through the shutters, but Grace didn't have the energy to get up and close them. They'd reached the hottest part of the day. Maybe a little doze would help her think more clearly.

A soft knock at the door woke Grace from a deep sleep, and for a moment she struggled to think where she was.

Who could that be? Maybe Elena had come to let her know what was going on. Grace lifted herself off the bed and opened the door. Anna was standing on the other side. What could she possibly want?

The girl looked very different from her usual glamorous self – no red lipstick, for one thing, and her hair sat lank on her shoulders. But it still didn't dim her beauty.

'Can I possibly come in for a moment and speak to you?'

The brash confidence had been dialled down too. Her voice was subdued, and the smile that captivated every man within range had disappeared.

Grace pulled the door further open without speaking and indicated for the girl to sit on the bed. It had taken guts for Anna to come to her, so Grace could at least do her the courtesy of hearing her out. They were colleagues, after all. Grace took the chair in front of the desk.

'I'm listening.'

'Charlie suggested that I came and spoke to you. I have nowhere else to go, and no one I can turn to…'

So, she had Charlie to blame for whatever this was. Grace knew he and Anna were close; they were both half-Greek, and had roots on the island. She wondered what Sarah thought about it.

The girl – she couldn't even think of her as a woman – raised her head and looked Grace in the eye. Grace wondered fleetingly what it must be like to be so staggeringly beautiful. Not easy at times, she'd imagine. Men wanted you, as she'd seen with her own eyes, and women didn't altogether trust you, which she'd been guilty of herself. While she'd gone out of her way to make friends with the other teachers, she'd always avoided Anna to some extent.

'I know you are aware of everything that has gone on.'

Grace wasn't going to let the girl off lightly, no matter what she'd come here for.

'You mean your affair with Giannis?'

'Yes.' Anna fiddled with her thumbnail. 'It's something I bitterly regret…'

'You don't need to explain yourself to me.'

'No, but it's important to me that you know I realise I made a mistake.'

'I'm not here to judge you. Giannis is the one who is married, and a father. He should know better.'

The girl's eyes started to water.

'I really thought he loved me.'

She looked so young.

'How old are you, Anna?'

'Twenty-three.' A strangled laugh came out of her mouth. 'Old enough to know better.'

Grace got up and passed her a box of tissues from the bedside table.

'Why did Charlie suggest you came to speak to me, particularly?'

'He said you were kind and wouldn't judge me.'

That was nice of Charlie, although she still wasn't quite sure what he'd landed her with.

'What wouldn't I judge?'

The girl took a deep breath.

'I found out a couple of days ago that I am six weeks pregnant.'

So, the affair with Giannis had been going on a while then, since before they'd started working together at the language school.

After she'd got the words out, Anna broke down sobbing, and Grace couldn't help but move to her side and envelop her in a hug. Anna was still a young woman in trouble.

'You poor thing. Let it all out.'

Anna's body shook with the force of her tears, and Grace held her tight until it stopped.

'I swear it's all over with Giannis. I was honestly about to end it before I found out about the pregnancy. He told me his marriage was over, but I now know that's not true, and I also know that he would never leave his wife. We rowed about it many times.'

Grace recalled the scene in the restaurant at the works dinner.

'That's a painful lesson to learn.'

Her eldest daughter, Lottie, had had a fling with a married man in her twenties, and been distraught when his promises came to nothing.

'Does Giannis know you're pregnant?'

'I told him yesterday when he returned from his trip.'

Giannis must have had quite a day of it then. Finding Elena in that state, and then hearing the news from Anna about the baby. He deserved everything that was coming. No wonder he'd been so angry earlier. It was like a plot from a Greek soap opera that she'd unwittingly got herself caught up in.

Anna twisted a piece of tissue round and round her finger and stared at the bedspread.

'I also told him that I don't want to have the baby.'

Anna met her eye.

'Are you appalled by that?'

155

Grace knew it was important how she reacted, but she still wasn't sure why.

'No, not appalled, particularly in your situation.'

Grace had also found herself pregnant at twenty-three, with her eldest daughter, Lottie. It wasn't planned, and she could still remember the shock that went through her body at the positive result. She and Phil had only been teaching for a couple of years and had plans to travel and work abroad. Doing what she was doing now, ironically. She'd ended up doing it for both of them.

But the difference was that she and Phil were married when she got pregnant, they had a home and, most importantly, she loved him. She'd never regretted her decision to have a baby. But it wasn't the same for this young woman.

'What are you going to do?'

'There are places in Athens where it's easy to arrange an abortion, if you have money.'

Was this girl going to ask her for money? She hated to disappoint her, but she wasn't a wealthy woman.

'It's not the money that's the problem.'

The girl had obviously read her mind.

'Giannis will pay. He respects my wish to do this.'

He's also got another life on the way was on the tip of Grace's tongue, but that wasn't her news to impart. Elena might not even have got round to telling him yet.

'The problem is that I have no one to help me.'

The young woman had gone white. Grace handed her a glass of water.

'Of course, I cannot tell my parents. They would be scandalised and so disappointed in me. It is a small island, and

Giannis and Elena are friends of theirs. Which is how I met him in the first place, and how I came to be working here.'

So, he'd taken advantage of the daughter of friends. It got worse. Grace frowned.

'Please don't think he forced me into anything.'

Anna lifted her head.

'If I'm being honest, I pursued him. He was good-looking, charming, funny, and so much more sophisticated than any man I'd met before.'

Grace thought more of the young woman in front of her for telling the truth. It would have been so easy for her for pretend that it was all Giannis.

'But I realised I didn't want to be anyone's dirty little secret anymore.'

'I can understand why you feel like that.'

'I just want this whole thing over with by the time I go back to London to do my Masters in September.'

'Yes, a fresh start is very appealing.'

After all, it was why she was here on the island.

'So, I have already booked the procedure for next Saturday.'

Now they were getting to the nub of it.

'I was just wondering if...' Anna's voice faltered. 'You would please come with me. It's a very early termination and there shouldn't be any problems, but I'm supposed to have someone stay with me overnight on the first night.'

'Me?' Grace wanted to pinch herself. 'Why me? Haven't you got any friends that could go with you?'

Anna shook her head.

'All my friends live abroad. I lost touch with my

schoolfriends here years ago as I went to an international school in Chicago where my dad worked. And I don't have any brothers and sisters.'

'What about Charlie?'

'We've grown close since we started working together. But I don't know him that well. And I'm not sure how happy Sarah would be. We'd have to share a room.'

Not very happy at all would be Grace's guess.

The first hint of a smile played around Anna's wide mouth.

'It will be twin beds for us, of course. I'll make Giannis pay for the best hotel in Athens, with room service.'

Grace ignored the 'us' for now.

'Does Charlie know who the father is?'

'No, I said it was a guy I had a one-night stand with. No one else knows, only you.'

It didn't feel like a privileged position.

Anna put her hands together in prayer.

'Please help me, Grace, you're the only one who has all the pieces of the puzzle.'

That was truer than Anna knew. There was Elena's baby to think about as well. When had she become the keeper of everyone's secrets? Staying in a posh hotel for the night was like being paid to do Giannis's dirty work. It didn't sit well with her.

'Plus, I trust you. I'm desperate to move past this.'

'If, and I say if, I agreed to go, how would it work?'

She wasn't saying she'd do it.

'We'd go straight after lessons on Saturday to catch the boat and come back Sunday afternoon. The language school classes finish next weekend anyway, and then there are only a few private clients to think about. Giannis has agreed to fill in and take my little ones for the month of August.'

Grace shared a smile with Anna at the thought of Giannis down on the floor playing games. Both he and Elena had started out as teachers before swapping to the business side and Giannis still taught occasionally to keep his hand in.

'Serves him right. I hope they're really difficult and bratty.'

'Me too. After we're back, I go off on holiday for a month with my family to the island of Paros, where we have a second home.'

Money obviously wasn't an issue for Anna. She was part of Giannis and Elena's world of big houses and expensive cars. It hadn't helped her a lot so far, but at least she had options.

'It sounds like you've got it all mapped out.'

Anna's big brown eyes with their thick lashes were trained on Grace. She could see how it might be tough for a weak man like Giannis to resist if Anna got you in her sights.

'There's just one missing ingredient, and that's you. I really respect you, Grace, as a teacher and as a woman.'

'You can cut the flattery. Just give me a moment to think.'

Anna really would go far. She could do so much better than Giannis. Grace conjured up pictures of her daughters at the same age, pregnant and far from home. She really hoped that there would have been someone who would step in and help.

'OK, and I'll probably regret this, but I'll come with you.'

'Thank you, thank you.'

Anna's arms were round her and Grace leant into the hug.

What had she involved herself in now?

Chapter Fifteen

Grace was outside, waiting on the pavement opposite the language school, at five to eight in the morning. The streets were quiet, and she could see all the way up the coast road. There wasn't a car in sight. Will was going to be late picking her up for their hike. Her eyes followed a black dot that was making its way down the hill at speed. As it got nearer, Grace realised that it was a motorbike. And a big one at that. She'd guess a Harley Davidson. Her father had been a motorbike fanatic and had made Grace and her sister experts at identifying bikes in the street, sometimes by sound alone. Neither of them had ever wanted to own one, to his obvious frustration.

The bike turned left along the port road. Will was definitely not going to make it on time. The machine came to a halt a few feet from where she was standing, and the helmeted driver got off and waved.

No, please no. He had to be joking.

Will took off his helmet and beckoned her over.

Grace was too shocked to speak. She'd envisaged a scenic car journey to the other end of the island. She hadn't been on a bike for probably thirty years. The memory of holding on tight to her dear dad as he navigated the Oxfordshire roads on his Triumph flashed into her mind. He'd taken her out for a spin most Sundays when she was growing up. Her sister had hated the whole thing, and her mum flatly refused to go. It had been her special time with her dad.

Will had his smirk on.

'Surprised?'

'You could say that.'

'No need for a car here if you can ride a bike. And nowhere to park it anyway.'

'It would have been nice to get a little warning.'

'Ah, that would have spoilt the surprise.'

Grace pointed at her shorts and T-shirt.

'But I might have worn something different.'

Will's eyes travelled the length of her body, down to her shoes. It was like being in an airport scanner. She wasn't asking him for a weapons assessment.

'No, you're fine.'

He opened one of the saddlebags and tossed her a helmet.

'Catch!'

At least he was wearing a helmet and had one for her too. From what she'd seen, a large majority of Greeks didn't bother with helmets, especially in towns. They also managed to talk on their phones, drink coffee, carry small dogs and huge bags of shopping and balance children on their laps while riding.

'Thanks.'

Will put his hand on the leather seat. She swore he gave it a little stroke.

'So, before we set off, I'd better give you a few basics about what to do and what not to do on the bike. The most important thing is that you lean the same way as me round corners.'

Grace snapped on her helmet and climbed aboard the machine with ease.

'No need. I was brought up around bikes.'

Will's face was a picture.

She clung on tight as they climbed back through the town. Thankfully, Will had given her plenty of solid muscle to hold onto. Privately, she'd been concerned that she might be a bit rusty on bike etiquette, but her muscle memory kicked in in seconds. It literally was like riding a bike.

Perhaps a change of scene would stop her worrying about the meeting with Giannis the following morning. Lying in bed last night, she'd realised that she wasn't ready to go home. Even if she was sacked, but decided to stay on for a holiday, it would be virtually impossible, and incredibly expensive, to secure any accommodation on the island in August. But she was racing ahead again.

The town dropped away as Will eased back on the throttle and the houses became more and more spaced out. She'd read that very few people lived in the north of the island, just a few farmers and the odd taverna owner. The land was rocky, and the road just a dirt track in places. As they wound up and down the hills, the slower pace let Grace take in the ancient stone terraces cut into the rock, which fell in layers to sea level.

The sheer isolation of the place gave it the feel of a lunar landscape. Grace wasn't sure she'd venture out here on her own. She held onto Will a little tighter.

The bike pulled up at a spot at the very tip of the island and they dismounted. Grace knew she'd ache like hell later, but she'd enjoyed it far more than she'd let on to Will. There was a small white building ahead and space for a few cars. Will pointed in the direction of what Grace could now see was a taverna.

'Fabulous place to go in the winter for people brave enough to make it out here. They have a fireplace with a big roaring fire and the most amazing roast pork.'

A part of her was sad that she'd never get to see that.

Will stowed their helmets and pulled a rucksack onto his back.

'Ready?'

'I'm always ready.'

He turned away, but not before Grace saw the smile. What was it about him that made everything she said sound like it came straight from a *Carry On* film script?

Will strode off towards the headland.

'We can see the whole way round the island from here. The views are amazing.'

Grace didn't want a geography lecture, but her thoughts were silenced by the beauty of her surroundings. She turned a full circle where she stood and took in the promontory running down to the sea, the secluded beaches that you could only get to by boat, and the other islands way off in the distance. The morning sun splintered into a million pieces on the sea as she breathed in the smell of wild garlic.

'We'll take that path'—Will pointed to his left—'and walk for a couple of hours before finding somewhere for our elevenses. It's single file most of the way as the path's so narrow. Does that sound OK?'

She wasn't sure anyone under the age of forty would use the word elevenses.

'Perfectly manageable.'

An hour into the walk, the urgent need to pee made her drop behind a little. Maybe she could just duck out for a moment and then catch up with him. She didn't want to make it obvious. Just as she prepared to nip off the path, he turned back.

'Everything OK back there?'

Grace indicated with her head towards the bushes.

'Just need to…'

'Why didn't you say? Thought you'd slackened the pace.'

Slackened the pace? As far as she knew they weren't on some army manoeuvre. Maybe she'd missed the memo.

Grace pushed back some branches and went as far away from Will as she could. She found a little clearing which seemed ideal. She was just pulling up her pants when the sound of something crashing through the bushes made her leap out of her skin.

She couldn't stop her enormous scream.

Seconds later Will appeared. Grace's shorts were still round her ankles. Rushing to pull them up, she managed to overbalance and stagger sideways into a tree.

Will turned his back to let her finish dressing.

'Are you all right?'

'Yes, I'm fine. I heard a strange noise.'

Grace stepped back into the light and spotted a wild goat rubbing his horns against the bark of a nearby tree.

'Look. It must have been him.'

Will took his rucksack off.

'You look a little hot. Do you want some water?'

If she caught even a hint of a smile from him, she'd lose it. Of course she was bloody hot. He'd missed seeing her with her pants down by a microsecond.

She took the water, downed half of it and gave it back to him.

'Thanks.'

'Thirsty?'

'Mmmm.'

The next section of the walk was completed in silence. Will took her down a steep path that led to a tiny, deserted beach.

'This all right for you as a picnic spot?'

'Looks lovely.'

She didn't have to pretend. It was absolutely gorgeous. Framed by black rocks, the beach was full of sand lilies, delicate white flowers that grew in clumps, and the azure sea stretched out beyond the sand as far as the eye could see.

Will even had some sort of lightweight blanket in his rucksack for them to sit on.

'Are you always this prepared?'

'You know what they say, fail to prepare, prepare to fail.'

Grace did a mock vomit.

'Did they teach you that in the army?'

Will smiled.

'Amongst other things.'

A variety of little bags appeared out of the rucksack, along with a carton of pieces of tomato, avocado, cucumber and carrot.

'My, you have been busy.'

'I'm not pretending I made the pies myself. There's a very good bakery on the way to the port.'

Will tore open the bags.

'We have traditional spinach and feta, cheese and ham, cheese on its own, chicken, and for the adventurous, nettle pie. I wasn't sure what you liked, so I got a selection.'

'Oh, I'll eat anything…'

Will raised his eyebrows.

Now she was making herself sound like a dog who scavenged round the bins. This man really did have a strange effect on her.

'Thank you for organising everything. This looks lovely.'

'There's water to go with it, or coffee in a flask, plus some ripe peaches to follow.'

They ate in a companionable silence for a while, staring at the sea. Will spoke again first.

'Just to let you know, we won't be able to do this again next weekend. Much as I'd prefer to be out and about, I've got to accompany the family to their holiday home in Antiparos for ten days and get them settled in. I leave tomorrow.'

'That suits me as well, as I'm actually going to be in Athens next weekend … with a work colleague.'

Grace was pleased that Will wasn't top trumping her. She had places to go and people to see, too. Somewhat sadly for all concerned, she wasn't off for a fun few days in the capital;

rather, she was accompanying a young woman to an abortion clinic. But he didn't need to know that.

'Oh, right.' A frown appeared on Will's face.

She'd said work colleague. He didn't think it was Thanassis she was going with, did he? Although it was none of his business, it was important to her that he didn't think she'd planned a weekend away with the man after finding out he was married.

'It's one of the young female teachers. She's going over for a hospital appointment, and asked me if I'd like to come, as I've never seen Athens.'

It was mostly true.

'Enjoy it, then. Athens is one of the loveliest capital cities in the world. I'll be back in the middle of the following week, and then I'm officially on holiday for a couple of weeks myself, while my deputy takes over.'

'Nice.'

She'd be working until the end of August, giving one-to-one lessons with regular clients in their homes, plus teaching Elena and Giannis's children. That was the current plan anyway.

'I'm having a party when I get back. My actual birthday's while I'm away, but as I'll be working, I'm throwing a moon-themed extravaganza the following Saturday. Obviously, you're invited.'

Grace didn't even know if she'd still be here by then. She'd managed to put off thinking about the summons to the boss's office for a few hours, but each minute brought it nearer.

'What's up? Parties not your thing?'

Will had obviously clocked her face.

'It's not that… I've got a meeting with one of my bosses in the morning, and I'm really not sure if I'm still going to have a job by next Saturday, or even be on the island.'

Will started to pack away the picnic.

'Is this to do with what you told me before?' He gave her a hard stare. 'Except it wasn't just anyone we were talking about, was it? It was your boss and his wife, wasn't it?'

Grace nodded.

'And you went ahead and told one of them, presumably the wife, whatever it was, and now the husband's gone ballistic.'

Grace nodded again.

'Well, I did warn you not to get involved…'

'That's all very well in theory. But he's behaved appallingly.'

She had to get Will to understand why she'd done it.

'This is in confidence, but he's been sleeping with one of the young teachers. I saw him slip out of her room in the early hours. And his wife's convinced herself she's going mad because he's denying it. Plus, it's not the first time he's done it.'

'And now, as I predicted, you've been caught in the crossfire.'

'But I had to tell her.'

'I'm sorry but no, you didn't. It was obvious she'd tell her husband straightaway. You've put your job at risk and made an enemy.'

His attitude got right under her skin.

'So, I was just supposed to forget about it? Let the woman go insane?'

He just didn't get it.

'Look, for what it's worth, he sounds like a complete shit,

and believe me, he'll carry on doing it. Once a shagger, always a shagger. I've met enough of them, guys who think it's just a bit of fun and to hell with the consequences for everyone else.'

'But doesn't his wife have the right to know what he's up to?'

'Still no.' Will had his serious face on. 'Do you actually want my opinion, or do you just want me to agree with what you've done, Grace? Those are two very different things. I'll say it one last time, I don't think you should have got involved.'

It was developing into their first row. But she wasn't going to sit there and listen to any more of his highhanded disapproval.

'Fine. You've made your point. Let's go.'

The walk back was completed in silence. Grace contented herself with making rude gestures with her fingers out of his line of sight. They were perhaps ten minutes from the bike when Grace heard what she thought was a feeble cry.

She stopped still and waited. There it was again. A tiny noise somewhere off to her right. She attempted to follow the sound. Steps behind her told her Will had noticed she'd veered off without permission.

'What it is? Too much coffee?'

'No. It most certainly is not.'

She wasn't going to forgive him for his earlier comments easily.

'What then?'

'Listen…'

Will did an impression of someone listening by holding his

ear on one side, which made Grace look away, but then he started to run in the direction of the sound.

'It's definitely an animal in pain.'

Grace struggled to keep up with him, but they didn't need to go far. Up against a rock just off the path was an open sack. The sound was coming from within.

Will put his hand inside and pulled out a ball of fur. It was a tiny tabby kitten. He put it carefully on the ground, but Grace could tell there was no hope. Its little body just lay there.

Will shook his head and reached in again. He brought out another one, but it was the same story. It was a little black one this time. Grace forced herself not to cry.

The pitiful meow came again. Will reached in with the utmost care and pulled out a grey kitten, its fur standing on end. It was barely alive, but it was still making a noise. It looked tiny in Will's large hand, like a toy.

'Quick, can you get the blanket out of my rucksack and the water, please.'

Grace snapped out of her frozen state and unzipped the bag. She poured some water into the lid of the bottle, and Will held the kitten's head over the water so it could reach. It seemed to understand what to do and lapped at the liquid with a tiny pink tongue. Will smiled.

'That's it, well done, little one.'

Will passed his bundle to Grace. 'The poor thing's totally dehydrated.' He bent down to pick up the blanket. 'Here, wrap this around it, and keep getting it to drink the water.'

Grace coddled the tiny scrap, while Will double-checked there was nothing else in the sack.

He carefully put the two dead kittens back inside, tied it up and hid the package under a bush.

'There's nothing we can do for them, but this little one has a chance. We need to get to a vet as soon as possible. I know someone who can help.'

Their squabble was forgotten just like that. The kitten needed them and they worked together as a team, without words. Grace got as much water into the cat as possible and kept it warm, while Will rang his contact to inform them they were on their way.

'You're going to have to hold onto me on the bike one-armed? Is that OK?'

Grace nodded and took off her cap to shield the kitten from the sun on the walk back.

Her rides with her dad proved their worth as her sense of balance kicked in and she was able to keep the kitten stable. It was still making the odd noise, thank goodness. When they reached the vet, Will took the kitten from her so she could get off the bike, and then handed the little bundle back. He seemed to understand she couldn't let it go.

'Will!'

A petite woman in a white coat rushed out and embraced him fully for several seconds, planting kisses on both cheeks. It seemed a little more intimate than the usual vet-and-client greeting, but maybe it was a Greek thing.

'Angeliki. You've got to help us.'

The woman gave Grace a cursory look and took the kitten out of her arms.

'Follow me.'

They were whisked into the surgery. Angeliki went through a door and indicated for them to take a seat outside.

'Wait here. I'll do an assessment and be back out.'

Will reached down and gave Grace's hand a squeeze.

'I think this little one has got a chance. He or she is obviously a fighter.'

Grace gulped back the tears.

'But why would anyone do that? Leave a bag of kittens to die out in the middle of nowhere.'

Will shrugged.

'All the islands have a problem with too many cats. It's cruel, but not everyone loves them. The feral cats are often diseased. And it costs money to have them put down, so sadly this isn't uncommon.'

Grace couldn't bring herself to speak. She'd lost her own cat, Clooney, in the spring, one of the reasons that pushed her to apply for the job in Greece. The big ginger tom had been the last tie to the house where Phil had spent his final years. They'd downsized to the tiny cottage when both girls finally left home, and Clooney had had a fabulous time in his later years, roaming the nearby fields catching mice that he liked to bring home to show them. He'd died in his sleep one night at the age of nineteen, and she'd found him, stiff and cold, in the morning. Those poor little kittens on the ground had had no chance at any kind of life. She didn't think she could bear it if the grey kitten didn't make it either.

'But there is progress.'

Grace tried to focus on what Will was saying. He was in his default position, fact mode.

'A group of vets, including Angeliki, have banded together

to sterilise as many cats as possible on the island. People pay what they can, and many cats are sterilised for free because of donations from others.'

Grace knew Will was just talking to keep her mind off what was going on in the other room.

'When a cat is sterilised, the vets cut a little triangle in its ear to show it's been done. You might have seen that and wondered if the cat had been in a fight.'

Grace had in fact wondered that very thing, but she wasn't going to admit it.

Will was still working hard to distract her.

'You do realise, that if this cat survives, we're going to have to name it after one of Will and Grace's best friends? It will be either a Jack or a Karen.'

He had managed to make her smile.

Angeliki bursting through the door made them both stand up.

'OK, she's very weak, and she'll have to stay with me for a couple of weeks, as she was really too young to leave her mother, but … I think she'll make it. Keep in touch, and we'll talk about the next steps.'

Will enveloped Grace in a tight hug, before thanking Angeliki profusely.

'That's wonderful. Of course, I'll cover any costs.'

Grace could hardly see through her tears of relief.

'Karen it is then.'

Chapter Sixteen

I t was time to face the firing squad. Grace had dressed in her smartest outfit, a navy cotton skirt and a white shirt. She knocked at the door so hard her knuckles hurt. She'd hate to sound half-hearted.

'Come in.'

Grace had to conceal her surprise when she realised that both Giannis and Elena were standing behind the desk. He'd given her the impression that it would be just him.

'Sit down, Grace.'

Giannis pointed to the chair in front of the desk, which made her want to ask where the hell else did he think she was planning to sit? On the ceiling? Maybe he was nervous too. There probably wasn't much call for sackings at the language school.

The couple took their seats, and Grace spotted that they were holding hands. What it meant for her; she had no idea.

'Elena and I have talked everything through...' Giannis

patted his wife's leg under the table, which made Grace want to gag.

'And we have decided that we'd like to keep you on until the end of your contract, as planned. You are an excellent teacher, and both the children and their parents seem to love you.'

It was as though Giannis was reading from a preprepared script. Elena sat mute through the performance, but she must have had a hand in what Giannis was saying. He'd been ready to get rid of her two days ago.

Part of her wanted to tell them both to stuff their job, but she kept quiet. There was relief mixed with her anger too. Knowing that she could stay on the island for another month meant she'd be able to find out what happened to the cat she'd rescued with Will. Karen needed them. His smirking face also flitted through her mind. She'd miss him if she left now. They hadn't done quite enough winding each other up. And it wasn't as if there was anything she needed to rush home for, which was telling in itself.

'However…'

'However' wasn't the best start to a sentence. Giannis looked at his wife again, who nodded.

'We won't need you to come to the house to teach our children anymore.'

There it was. Giannis didn't want her appearing in his kitchen any time soon. Grace was a constant reminder of his relationship with Anna, as she was for Elena as well. His wife had obviously agreed to the ban. Maybe it was one of her conditions for them to stay together. Grace found that she really didn't care. They were welcome to each other.

'We will make sure you don't suffer financially.'

Grace was tempted to chuck in the towel again and resign. Surely this man didn't think it was about money at this point. She'd been keen to teach their children because they seemed like nice kids, rather than seeing them as a pile of euros. But one thing she'd learnt to her cost was that the rich always thought everything was about money. In most cases, that's why they were rich.

'Rose will be teaching our children instead, and you will be given her clients during August, so it should all work out fairly.'

There was nothing fair about this arrangement. The only saving grace was that the language school would be shut, and she'd be visiting the students, children and adults, in their own homes. She wouldn't need to see Giannis and Elena at all if she didn't want to. And she really didn't want to.

For one insane second, she considered breaking the news that she was accompanying Anna to an abortion clinic at the weekend, just to take the fake smiles off both their faces, but what would that achieve? Jumping in with both feet hadn't worked out too brilliantly for her up until now.

'So, is that acceptable to you, Grace?'

He wasn't really asking her a question. It was this or nothing, something all three of them understood.

'Yes, I'd like to stay on. And it will be interesting to teach some new faces.'

She'd also been genuinely keen to have a good old nose around some of the town's houses as well, so this would give her plenty of opportunity.

'Excellent news.'

Giannis gave his wife a loving look. Grace wasn't sure how the woman could bear it.

'Also, we have some good news of our own. You're one of the first people to know that we're expecting a much-wanted fourth child.'

Elena's pleading eyes met hers. Grace was desperate to tell the man that she'd known before him. But spilling the beans was just a fantasy. She knew she'd never do it. Elena still looked pale and pinched. Having a baby in her mid-forties would be no picnic, even though they could afford all the help they'd ever need. Anastasia would probably go along to the antenatal classes. The thought of Anastasia, in her uniform, sitting behind her mistress telling her when to breathe made Grace smile. She could afford to be generous.

'Congratulations. I'm sure that your children will love having a baby brother or sister.'

Elena's face relaxed at last and lost some of its vulnerability. She gazed up at her husband, and Grace had to accept that she looked happy, much as it pained her.

The baby was the important thing here. Grace really did believe that giving a child a happy and settled home, whatever form it came in, was the best thing. All relationships involved compromises. Staying with a cheating husband like Giannis would be a compromise too far for her, but it wasn't her marriage. She didn't even have a marriage anymore. It was dead and buried, alongside her husband. Well, cremated if she was being accurate.

'Thank you, Grace. The children are very excited and already arguing about names.'

Elena nodded her thanks and put her hands together in

prayer when Giannis looked away for a moment. Grace acknowledged the gesture with a smile.

Giannis took his wife's hand and helped her up.

'Class will begin soon. So, let's all hope for a rewarding and productive last week.'

'Yes, let's.'

Grace had reached the door before she turned back to see the couple in a full-on snog. She closed the door softly and left them to it.

In her lunch break, Grace was too restless for a siesta. She needed to stretch her legs. At the bakery she bought a slice of nettle pie, which Will had given her a taste for on the picnic, and she picked a bench facing the yachts to eat it.

A text from Will came in just as she was about to take a bite.

> On the boat to Antiparos. How did it go this morning?

> Escaped by the skin of my teeth. You'll have to put up with me a while longer.

> Good, I think.

> You think???

> Good then. Any news on Karen?

> Going to pop in there once I've eaten my pie.

> What flavour?

> Nettle. But don't let it go to your head.

Yes!!!

> Let me eat it in peace. I'll send patient condition check later. And remember, I'm paying half the vet fees.

Maybe, but I do get a very special discount.

Grace wondered again if there was something more between Will and Angeliki. Or had been, at any rate. But again, none of her business. He was typing again.

> Instead of paying half … when I'm back, you can buy me dinner.

Deal.

The island would definitely seem like a quieter place without him over the next week or so.

Grace waited at reception for Angeliki to finish treating whichever animal was closeted in with her. Luckily, because it was lunchtime, there were very few people about, and only one elderly Greek woman sitting there. Every now and again she would rake her hands over her worry beads on a string. Grace wasn't sure if the woman could speak English. It certainly wasn't a given for the older residents, although anyone under forty-five was more or less guaranteed to speak it well. The woman's breathing was quite laboured, so Grace took the seat next to her.

'Don't worry, I'm sure it will be OK.'

The woman just let out a low moan.

Grace started an elaborate mime, pointing inside the surgery, doing a double thumbs-up and smiling like a maniac.

The woman just stared at her.

She was in the middle of repeating it, when the door opened and an ancient dog trotted out on rickety legs, the white hairs around its eyes giving it painted-on spectacles. The woman sank to her knees on the floor, her arms round the dog's neck.

Angeliki emerged from behind the dog and helped the woman to her feet, speaking to her quietly in Greek, before taking her arm and guiding her to the door.

Grace waited in the corner.

'Oh, hello. You're Will's friend, aren't you?'

'That's right.'

Grace stared at the departing woman.

'Will that dog be OK?

'Yes. The stupid thing swallowed a rubber ball on the beach. Managed to get it to pass through with a bit of help.'

'Oh, good.'

Grace didn't hugely want the details. Not so soon after her nettle pie.

'What can I do for you?'

'Is it possible to see Karen at all?'

'Karen?'

'Sorry, the kitten we rescued. Which is called Karen for a reason too boring to go into.'

Angeliki waved her arm around the waiting room.

'As you can see, I'm not exactly rushed off my feet, so come through. My receptionist's at lunch, so I really should close the shop, but I can't bear the thought that I might miss an animal in need. They're so much nicer than humans, you know.'

On the whole, Grace agreed with her, especially after this morning. She could warm to this woman with her wild curly hair and practical bedside manner.

Karen was sitting calmly in her cage. As Angeliki approached her, she put her front paws up to the bars, and the vet stroked the tips through the grid.

'She's a real cutie. Would you like to hold her? I'm trying to get her as used to people as possible, so it will be easier for whoever adopts her. Most wild cats don't really want people touching them.'

'I'd love to.'

Grace sat on a stool that Angeliki placed in front of the cage and waited for the kitten to be put on her lap.

Karen was light as a feather and Grace barely dared breathe while the kitten pawed at the fabric of her shorts.

'Go on, it's fine to stroke her. She won't break. She's tiny but tough, like me.'

Grace hadn't held anything this delicate in her arms for a very long time. She moved her hand over Karen's back, making sure she went with the direction of her fur, and was rewarded with a tiny sound.

'She's purring!'

Angeliki smiled.

'She is indeed. Tell you what – shall I make us a coffee and you can tell me all about this rescue?'

'That would be lovely, thank you.'

Grace had a few minutes on her own with Karen before Angeliki came back. The kitten's eyes were green, as far as she could tell. She was such a pretty cat. Once she'd had her injections, she'd be snapped up by someone in no time. The thought didn't fill her with joy the way she thought it would.

Angeliki returned with two mugs.

'Pop her back in the cage then, and you can wash your hands at the sink.'

Grace gave the kitten an extra stroke before saying goodbye.

'Can I come and see her again?'

'If there's no one else in, then sure. Lunchtimes are always good. Pull up a stool.'

'Thank you. Your English is excellent, by the way.'

'I trained in Britain, in Liverpool, and I worked at a practice there for ten years, so I can even do a Scouse accent.'

'Crikey, I don't think we need to go that far.'

There were the inevitable handmade cookies to go with the strong coffee, which Angeliki consumed at a rapid rate. Grace wondered if the woman ate properly. She repeated the story of the dramatic rescue and the hazardous journey home on the bike.

'You did a good thing. And how do you know Will?'

There was more than casual interest in the woman's query. Angeliki's eyes were alive with interest.

'I don't really. Not that well. We bumped into each other the day I arrived on the island. He screamed at me for taking a shortcut across the garden of the villa where he works.'

'Ah yes, Will takes his job very seriously.'

'And how about you? Have you known each other long?'

Grace kept her voice light but she was curious to know the truth as well. Angeliki laughed into her coffee.

'Around eight years. It's no secret around here. We had a thing going for a couple of years, but it would never have worked out. I'm a workaholic, and Will's not big on commitment.'

'Ah. I really don't know him that well.'

But she'd been right that there was more to his relationship with Angeliki than met the eye.

'We managed that awkward transition to friendship, thank goodness. I adore Will, as a friend, and we look out for each other. We really weren't meant to be. But the person who eventually ends up with him will be a lucky woman.'

Grace put her hands up. 'It won't be me, honest.'

Angeliki subjected her to a long stare. 'Well, we all need friends.'

At the ring of a bell, Angeliki leapt up. 'I'm on. Got to go.' She gathered the coffee cups with one hand and chucked them into the sink. 'Please come again. I've enjoyed our chat. And come and see Karen whenever you like.'

'Thank you, I will.'

As Grace emerged onto the street, a man carrying a small dog with its leg bent at an unnatural angle brushed past her and disappeared inside.

Angeliki was the sort of woman she could imagine being friends with. She had a touch of Sofia about her with her fearless attitude. She wasn't sure how Will would feel about her taking up with his ex-girlfriend. Not that it really mattered, as she'd be leaving in a month's time anyway. She quickly updated him on Karen by text, before returning to the school for her next lesson.

An afternoon with her adult students talking about the

history of the island, asking them to describe artefacts and equipment she'd taken photos of in the town museum, passed quickly. Many could remember their own parents and grandparents using the kitchen and farm implements on display and were eager to join in the discussion.

Now there were only a few days left until August, the town was busier than ever, and when Grace finally got to sit on her balcony, she could hear French, German and Scandinavian voices floating up from the street. She'd go out later and get something to eat, when things had calmed down a bit. It made her long for the peace of the cove, but she was too tired to attempt the forty-minute walk.

The ping of her computer reminded her that she had an online meet with her youngest daughter anyway. They'd missed their usual Sunday slot, as Flo and Jilly had gone away for the weekend. Flo's face appeared on screen, wreathed in smiles.

'Hi, darling.'

'Hi, Mum.'

'No Jilly?'

'No, she's out in the kayak. It's a beautiful evening here.'

'Here too.'

Flo hadn't stopped grinning, which was slightly unusual in itself. Her daughter was more often than not a glass-half-empty person, like her father.

'What are you looking so happy about?'

Flo left it a beat.

'We've decided that we're going to have a baby!'

Grace sat in stunned silence. So many thoughts were racing through her mind.

'I'll be the one giving birth, and Jilly will go back to work. I'll get a whole year off, so we can time it with the university schedule.' Her daughter's words were all running into one.

'Wow.'

'Is that all you can say, Mum? You were all over Lottie when she announced that she was pregnant. Why is it so different for us?'

Her youngest child had always been the more sensitive of the two. Grace was just trying to get her head round how it would all work. Where would they find the sperm donor? Would it be someone they knew? Would he have any involvement with the baby's life? She'd better not rush in with too many questions.

'I'm thrilled for you both. It's really exciting. But take it slow, and remember, you're not actually pregnant yet, darling.'

As soon as she'd said it, Grace knew she'd made a mistake.

'That's right. Pour cold water over the whole thing. Just dismiss our dream.'

'No, no, it's a lovely idea. You'll make a great mother.'

But the screen had gone blank.

Grace pressed the redial button twice, but there was no answer.

She knew from experience that she'd be better off leaving her daughter alone for a while. She took a bottle of white wine from the fridge and poured herself a large glass. What a day! She'd almost been sacked this morning because she'd felt the need to rush in and tell Elena what she really felt. Now she was getting grief from her daughter for not being enthusiastic enough about her plan to have a baby. Was she ever going to get it right?

Chapter Seventeen

The last day of term looked like being a lot more emotional than Grace could have imagined when she'd started at the language school. Just the sight of the kids sitting quietly in front of her was almost enough to set her off. She was ending with her favourite Saturday class of eight- and nine-year-olds, Stelios among them.

All week long she'd been plied with homemade treats from parents, most of which she'd taken straight to Angeliki to share at lunchtime. Grace had seen how hard the poor woman worked. She never turned anyone away. The vet barely had time to breathe, let alone eat, and Grace had become her unofficial coffee maker and food provider, forcing Angeliki to take a break each lunchtime.

Karen the kitten was getting stronger by the day, and her playful personality was emerging. Grace had bought some cat toys for her from one of the many pet shops in town. She'd had Angeliki in fits of laughter as she dragged the fake mice along the ground and Karen timed her pounce exactly. Grace had upgraded her messages to Will from texts to videos of the cat they'd rescued together. He sent videos back of the various beaches and yachts he'd been on. Plus, one of a birthday cake and a bottle of champagne. Obviously, a tough gig.

'Will you be teaching us again next year, miss?'

It was Stelios who had his hand up. The boy had become so much more confident in the past few weeks. He'd been allowed to bring Mikey in for the final lesson, and the dog was lying calmly by his side.

'I hope so, Stelios. I'd love to see you all again next year.'

She meant every word, but she had absolutely no idea what she'd be doing next month, never mind next year. The idea of returning home to tutor spoilt children back in Oxfordshire didn't hugely appeal, but she wasn't sure what she'd replace it with.

'We're going to do some work on animals from around the world today, and then I have a treat for you all.'

After a quiz where the kids had to identify the animals on the cards, suggest what they might eat and then match them with the countries they came from, the noise level was rising. Grace had timed it just about right.

'Now, children, we're going to watch a film to finish off, called *Lassie*.'

Much as she'd like to, she wasn't going to subject them to the black and white version, featuring the original dog, Pal, who'd lived to the ripe old age of eighteen. Instead, it was a later version in colour with a new dog, Mason, ably assisted by the actor Peter O'Toole.

Although the film didn't have Greek subtitles, Grace was confident they'd pick up the story. They sat entranced throughout, eyes shining, and cheered loudly when Lassie finally made it home to his schoolboy owner, Joe.

Grace had to turn and wipe away a tear before she faced the children. The story always got to her, however many times she'd seen it.

'Children, gather up your things, and go and meet your parents. I'll be seeing some of you over the next few weeks, but for those who are going off on holidays, have a wonderful time and forget about school for a while. That's an order.'

Grace stowed the last of the parents' gifts in her room. She put some homemade courgette balls with tzatziki and a few pieces of delicious-looking baklava into cartons for the journey and added them to her packed holdall. She was meeting Anna downstairs in five minutes. At the last moment, she remembered her Kindle in case she needed something to do while she waited around.

Anna was already there, bag slung over her shoulder. They watched Elena and Giannis walk together to his BMW. He rushed round to open the door for his pregnant wife, which brought forth a snort from Anna. Grace was certain that neither she nor Anna wanted to bump into the dynamic duo if they could help it, so they hung back until Giannis's beloved car had left the car park. There was plenty of time before their ferry left.

The cage-like waiting area was packed with passengers. The heat was intense, and some people had madly opted to wait in the sun. Grace managed to find two seats in the shade on one of the concrete benches.

Anna was quiet, which wasn't exactly a surprise. Grace was still wondering why on earth she'd agreed to accompany her colleague to Athens, but there was no going back now.

After an uneventful boat journey during which Grace shared her snacks with Anna and they both had a little snooze, they arrived at the port of Piraeus to a teeming mob of people.

Grace followed Anna down the gangway into frenzied crowds fighting to be first to get on the boat. The port police blew their whistles as hard as they could, and the cars driving off the ferry tooted their horns to try and force a path through the mass of people. Children were crying all around her. A man going the opposite way managed to bash Grace's leg with his suitcase and didn't even glance back. It was utter chaos.

'Sorry, Grace. I didn't think. I have brought you to Athens on one of the busiest days of the year. Everyone is trying to leave for their holidays.'

The girl looked close to tears. It wouldn't benefit either of them if Grace had a hissy fit.

'Don't worry. Let's find a taxi, shall we?'

Grace had to smile as Anna bartered with the taxi driver over the price of the fare. Even the wealthy Greeks she'd met loved a bargain.

As they left the port behind, Grace stared out of the window at the furniture shops, cafés and petrol stations that lined the route. There was nothing out of the ordinary so far. The journey to the clinic in central Athens would take them a good forty minutes. It was still incredibly hot outside, and although the taxi had air conditioning, the car seats were boiling to the touch where the sun hit them. Another little doze wouldn't hurt.

It seemed like the phone rang the second she shut her eyes.

It was Flo. She had to take it. They'd not spoken since the row earlier in the week. Grace had tried to message her, but there'd been no response.

Her daughter's voice came through loud and clear.

'Mum… I'm sorry for overreacting.'

'And I'm sorry too, sweetheart, for not reacting enough. I really am thrilled about your news.'

'I know, and I know you had loads of questions you wanted to ask.'

'Well … a few.'

'I can answer the one you were desperate to know the answer to. A friend called Max, who's also a lecturer at the uni, is going to be our sperm donor. He's gay too and wants to help us. He says he's happy not to play any part in the child's life unless we want him to.'

'Sounds good.'

Grace wondered what the legal implications were, but she wasn't going to voice that aloud, especially after they'd only just made up. She hated falling out with either of her daughters, even for a day. They only had each other.

'I can hear that tone in your voice, Mum. You're worrying that Max is going to change his mind and apply for custody or something.'

'Of course not. I'm sure he's a lovely guy.'

'Mmmm. Anyway, remember Jilly is a law lecturer, so we'll probably have some sort of document drawn up.'

'That does make me feel better.'

'See. I knew it.' But there was a smile in her daughter's voice. 'We're going to get on with it as soon as we're back for the new term. I'd love to be pregnant by Christmas.'

Grace stopped herself from speaking.

'And … before you say it, I know it isn't always that easy. And that I might have to be patient.'

'I wish you all the luck in the world, my darling.'

'Thanks, Mum.'

The taxi driver was talking loudly in Greek to Anna.

'What's that noise? Where are you?'

'In a taxi on my way into the centre of Athens, with a colleague. Official lessons finished today, so before we start the private ones, we've nipped over for a night.'

'Oooh, lovely. I'll let you go then. Love you.'

'Love you too. Speak soon.'

Anna had obviously listened to the whole conversation. Or Grace's side of it at least. There was a puzzled look on her face.

'If I'm not being rude, can I ask, who was that?'

It was a little bit rude, but Grace could hardly complain – they were sitting so close to each other that it would have been virtually impossible for Anna not to hear her call.

'My youngest daughter, Flo. Both she and her sister, Lottie, are older than you are.'

'Wow. I had no idea that you had grown-up daughters. Sorry if I'm being nosy here, but it sounded like you were making up after some sort of row.'

'Correct.'

Grace wasn't going to give Anna any more information than that. She was in a surreal situation, accompanying a young woman she barely knew to have an abortion, while encouraging her own daughter to go ahead with a potential pregnancy that could be fraught with problems.

It was time for her to be a little nosy too.

'Do you get on well with your parents?'

Anna put her head on one side.

'Yes, as long as I do and say what they want. They are very strict. We would never have a conversation like you've just had with your daughter. I know they love me, but they're a bit … formal.'

'What do they do for a living?'

'They're both in international finance. We have lived all round the world, which sounds glamorous, but often means that you don't really spend enough time anywhere to put down roots. Hence my lack of friends to come with me now.' Anna smiled. 'I sometimes wonder if my parents should even have had children. Their life is all work, travel and expensive dinners.'

Grace patted the young woman's arm.

'You mustn't say that. I'm sure they love you to bits.'

'Yes, I'm being a bit mean. It's just a lot of pressure. They'd like me to follow them into their world when I finish my Masters.'

'What are you studying?'

'Economics, which of course is perfect … for them.'

'And what about for you?'

Anna sat back in her seat and closed her eyes against the sun.

'I've realised these last few weeks that I'm falling in love with teaching. Because of my degree and my contacts…' Anna opened her eyes again. They both knew what contacts, or rather contact, she was talking about. 'I was given the chance to teach the little ones this summer, which was fun. But I've watched the other teachers, including you, Grace, and I'd love to teach different age groups too, all the way up to university level.'

Grace had a little smile to herself at the effect Anna would have on teenage boys. They'd certainly turn up for lessons.

'Well, your degrees won't be wasted if you eventually become a teacher.'

'It's not that.' Anna opened her eyes and Grace could see the sadness in them. 'I don't think my parents would ever allow it.'

At Anna's age, Grace had already been working for two years, and was living in a rented flat with her husband. She did worry that young people grew up a lot later these days.

'Have you tried talking to them about it? You may be surprised. I'm sure they'd want you to be happy.'

'Mmmm, maybe.'

The taxi pulled up outside a small but obviously expensive hotel, and a uniformed flunkey rushed to open Anna's door.

'We're here.'

In their room, which had two enormous beds, each the size of a double, plus a generous seating area with blue velvet sofas, the curtains were shut tight against the sun.

Anna drew them back with a flourish.

'Surprise!'

Grace caught her breath at the view. In front of them in the distance was the Acropolis in all its ancient glory, with the columns of the Parthenon rising against the blue sky.

But Anna hadn't finished. She flung open a door that had been hidden behind the curtains.

'And look, we've got our own balcony!'

There was room for a table and four chairs, as well as two sun loungers. Grace hated to think how much it was all costing. But she remembered Giannis's face at their meeting earlier in the week and decided just to relax and enjoy it.

Grace put her bag down on one of the beds and went to check out the bathroom. It had both a bath and a shower so large it could accommodate four people within its marbled walls.

When she came out, Anna was waiting, handbag already over her shoulder.

'Sorry to rush you, but we need to go. The clinic is just round the corner.'

The young woman obviously wanted the whole thing over with as quickly as possible. Not that she could blame her.

The clinic was like a luxury hotel in itself. After a rapid exchange with the receptionist in Greek, Anna came back to where Grace was sitting.

'She says that you definitely won't be needed for two hours. Why don't you go out and explore?'

'Are you sure?'

'Please, it would make me feel better about dragging you over here. They have your number, if there's a problem…'

Grace enveloped her charge in a hug.

'There won't be. I'll see you back here at six.'

The busy streets of Athens were an assault on the senses. Everywhere Grace looked there were restaurants and cafés with tables on the street. The smell of frying fish, sizzling meat and herbs filled the air. Four in the afternoon was peak lunchtime, and noisy groups laughed and shouted across tables to each other. The atmosphere was lively but good-natured. Every now and again Grace would glimpse the Acropolis or some other ancient monument looming above the diners at the end of a street. The avenues were lined with trees, some dripping with oranges, although she'd been told by Anna on the boat that they weren't for eating, far too bitter. It seemed a shame that passersby couldn't just reach up and pick one, but if they did, they'd get a shock.

Turning into Syntagma Square, the famous plaza located in front of the old Royal Palace, Grace took a moment to watch the guards in traditional dress. Their strange garb below the waist reminded her a bit of rah-rah skirts from the eighties, with white cut-off leggings underneath, but she was sure the Greeks would be just as bemused by the ridiculously tall fur bearskins of the King's Guards.

In a little parade of shops off the square Grace spotted some hand-crocheted cat key rings. She bought a grey one for Will, to remind him of Karen, and two ginger ones for her girls in memory of their old cat Clooney. She'd wanted to buy Will something for his birthday, but nothing too flash or expensive that might give him the wrong idea, so this was ideal.

After she'd been walking for an hour, the heat was, if anything, intensifying, and Grace turned into a quiet side street. A café with a long line of tables covered in red checked tablecloths attracted her attention and she took a seat in the shade. A shower of mist raining down from the awning was an ingenious way of keeping the customers cool in the summer heat. Grace ordered an iced latte and a plate of loukoumia, which was very similar to Turkish delight, not that she'd be saying that out loud.

Athens was indeed fascinating, and she'd love to return, just not in August. It would be a treat to wander the streets with fewer people around and no queues for the ancient monuments. Grace had another quick glance at her phone to check that there hadn't been any messages, before setting off to meet Anna. The young woman was already waiting outside the clinic and greeted her with a huge smile.

After a delicious room service meal served on their balcony – for Grace, stuffed squid, and for Anna, seafood risotto – they sat and watched the sun go down over the Acropolis, before turning in for an early night.

Grace woke just before dawn to hear Anna softly moaning and took her a glass of water and some painkillers, but otherwise the young woman seemed fine, thank goodness. After a leisurely breakfast back on the terrace, they braced themselves for the return journey.

But the port was much quieter, to Grace's relief. Safely on board, she realised she was keen to leave the capital city behind and get back to her sleepy little island.

'I'm looking forward to going home, aren't you?'

Anna gave her a funny look.

'Is that how you think of the island, as home?'

Grace thought for a moment. Such a lot had changed in such a short time. Since leaving Oxfordshire and her reliable but – she had to agree with Sofia – rather dull life, she'd met so many new people, and experienced the best that Greek culture, food, weather and good-natured hospitality could offer.

'Yes, I really think I'm beginning to.'

Chapter Eighteen

K aren the kitten definitely recognised her now, there was no doubt about it. Grace put her hand into the cage and pulled out the kitten, who purred the moment she touched her.

'You're getting very attached to her, you know.' Angeliki's voice held a slight edge of disapproval. 'She's almost at the point where she could be rehomed.'

Grace's stomach lurched. She knew it was coming, but she couldn't bear it.

Angeliki put their coffees down on the bench.

'You can't take her, obviously, in your situation, so is there anyone you know who could?'

Grace shook her head. Or was there? Will had his own house, and he'd be on holiday for a couple of weeks soon, so he could easily settle her in – and he had a vested interest in Karen's welfare.

'Why are you smiling? Have you thought of someone?'

She'd have to find the right time to carry out her cunning plan.

'Maybe…'

Grace gave the kitten a kiss on the head and put her back in the cage. Her open bag on the floor reminded her that she had something for Angeliki.

'Here, I've got you a present. Some nut loukoumia.'

'Yummy.'

Angeliki's eyes shone as she ripped open the packet.

'Let's have some now. I can't wait.'

A woman after her own heart. Grace savoured a piece of the sweet treat and watched Angeliki roll her eyes in ecstasy.

'This is fantastic. Are you going to Will's party on Saturday?'

Grace couldn't quite see the connection between the two things.

'Yes, are you?'

'You couldn't keep me away.' Angeliki put her hands either side of her own face in an imitation of a waif. 'I don't get out much.'

'You poor little thing. Why don't we get a cab together? I don't fancy walking if I'm going to get dressed up. Arriving all hot and sweaty isn't a great look.'

Angeliki raised her eyebrows. 'Not if you want to impress.'

'I'm not looking to impress anyone. It's just nice to wear something other than shorts and a T-shirt.'

'Agreed. I like to get out of my white coat now and then too. Let's liaise on timings. In fact, why don't you come to mine first and we can get ready together? I'll send you the address.'

'I'd like that. I might even buy something new. I'm not sure I've got anything suitable for a space party.'

———————

Grace made her way back down the hill from the vet's in the direction of the language school and her room. She'd taught one of Rose's clients earlier in the afternoon for a one-on-one lesson, a chatty Greek businessman called Nick, but her evening was her own.

She debated whether to go for a swim at the cove. Will wasn't back for a few days, and in many ways she preferred swimming there when he wasn't around. Knowing that he could appear out of the sea at any moment wearing very little was a bit unsettling. Now she had a solid tan, she'd graduated from the hold-it-all-in swimsuits to the bikinis she'd brought with her.

Grace loved how free the Greek women were on the beach. Everyone wore bikinis, from teenagers to ninety-year-olds, and in all shapes and sizes. She'd worried she might be too intimidated by the perfect bodies on show to ever take her bikinis out of the case, but she'd proved herself wrong. She'd bought a couple of sarongs in town too, printed with sea creatures and coral, and now there was no stopping her. The cove sounded like a good idea, once the heat started to disappear from the day.

A man running in her direction carrying something in his arms caught her attention.

As he got nearer, she realised it was Charlie, and, God, no, Buster.

'Charlie!'

He didn't react, just kept running. Grace rushed after him back into the vet's.

The receptionist tried to stop them going straight in to see Angeliki.

'Can you and your … son please wait outside.'

Grace didn't have time to explain.

She pushed open the door. Angeliki held a large rabbit in her arms, but as soon as she saw the dog, she pushed it back into its cage and pointed to the operating table.

'Put the dog here.'

Charlie's eyes were blank. Grace pulled at his arms, so that Buster rolled gently onto the table. Angeliki gave the animal's head a stroke.

'What's the dog's name?'

Grace answered as Charlie was still in a daze.

'He's called Buster.'

'What has happened? Tell me, quickly.'

Charlie stood there, mute.

Grace reached round and held his face in her hands to make him look at her.

'You must tell her. I don't know the answer, and she can't help Buster otherwise.'

Charlie's eyes filled with tears as he faced the vet.

'He's eaten chocolate, tons of chocolate.'

'What sort of chocolate?'

'Dark chocolate.'

Grace couldn't miss Angeliki's wince. Even she knew that chocolate was bad for dogs. And dark chocolate was really bad.

'How long ago?'

'About an hour, I think.'

'OK, we've got to make him sick. It's his only chance. And we've got to do it now.'

At that moment, the dog had a seizure on the table, and Charlie's howl filled the room, bouncing off the walls and going directly to Grace's heart.

Angeliki held the little dog down as his legs thrashed around.

'I need someone to help me. Charlie?'

But the man was frozen to the spot.

'Grace, it will have to be you. Can you hold his head for me?'

Grace stroked the little dog while Angeliki prepared the equipment. It seemed like only yesterday that Buster had performed his tricks in the classroom for Stelios. He was so full of life and such a trusting little thing. The vet filled a syringe and Grace held onto Buster's head while Angeliki squirted the liquid down his throat.

'Grace, fetch the bucket over there. It won't be long.'

Charlie was bent double on the floor, making a sound that was barely human. Angeliki gave her a thumbs-up as she placed the bucket below the dog's head.

'Hold onto his legs now, Grace, and I'll take his head.'

Minutes later Buster's whole body convulsed as the first of the chocolate-stained liquid hit the bucket and went all over the floor and both of them.

Again and again the little dog vomited. Grace ran to empty the bucket in the sink and put it back again.

Gradually, the force of the vomiting lessened, and became just a few little dribbles.

Angeliki stroked Buster's head again and got a weak bark in response.

'Good boy, well done.'

Grace had to lean in to hear what Angeliki was whispering to her.

'I think we're over the worst, but I need to do some checks to make sure.' She pointed at Charlie on the floor. 'Can you get him into the waiting area, please, and I'll be out in a minute.'

Grace tapped Charlie on the shoulder.

'The vet has to do her checks. We need to wait outside. Come with me.'

Grace held out her hand, and half-pulled Charlie up to a standing position. They were roughly the same height, which made it easier. She'd never be able to pull Will up like that.

Before he allowed her to lead him away, Charlie rushed to his dog's side and gave him a tender kiss on the head.

'Hang on in there, buddy. Please, for me.'

Charlie turned to Angeliki with red-rimmed eyes.

'Is he going to make it?'

'I hope so. But I need to give him the best possible chance. Please wait outside.'

Grace led Charlie into the waiting room. A couple of people had turned up and gave them both a curious stare. Grace realised she was splattered with brown sick, and she smelt dreadful. Not that it mattered. She knew how much Buster meant to Charlie, and she'd do anything to help.

She was still holding Charlie's hand. The receptionist beckoned her over.

'Can you please give me your or your son's details.'

'Oh, no, he's not my son.'

They were the only natural blondes in the vicinity so she could see why the woman had made the assumption. Charlie got up and shuffled to the desk like an old man.

When he sat down again, he grasped her hand.

'It was terrible, Grace. I only went out for an hour to teach. Sarah is away on a photoshoot in Rome. Usually, one of us is with him. She loves dark chocolate, and she keeps a big stash of it in the cupboard.'

He obviously needed to talk, so Grace just nodded.

'Buster managed to get up on the worktop from one of the chairs, and get the door open somehow. You know what a pig he is for food.'

Grace did know. He'd wolfed down her slice of spanakopita on the beach in seconds.

'When I came in, there were wrappers and bits of gold foil everywhere, all over the floor, and Buster...'

Charlie stopped and wiped a hand over his eyes.

'He was just lying there. I thought he was dead. It was the worst moment of my life.'

It looked like Buster would survive his ordeal, and Grace hoped that nothing worse would happen to Charlie for many, many years. She'd grown extremely fond of the young man in the short time she'd known him. She had daughters, whom she adored, but if one of them had been a boy, she'd have been quite happy if he'd grown up to be like Charlie. It would probably freak the guy out if she said it out loud. Instead, she patted the hand that was still entwined with hers.

'I think he's going to make it.'

Charlie smiled for the first time since he'd arrived.

'Thank you for being here. I know I was a bit useless.'

Grace smiled back. 'You were a bit.'

'You know you stink, don't you?'

'Thanks.'

Angeliki emerged from the back room and Grace leapt to her feet at the same time as Charlie.

'We're not out of the woods yet. But I'm hopeful Buster will make a full recovery. I need to keep him in overnight, and he must eat plenty of activated charcoal to soak up any remaining toxins. Prompt action on your part has saved his life this time, but please lock your chocolate away in future.'

The vet had barely finished her sentence before Charlie picked her up and swung her round. She was tiny in his arms.

'You beauty!'

The vet tried and failed to look disapproving.

'You can see your dog now, but don't get him all hyped up.'

It was definitely time for Grace to get out of her sick-stained clothes and go for a swim.

———

After her busy weekend as a chaperone and the excitement at the vet's, Grace was looking forward to a quiet couple of days. Buster was doing well, and she'd had a big bunch of flowers from Charlie to say thank you for her help. A delivery of posh chocolates from Anna had also arrived, along with a WhatsApp of her sunning herself on a neighbouring island. Grace wished the young woman well.

Now the language school was shut for a month, the

private lessons gave her some free time during the day. There was virtually no involvement with Elena and Giannis, as she received her timetable by email, which suited her down to the ground. And because she'd taken over Rose's clients, while her colleague taught the couple's children, she was meeting some new people, as well as teaching her own regulars.

Nick the businessman had booked a block of lessons while his company was on summer break, and she'd got to have a good nose round his apartment at the top of the town. It boasted high ceilings, faded turquoise plaster walls, and a cute balcony covered in plant pots filled with a riot of colourful flowers, as well as a view of the sea. After today's lesson he'd invited her out onto his balcony for coffee. A coffee in town was her plan anyway, so she was happy to stay a few minutes longer.

Although she'd managed to have a good look round the downstairs of the apartment on the pretext of needing the toilet, she hadn't been upstairs, but she got the very definite feeling that Nick might be keen to show her his bedroom. Not that he'd been creepy in any way, just a little too enthusiastic. And she'd caught him looking at her ring finger.

The businessman owned some sort of import–export company, the details of which she'd failed to grasp, although he'd spent quite a while trying to explain it to her, as part of one of her lessons on workplaces. It wasn't that his English was bad, it just sounded extremely boring. He most definitely lived alone; there were no female touches anywhere in the apartment, and a single cup and plate on the draining board backed up her theory. He'd spoken of an ex-wife and grown-up daughter who lived abroad, but she'd learnt to her cost that that was no guarantee.

Having had her fingers burnt with Thanassis, Grace was wary. Nick was nice-looking, typically Greek, dark-haired and solid, of medium height and build, around her age and perfectly pleasant. But there was no spark.

She regretted mentioning Nick to Sofia in their weekly calls, as her friend had asked for an update and urged her to go for it if he asked her out. For some reason that she herself wasn't totally sure of, Grace hadn't got around to disabusing Sofia of the idea that Will was gay. Given Sofia's reaction to Nick, she'd never hear the end of it if she did. Sofia would be urging her to sleep with Will at the earliest possible opportunity.

Trying to shake off thoughts of what Will would be like in bed, Grace was saved by a ringing phone. Her heart missed a beat when she saw the name.

'Charlie. Is everything OK with Buster?'

'Yes, he's fine. My mother's staying with us and spoiling him rotten. But you might not be so good when I tell you why I'm ringing.' He left a pause. 'You're on tonight! I've found the perfect spot for you.'

'What! Don't be ridiculous.'

'I knew you'd freak out if I gave you too much notice. I didn't say anything, but that last session was really a dress rehearsal. You're more than ready. Meet me at the Star Bar, nine-thirty sharp. Are you up for it?'

She couldn't pretend she had anything else on. Her stomach contracted into a tight ball.

'I suppose so.'

Grace stepped into the bar at the allotted time. She spotted Charlie seated at the counter, talking to a dark-haired woman of around her own age who was serving. She walked towards him.

'Hey, Grace.'

'Charlie.'

The woman lifted her head to smile a greeting too, and Grace realised with a jolt that it was none other than Suzie Sessions, who'd been big in Britain back in the eighties, with a unique sound that successfully combined rock and pop. After a string of hits, she'd vanished, and now here she was, in front of her, serving in a bar on a little-known Greek island.

'Hi, I'm Suzie, can I get you a drink?'

Grace snapped out of her daze.

'Yes, please, a Mythos.'

The woman passed over the familiar green bottle and a glass. Grace reached for her purse, but Suzie waved it away and smiled.

'This one's on the house. Any friend of Charlie's is a friend of mine. He's a good boy. Man, I should say. We're not allowed to call them boys anymore, are we?'

Grace smiled back.

'No, we're absolutely not.'

Obviously, Suzie must be nearly forty years older than when she'd been plastered on posters in boys' bedrooms across the land, but her smile and the twinkle in her eyes were still the same. Her spiky dark hair and petite frame hadn't changed either.

Grace raised her bottle in the woman's direction and mouthed 'Thank you' before Suzie moved on to serve someone else.

As soon as she was out of earshot, Grace couldn't wait any longer.

'What's Suzie Sessions doing here?'

Charlie took a long slurp of his beer.

'I just know her as Suzie. I've been mates with her sons all my life. I used to spend all my summers on the island, and the three of us are tight.' He grinned. 'I mean, I knew their mum was some sort of pop star way back, but it was before I was even born. None of the foreign tourists know who she is, and now it's just the odd Brit of a certain age who recognises her...'

Grace gave him a playful punch on the arm for that one.

'Ow. She's run this bar for well over twenty years, and she just loves music, so there's something on most nights.'

Charlie jumped off his stool and motioned for Grace to follow him through an archway.

'Bring your beer. You need to get familiar with the place.'

Grace was desperate to ask some more questions about Suzie but went with Charlie into a large walled space with low brick seating round three sides, open to the elements.

She stood in the middle and looked up and all around. The reason it was called the Star Bar became obvious. There were hundreds of them above their heads, twinkling in the darkening sky.

At one end was a raised platform with a mixing desk. Grace's heart leapt into her mouth. It was impossible to believe she'd be performing there in a couple of hours. Why had she agreed to do this?

As she was a soul girl through and through, she'd painstakingly put together a set of eighties soul classics with his help. She'd included plenty of Luther Vandross, George Benson and Diana Ross in the mix, but she'd stretched it a little on the timeline for the King and Queen of Soul, Marvin Gaye and Aretha Franklin. As vinyl records had been pushed aside in favour of digital formats, Charlie had programmed everything in for her in advance, but there was still plenty to do.

She'd be going on in the middle of Charlie's session. What if everyone drifted back to the bar the second one of her records came on?

'Earth to Grace.'

Charlie's hand on her arm forced her to look at him.

'You're panicking, aren't you?'

Grace nodded.

'There's nothing to worry about. You're well prepared. People are going to love you. Come here, you.'

Charlie pulled her in for a hug. Grace smiled to think that one of her closest friends on the island was a guy in his thirties. Not something she'd imagined when she left Oxfordshire. She wasn't going to even try and fit Will into any category. Far too complicated.

The next couple of hours flew by as Charlie did his thing and the outdoor arena filled up with people. Because it was an eighties night, there was a huge age range in the audience, from twentysomethings to seventysomethings, which helped calm her racing heart.

At midnight Charlie beckoned her over and told her to prepare while he played his last record of the set. The next three minutes went by in the blink of an eye, and Grace gulped when Charlie spoke to the audience.

'And now, we have a special treat in the form of a guest DJ. She loves soul music…'

There was a reassuring cheer at the words.

'And she's put together a set I know you'll love. Give it up for … Amazing Grace.'

She took his place at the mixing desk and looked out at the sea of people. For a moment she faltered, but a nudge in the back from Charlie brought her round.

'Hello, everyone. I hope you love these artistes as much as I do. So, let's get it on, as Marvin would say.'

Once the first notes filtered out into the night, Grace let go of the breath she'd been holding.

Song after song came and went, and the audience danced their hearts out and sang along to the lyrics. It was only when the last song started to play an hour later that Grace was finally able to relax. She stared out into the audience and into some of the faces of people who'd definitely appreciated the music. It was such a rush to give pleasure to so many people at once. She spotted Charlie's girlfriend, Sarah, in the gloom, and Angeliki. She glanced back towards the bar and Suzie Sessions gave her a thumbs-up. Suzie Sessions!

The last song ended, and Grace took a deep breath. She'd done it. Performed as a DJ. And it hadn't gone horribly wrong. In fact, it had gone so well, it had turned into one of the best experiences of her life. If someone had suggested six months ago that soon she'd be a guest DJ at a bar on a Greek island, she'd have laughed in their face.

Charlie came to stand beside her.

'That was fantastic, Grace. I'm sure that won't be the last we'll see of you on the decks. Let's all show our appreciation.'

The wall of sound that greeted her was deafening. Grace took a bow and made her way towards Angeliki, who had a bottle of beer and a hug waiting.

'Well done, girl. You smashed it.'

'Thanks. Did you manage to take a video?'

'Sure did.'

Will wouldn't know what had hit him.

Chapter Nineteen

After a late night partying to the rest of Charlie's set, and a busy day teaching, Grace was finally about to press send on the video to Will when a message came in from the man himself.

> I'm back. Can we meet for a drink?

> When?

> Now, if possible.

> Where? I'm in town.

> Not in town, please. Can you come to the bar on the headland above the cove?

It was all a bit mysterious. Grace knew the place. It was very out of the way. She'd better start walking. She was excited to show him her DJ debut in person and maybe this would be her chance to talk to him about adopting Karen.

Ok, half an hour?

Fine.

When she arrived at the bar, Will was already seated at a table outside and waved her over.

As soon as she sat down, Grace could tell that something was wrong. For once, Will looked tired. He was unshaven, there were dark circles under his eyes beneath the tan, and when he spoke, she could smell alcohol on his breath. He'd definitely started without her. And a little while ago. The guy was admittedly on holiday and allowed some downtime, but the familiar smirk was missing completely. DJing and cat adoption would have to wait.

'Beer?'

'Yes, please, Mythos.'

Will raised his hand at the barman.

'Two more please, Theo.'

There was only one other couple sitting outside, but Will looked around as if he was scanning the place for potential enemies. They sat in silence for the first few mouthfuls of beer, until Grace could bear it no longer. He was the one who'd invited her here for a drink, not the other way round.

'Is everything all right?'

Will turned his face to hers, and Grace put her bottle back down on the table with a bang when she saw the look in his eyes. She knew that look only too well. It was the pain of loss. His eyes were the colour of conkers just after their green spiky shells had been broken open. They were usually as shiny too, but tonight they were dull.

'What's happened?'

Will took another sip of beer before speaking.

'I've just heard that a good friend of mine has died.'

There was no satisfaction for Grace in being proved right this time.

'That's awful. I'm so sorry.'

Grace stopped herself asking any more questions. Will was the sort of man who would only speak when he was ready. There was no point pushing him. She concentrated on downing her beer instead.

'We served together. Afghanistan, Iraq, Northern Ireland.'

Grace nodded.

'It was years ago, but you never forget. Those men are family.'

It was what they were always promoting in the recruitment ads for the services, the idea that if you joined up, you'd be part of a new family, but up to now Grace hadn't known whether it was true. She didn't know anyone who was or had been in the army, navy or air force. And if she was being honest, she wouldn't have been too keen on either of her daughters ending up with someone in the services either. Not that she could explain why, exactly; it just sounded like a tough life all round, both for those posted abroad and possibly having to fight and for those left at home.

Will lifted his hand at the barman.

'Two more beers over here, please, Theo.'

Will was certainly going for it. He needed to talk, that much was clear, and for some reason she had been picked as the one to listen.

'His name is … was Barney. Just a couple of years younger than me.'

Will's hand tightened on the beer bottle.

'Such a bloody waste.'

Grace leant over and stroked his other hand.

Will looked up in surprise. It was almost as if he'd forgotten she was there. Grace took her opportunity.

'Shall we order some food? I'm hungry.'

She wasn't really, but she thought that Will could do with something to soak up all that beer.

'Yes, please get whatever you want.'

Grace left Will staring out to sea, while she wandered over to the barman.

'Can we please have some fried calamari over there, a Greek salad, some bread, and a big bottle of water with two glasses.'

'Of course.'

'I'll take the water now.'

The barman reached behind him to get the bottle of water out of the fridge.

'Is Will OK?'

Grace couldn't pretend to know Will well, but one thing she did know was how private he was. He'd hate to think that people were gossiping about him. She could see why he hadn't wanted to meet in town. It was all too easy to bump into someone you knew.

'Yeah, he's fine. Just a bit of a rough day.'

'Ah, we all have those.'

Grace smiled her polite smile and headed back to the table

with the water. She poured out two glasses and put one in front of Will. She wouldn't force him to drink it. He wasn't a child, and if he didn't want it, it was up to him.

Will ignored the water and reached for his beer.

'Barney struggled when he left the army … he never settled to anything. Got a bit too fond of the drink.'

Grace tried not to look at the bottles mounting up on the table.

'His wife eventually left him, and he rarely saw his kids. But in the last couple of years, he seemed to be doing better. He got sober and was working as a night security guard. Sent me pictures of himself every week at the football with his sons.'

Will drained the dregs of his beer.

'I offered him a job out here at the villa in the early days. But he told me he could never leave Manchester again. If only he'd taken it…'

Will raised his hand yet again for the barman. Grace had barely touched her second beer.

'Not for me, thanks.'

The man was on a mission. It wasn't her place to stop him drinking, but she just hoped the food would arrive soon.

Will stared at the bottle of beer as if he'd find the answer to his problems in the contents of its green glass.

'The landlord found him. No one had heard from him for a couple of days.'

Grace heard the break in his voice.

'He'd hung himself in his room…'

Will turned to her and Grace saw that pain again in his eyes. The pain that was in hers every time she looked in the mirror. His eyes were full of unshed tears, and Grace welled up too. A couple of her tears escaped onto the tablecloth, and she dried them with a serviette before speaking.

'Poor guy. To die all alone like that.'

Will wiped his eyes with the back of his hand.

'Hey, I'm sorry. I didn't mean to upset you. I didn't think…'

Grace didn't want to bring Phil into it. This wasn't about him.

'No, it's fine. You need to grieve for your friend, it's important.'

The food arrived and by unspoken agreement they both plastered on a smile for the barman. Will raised a hand.

'Thanks, Theo.'

Grace dealt herself a plate with a bit of everything and put some squid in her mouth.

'Mmmm, delicious. You should try some.'

Will looked at her with some of the old scepticism. She had said it like she was taking part in an advert.

'Are you suggesting I eat before I fall over?'

'Something like that.'

Will tore off a piece of bread and put it in his mouth.

'Happy?'

'I think you'll need something a bit more substantial than that.'

Why was she giving in to the urge to mother him? He was a grown man, and how much he ate was his concern. The need to constantly feed people was very Greek, so maybe she was going native.

Will tore off another piece of bread but left it on his plate.

'I just wish there was more help available for guys like

Barney. Guys who put their lives on the line day after day, and who are suddenly left out in the cold. One day you're a hero, the next, no one wants to know.'

They were venturing deep into personal territory. This was a very different side to the Will she'd known so far.

'But aren't there organisations or charities who can help ex-service personnel?'

She was sure she'd given money to people collecting for the services in the past. Grace thought about her own position. She'd always seen the armed forces as something the country needed, but at the same time she abhorred the idea of violence or actual killing. Perhaps naively she hadn't thought much about what happened when you were no longer part of a team who'd been through such intense experiences.

'There is some help available, and it's a damn sight better now than it was years ago, but it's not enough. People try, but they don't always understand what we've been through.'

Grace noted the change from 'they' to 'we'. This was more than a simple mourning of a friend.

'Mental health is a major issue. What we have to do messes with your head. And the longer it goes on, and the more tours you do, the worse it gets.'

Will turned to face her.

'I knew I had to get out when I started being sick every morning before going out on patrol. I'd look at myself in the mirror and it was pure fear that looked back. What use is that to the men you're leading? You could put someone's life in danger. Keeping your men safe is more important than anything.'

Grace stayed still and silent. Whatever this was, Will

needed to push through it. She knew from bitter experience that you couldn't keep repressing feelings, because they'd come back to bite you. Immediately after Phil's death, when people had asked her if she was feeling OK, she'd nearly always said yes, because that's what they wanted to hear. It made them feel better. What she really wanted to do was stand up, scream and say, 'Are you out of your mind? Of course, I'm not OK. How could I possibly be OK when I've just lost the person I've loved for the whole of my adult life and all our plans for the future are destroyed?'

Of course, she'd never done it – someone would have probably tried to have her committed – but it had only been with Sofia that she could tell the truth about how bad things really were. Three years on, the raw grief had almost gone, but there was still a dark corner of her bruised heart that made itself known every now and then. At least she had Sofia to talk to. She didn't like to assume, but Will, being a man, was probably less likely to talk to someone about his experiences, especially as he lived alone.

Grace tuned back into what Will was saying.

'And becoming a parent while you're serving in the forces affects you even more. I saw an extra level of fear in the eyes of the men who were fathers. It makes you a whole lot more vulnerable too, which is dangerous in itself. I used to think about my son every time I left the camp, wondering if he was going to be left fatherless.'

Will missed the table completely when he tried to put the bottle down, and Grace bent to pick it up from the stone floor, where it was spilling its contents, miraculously still intact. She stopped worrying about being seen as motherly and put some calamari and salad on a plate.

'Here, eat this, before you smash something.'

His salute held a bit of the Will she knew.

Grace waited until he'd eaten everything on the plate before speaking.

'Have you ever thought about getting involved in some way with veterans yourself? Working with one of these charities? You'd probably have to do some training, but you'd be a damn sight more useful to people who were struggling, like your friend, than someone who knew all the theory but had never served.'

They needed to get away from subjects that were dragging them both under. She'd given Will pause for thought with her question.

'I've never really considered it. When I left the army twenty years ago, I'd had more than enough of the whole bloody thing, and I didn't look back. My marriage was well and truly over, my son was more or less lost to me, and the last thing I wanted was to be tied to an office job.'

A vision of a suited Will lashed to a desk was a disturbing thought.

'No, I can't see you in an office environment.'

'So I became a close protection bodyguard instead, to anyone who'd have me, ambassadors, billionaires, celebrities, you name it.'

'It sounds fascinating, but I'm sure it isn't always.'

'No, it's a job like any other, but with the added possibility that you need to be prepared to kill or be killed.'

Grace took a deep breath. She was going to say it.

'Have you ever knowingly killed anyone?'

Will took another swipe at the beer Grace had rescued from the ground. He looked her straight in the eye.

'Yes, in self-defence, while under fire. To protect the life of the person I worked for.'

Grace took a moment. She had asked the question. What did she expect? Could she ever be with someone who'd killed another human being as part of their work? Not that she was thinking of getting together with Will – it was just theoretical.

'How? Did you shoot them?'

'Yes.'

'And why did you have a gun?'

'You're allowed to carry a gun outside the UK if it's been approved. We always flew PJ – private jet – so the guns are checked in and out each end.'

Will forced out a weird chuckle.

'When I first started as a bodyguard, and the other guys were talking about PJs, I thought they meant pyjamas at first…'

Grace didn't laugh along. It was a world she knew nothing about, and she wasn't sure how much more she did want to know. But she couldn't stop herself.

'Are the threats of kidnap real?'

'In some parts of the world, very much so. Particularly for billionaires and their children. And even in London they don't like to take any chances.'

Her curiosity got the better of her.

'And do these children go to normal schools?'

'Some are home tutored, but in one family I worked for, the

children were at an ultra-exclusive private school in the city. We took it in turns to go in with them.'

'And then what did you do? Hang around until they finished lessons?'

'No … sit in the classroom with them.'

'Hang on, you mean you had to sit with them all day?'

'Yep.'

'And were you the only one?'

'No, there were other bodyguards too.'

Grace thought her head would explode.

'So, let me get this straight. There was a line of bodyguards sitting at the back of a classroom, where, presumably because the parents are already paying astronomical fees, there were only a few children anyway?'

'Basically, yes.'

'That seems ridiculous.'

Will shrugged.

'As a teacher, I can tell you it's not healthy. Is that the sort of life you'd want for your own children? Anyone's children?'

'No.'

At least she'd slowed down Will's drinking.

'How do you get into a job like that? Are they advertised?'

'Not really. Everyone is basically ex-forces or police weapons trained. It's all word of mouth.'

'So they don't let just anyone fly around the world using a gun whenever they feel like it? That's a relief.'

Will ignored her outburst.

'I got fed up with the travelling too. It may sound glamorous, flying to these people's homes in the Caribbean or the Swiss mountains, but you're always on duty. You're not on holiday.'

'Is there anything you do miss about it?'

Grace unloaded the last of the calamari and bread onto his plate in the hope that he'd finish it off.

Will forked a baby calamari into his mouth.

'The food. The guy I worked for in London had a team of top chefs and each day one had to get the ingredients and prepare six potential meals for the boss and his partner. Then during the day they'd narrow down the choices to one.'

'What a terrible waste.'

Will smiled for the first time that evening.

'Oh, nothing was ever wasted. We got to eat food made by Michelin-starred chefs on a regular basis. That's why it paid to be mates with the chefs. Get in there first before the nannies.'

Grace finished off her second beer.

'What a strange life. For everyone involved.'

'Agreed. I got fed up with it in the end. Wanted to be in one place for more than a couple of weeks. I came here on holiday and never left. Picked up the house for a song and did it up myself. Picked up a job at the same time.'

Will made inroads into the final beer on the table.

'It's suited me down to the ground.'

'Why are you saying suited instead of suits? Is it about to come to an end?

'Sadly, yes. I retire at Christmas. You don't get many heads of security over the age of sixty.'

'Oh, I see. And is that what you want?'

Will didn't seem anywhere near old enough to be giving up

work. He was obviously still very fit; she'd seen enough of his body to attest to that.

'Not really. I'm not the type to give up work completely and sit twiddling my thumbs. I just need to sort out what the next phase will be.'

You and me both, thought Grace. Her life had split wide open over the summer. Before Greece was done and dusted, but she really wasn't sure about After Greece yet.

Chapter Twenty

G race did a twirl for Angeliki and peered at herself in the full-length mirror. The one in her room at the language school offered a view that only reached the waist, and she was desperate to see how her new dress looked.

She'd bought the garment in the few minutes she'd had between lessons in town earlier, mainly because it had big splodges of silver everywhere over the white linen, and she wanted to at least make an effort for Will's space-themed party. It had looked approximately her size on the rack, but she hadn't had time to try it on, so she'd come straight to her friend's apartment near the port after her final lesson. Unfortunately, for her bank balance anyway, she'd also happened to pass the shoe shop where she'd bought the horribly expensive espadrilles with Sofia, and had persuaded herself it was an investment to get a pair in silver too.

The sound of Angeliki clapping made Grace smile.

'Bravo! The dress is dynamite. And the shoes are gorgeous.'

Grace didn't class herself as vain, but even she was thrilled with the way the thin spaghetti straps showed off her tan and the cut of the simple knee-length shift dress hugged her curves without being too suggestive. It had hit thirty-two degrees during the day, not unknown for early August, and it hadn't cooled down that much by the evening. It was impossible to wear anything that wasn't loose and lightweight, otherwise she'd start to sweat – not a great look. She bowed low at her friend's applause.

'Phew, it fits.'

'It more than fits, baby. It's going to make you the belle of the ball.'

Grace took the glass of wine that Angeliki offered her.

'Let's have a little freshener first. You drink this while I get changed out of my white coat. There's more in the fridge if you run out.'

Grace wolf-whistled when her friend came back twenty minutes later, wearing a tight-fitting silver jump suit and high silver heels, with her long curly hair down for once and her face made up.

'Wow. You look like one of Charlie's Angels. No one's going to recognise you.'

Angeliki completed her own twirl.

'That's the idea. Normally they see me lightly splattered with blood, vomit or worse.'

'Yuk. TMI.'

'Exactly. So, this is my chance to appear somewhat normal.'

Grace applied a little more pale pink lipstick in the mirror.

'Well, I hope Will appreciates what a big effort we've made. Unlike him, we've both been working all day.'

Angeliki nudged her in the side. 'Oh, I think Will most certainly will.'

'Stop it. I'll admit that he and I are friends now. But that's it. Nothing more.'

She hadn't told anyone about Will's uncharacteristic meltdown at the bar, and she wasn't planning to.

Angeliki tapped her nose. 'If you say so…'

'I do. Let's order that taxi.'

Will had sent her several texts over the last twenty-four hours, thanking her for rescuing him, for getting her taxi driver to drop him off first at his house, and for paying for their food and drinks. It was like the evening had come back to him in stages, which it probably had, given the amount he'd drunk. He'd had nearly two days to sober up, so she hoped he was ready for his party. She and Angeliki certainly were.

The light was fading fast when they climbed out of the taxi on the road above Will's house, and the first streaks of orange in the sky promised a spectacular sunset. From the level of chatter and music coming from below, they were far from being the first guests.

Grace and Angeliki walked down the path together towards their host, who had his back towards them, deep in conversation.

The slam of a car door made him turn, and Grace noticed that he took a step back at the sight of the two of them, before remembering his manners.

'Grace! Angeliki! You came … together.'

Will knew she'd been spending time at the surgery, visiting Karen and sending him updates, but she'd probably failed to mention quite how well she'd been getting on with his ex-girlfriend. Angeliki was firmly in friend territory now too.

'We did.'

Angeliki gave Will a quick hug and skipped past him onto the veranda, the roof of which was festooned with silver balloons, fairy lights and a couple of toy spacecraft.

Will gave Grace another of his airport-style top-to-toe scans, which always made her feel like she was standing there in her underwear.

'Nice dress.'

'Thanks.'

'Love the touches of silver.'

Will himself was wearing a white shirt with bands of silver randomly highlighting areas of his chest, teamed with smart grey shorts and deck shoes. She was pleased to see he was wearing socks with them. It was one of her bugbears, men wearing deck shoes without socks, particularly if they wore them with those half-mast trousers that exposed bony ankles; it just looked like the trousers were missing a chunk of material.

'And that's a fun shirt.'

'Fun? Not sure that's what I was aiming for.'

Will leant in close.

'Thank you again for the other night. I know I was pretty out of it…'

'Don't mention it.'

'Let me know if there's ever anything I can do for you in return.'

Actually, there was, but now wasn't the time.

More guests were coming down the path, and Will smiled and waved in their direction. He was in mine host mode again, and there was no sign of the man who'd opened himself up to her two nights ago.

'Welcome, everyone. Drinks on the table behind you, and snacks inside. Please help yourselves.'

Grace poured herself a glass of wine and wandered inside the house, keen to see what Will had done with it, since he'd told her it was all his own work.

What had probably been several small rooms was now one big open-plan space, with a traditional cone-shaped open fireplace in one corner, into which someone, presumably Will, had put a red metal wood-burning stove.

Pale blue fabric sofas in an L shape and a faded yellow armchair faced the fire, with a large jute rug between them on the terracotta-tiled floor. A floor-to-ceiling built-in bookshelf, in what looked like oak, covered half of one wall, and there were paintings in oils and watercolours of sea scenes dotted around the white plaster walls.

It was all quite tasteful, without being ostentatious, and, to her surprise, Grace was impressed. She wasn't sure what she'd been expecting – maybe something aggressively bachelor, with swathes of black leather and hints of gold.

The wooden kitchen units, painted in the same pale blue as the sofas, looked handmade. A dining table in a more vibrant shade of blue had been pushed back against the wall and was covered in bowls of crisps and nuts and plates of canapés, plus little dishes of food that had obviously been brought by guests. Grace helped herself to some crisps – avoiding salt and vinegar, which always gave her indigestion – and a couple of falafel-type balls with a yoghurt dip, which she'd learnt were called keftedes in Greek.

She was surprised to find Will standing behind her just as she popped one in her mouth. Surely he had hosting duties?

'So, what do you think?'

Grace swallowed and took a gulp of wine.

'Of the keftedes?'

'No, the house.'

He seemed a little nervous, as if it really mattered to him what she thought.

'It's charming.'

His face relaxed into a smile.

'Glad you like it. I made the bookshelf myself and the kitchen units as well as the dining table.'

'I take it you're good with your hands then?'

As soon as she'd said it, Grace wanted to stuff the words back into her mouth. Will's eyes met hers, and she could see the laughter in them.

'I have my moments…'

Before Grace could think up a suitable retort, a pair of arms with long red fingernails at the end of them went around Will's waist.

'Will, darling.'

He spun round and the owner of the arms and the French accent was revealed to Grace as a dark-haired woman whose deep tan was the kind her daughters had warned her about. She wore a red mini dress which bore no relation to the party theme but did a lot for her slim figure. She'd completed the outfit with a pair of deely boppers with little silver moons on the end.

'Celine!'

Will didn't seem quite as thrilled to see Celine as she had sounded to see him. But it was none of Grace's business. She'd better go and find Angeliki.

'Grace. Can we…?'

Will was trying to ask her something, but she stepped out onto the terrace without a backward glance.

Angeliki was leaning against the wall chatting to an older man with sparse grey hair. Grace hadn't asked her friend how old she was, but Angeliki had volunteered the information that she was in her mid-fifties. She had married young and divorced ten years later; it was work that had been the constant companion in her life. They'd skated over her time with Will, neither wanting to go into detail. The guy currently towering over Angeliki looked like he was in his seventies, or even eighties. Far too old for her glamorous friend. They'd agreed a signal if one of them was being bored to death; a stretch of the arm towards the sky as if cramp had set in. Angeliki was doing it now.

Grace stepped into the circle.

'Excuse me. Angeliki, I'm sorry but I really need to talk to you about my … hamster. It's urgent.'

Her friend managed to keep it together somehow.

'Of course, let's go somewhere quieter.'

Round the back of the house was a small vegetable garden with views up into the hills. Angeliki led Grace by the hand until they were out of earshot, and they both collapsed laughing onto a bench.

'My hamster?' Angeliki struggled to catch her breath.

'Don't be harsh. It was the first thing that came into my mind. You looked as though you needed rescuing.'

'I most certainly did. He was asking me if I knew how to make bekri meze, drunken pork stew.'

'Sizing you up as a potential wife?'

'Housekeeper more like.'

'You're well out of that then.'

'Agreed.'

Angeliki picked at some flaking paint on the arm of the bench.

'Watch out for the lady in red.'

'Celine? Yes, I've already had the pleasure. Who is she?'

'Another ex of Will's. Owns a boutique in the town. But unlike me, she's not at all happy to be friend-zoned. Won't accept it's over.'

'Okaay. And you're telling me this because?'

'Because I can see Will likes you.'

'As a friend, maybe.'

Angeliki stared at her so long that Grace had to turn away.

'Whatever. But she's trouble.'

'OK, thanks for the warning.'

Had Will invited a whole harem of exes to his party? Was he going to line them up at the end of the night and introduce them one by one? Or give them marks out of ten? And why should she care if he did? Grace stood up.

'Let's go back in. Maybe we can find someone for you who isn't old enough to be your father.'

'That would be nice.'

Grace offered to go and get the drinks. But she wished she

hadn't when the first person she bumped into was Thanassis, with an elegant woman around his own age.

'Grace! I must introduce you to my wife, Maria.'

Since Maria was the housekeeper at the villa where Will worked, Grace kicked herself for not realising that they might be here. She didn't need a mirror to know that her face and neck were going bright red.

'Lovely to meet you, Grace. Thanassis has told me all about you.'

Not all about me, she hoped, especially the bit where I almost got off with him.

'He tells me what a wonderful teacher you are.'

'Thank you. It's lovely to meet you too.'

The woman seemed perfectly sincere, but when Thanassis moved off to get his wife a drink, she moved in close, and Grace's heartrate soared. Maria lowered her voice so only Grace could hear.

'And thank you for speaking to my husband and telling him to focus on what's important in life. The children and I are grateful to you.'

It wasn't the evening heat that was making her sweat. She needed to move away, and fast. Thanassis was on his way back.

'You're welcome. I must go and get that drink I promised my friend.'

When Grace looked up, Will was staring straight at her and Maria. Of course he was. The only other person who'd been present that disastrous night with Thanassis. Between Will's ex-girlfriends and her near miss, the party was becoming a minefield.

She spotted Angeliki in a mass of people at the other end of the terrace and filled two wine glasses to the brim. But she'd only gone a couple of steps when someone familiar stepped out and touched her on the arm.

'Grace!'

'Nick!'

What the hell was he doing here? He had on some sort of silver bomber jacket. Grace hoped there was something underneath so he could take it off later, otherwise he'd melt.

'It's so funny to see you here, Nick. How do you know Will?'

'We met a couple of years ago when he bought some stuff from my company.'

'Ah.'

Grace didn't want to hear any more about the intricacies of his work. She'd had enough of it in class.

'We went for a drink to seal the deal. And we've been doing it regularly ever since.'

'I see.'

'And you? How do you know him?'

Grace glanced up for a moment and caught Will's eye. He was still looking in her direction. Celine was at his side, and she reached up to brush something off his shirt. For a mad moment, Grace wanted to lean over and kiss Nick on the mouth. Not because she fancied him, but just to annoy Will. But it was hardly fair on Nick to lead him on. She turned back to her student.

'Oh, we both like to swim at the beach down here and got chatting one day. I've realised it's virtually impossible to be on the island and not bump into the same people all the time.'

'So true.'

Angeliki appeared at her side and took one of the wines.

'I think that's got my name on it. I'm dying of thirst here.'

'Hardly.'

Her friend looked at Nick expectantly.

'Of course, sorry. This is Nick, one of my students. Nick, this is Angeliki, our friendly local vet. You two haven't met?'

Nick's appreciative glance at her friend told her it was unlikely. It was like he'd found buried treasure.

'I think I would have remembered meeting someone so lovely. Alas, I don't have any pets, so we have never come into contact with each other … until now.'

Angeliki returned his look with one that told Grace close contact with Nick would possibly be welcome.

'Shame.'

Angeliki leant in.

'So, what is it you do on the island, Nick?'

It was Grace's cue to get away.

'I'm just off to check out the food. You two have a good old chat.'

Before she'd taken even a step, the two of them were nattering away in Greek. They'd only kept up the English for as long as she'd been there. It was perfectly understandable but made her feel a little left out. She was the outsider here after all, the only Brit at the party as far as she could make out – apart from the host, but he'd been on the island for years, so he probably spoke perfect Greek too.

As the evening wore on, Grace chatted to several of the locals and threw herself into the party, dancing to every type of music, despite a slight feeling of melancholy at the sight of couples old and new flirting with each other. Angeliki had rushed up to her at the food table and checked that Grace hadn't got any designs on Nick.

'Not at all. He's a lovely guy, but not for me.'

'Great. Thought I'd better check. I really like him.'

Her friend had rushed off again, back to Nick's side. The more she thought about it, the more she realised they'd be good for each other. Both busy people with a sweet side. You couldn't push these things, but she had high hopes.

During the evening she'd locked eyes with Will several times, and he'd sent her a rueful smile each time. He was always in the middle of a crowd, usually with Celine or another well-dressed woman at his side. Grace wasn't about to barge her way through that lot to go and talk to him.

A big cheer went up when a delivery of gyros from Tony's arrived, and the chatter quietened down while everyone ate their fill. The cheer was even louder when a giant moon-shaped cake was brought out, complete with craters and grey icing.

The whole place sang 'Happy Birthday' to Will, followed by the Greek version, 'Chronia Polla', and the champagne corks popped regularly as the music cranked up. Will had invited all the neighbours, which was a sensible idea, as no one was getting any sleep tonight anyway.

After some energetic dancing with Angeliki to Abba, Grace needed the loo. The one downstairs was occupied, but Will had told everyone to use the upstairs bathroom too. While she was up there, it wouldn't hurt to have a quick look at the bedrooms, surely.

She popped her head into the first one, which was obviously a spare. It held just a bed with a blue cover and a wardrobe. The one at the front with the balcony was the main bedroom. You couldn't call it the master anymore, which, Grace had been told by her daughters, had connotations dating back to the days of slavery. So many things to remember that she couldn't say anymore.

The bed in here was massive, with a blue-painted headboard, and there was room for a little sofa and a coffee table, facing the water. The view over the cove would certainly be spectacular. Grace crossed the room in the dark to look out at the sea. Tiny lights twinkled far away, and she imagined the fishermen hard at work hauling in their catch.

A noise behind her made her start.

Will stood in the doorway, arm on the top of the door, his bulk blocking her escape route.

'Lost, are we?'

'Just looking for the loo and took a wrong turn.'

He pointed into the corridor.

'That way.'

Grace dipped under his arm, brushing up against him as she did so, releasing a burst of his lemon aftershave, and ran to lock herself in the bathroom. Why did he have to come upstairs at that moment and catch her in his room? When she opened the door again, he was gone.

As dawn began to break over the sea below, the guests started to drift off, and the music changed to chill-out jazz and slow dance numbers.

Grace spotted Angeliki sharing a smooch with Nick and gave her friend a thumbs-up. She should think about leaving soon. Whether Angeliki would be coming with her was another matter.

Will appeared in the doorway and held out his hand towards her.

'Dance?'

The smoochy music was still coming out of the speakers.

'I'd prefer something a bit more upbeat.'

'Oh, come on, just one dance.'

'OK, just one.'

Will took her hand and led her onto the makeshift dancefloor on the terrace. He held her close, too close, and Grace tried to separate her body from his by leaning back, but Will gently pulled her in tight again. Grace forced herself to relax. Her body fitted his perfectly and the pressure of his hips against hers felt disturbingly good. She hadn't been in another man's arms like this for years.

He was a good dancer, she had to admit, but it was just wrong. It should be Phil's arms around her. Not the strong arms of a man she'd only known for a couple of months. A man who seemed to have women falling over themselves to be with him. As soon as the music ended, she slipped out of his arms and headed for the kitchen and a glass of water.

There was a mess of dumped glasses and plates everywhere, and it was hard to find a clean glass. Grace automatically filled the dishwasher and washed a glass for herself in the sink. Anything to stop thinking about how close her body had been to Will's. When she looked up from the tap, Celine was standing a few feet away.

'Keeping house, are we?'

'Excuse me?'

Even the way the woman said 'owse' in her French accent set Grace's teeth on edge.

'That's not the way to Will's heart, being the housewife.'

Shut up, you silly French bitch was on the tip of Grace's tongue, but that would be playing into her hands. Grace satisfied herself with a glacial smile.

'It's a good thing that I'm not looking for a way to Will's heart then, isn't it? Knock yourself out.'

Grace strode past the woman and straight past Will who had come into the room. She couldn't be sure if he'd heard that little exchange, but she didn't much care. Angeliki was on the terrace, exchanging numbers with Nick.

'Are you ready to go, Angeliki?'

'Taxi's waiting. I was just coming to find you.'

'Perfect.'

Chapter Twenty-One

G race's hangover had already started to dissipate by the time she got out of bed at two in the afternoon. She'd remembered to drink water and take painkillers before she went to sleep, so things could have been a lot worse.

Celine's thin face came back to haunt her as she showered. The woman had a bitterness about her that would never be erased. And all because of Will. She didn't know the ins and outs of his relationship with the Frenchwoman, and she had no desire to, but it obviously hadn't ended well. Celine was one unhappy woman.

Was it really worth volunteering yourself for the battlefield that was relationships? She'd had a long and happy marriage, and for many people that was enough for one lifetime. Was she being greedy if she hoped for another connection as strong as the one she'd had with Phil?

It came to her that she'd forgotten to do anything at the party about asking Will to adopt Karen. In the taxi, Angeliki had again mentioned that the young cat was ready to be rehomed.

Karen had had all her injections, and her slight eye infection had cleared up. Angeliki needed to free up space in her surgery as soon as possible. But Grace had let the night get away from her, not helped by the fact that Will had been surrounded by various women most of the time, and not available to chat. Slammed up against his chest during the dance and having to whisper in his ear wouldn't have been quite the right time to broach it either.

Her phone had been on silent while she slept, but when she checked it, there was a message from the party giver.

> Hope you enjoyed the party. Still not thanked you properly for the other night. Know you'll have work tomorrow. Care to meet me at four down by the port? Usual café?

She wasn't quite sure what was on offer, but a leisurely coffee and maybe a club sandwich would do.

> Yes, fine.

> Fine? Let's aim for something a bit better than that. Make sure you've got hat and swimming stuff.

Just what was she letting herself in for? Grace thought about making an excuse – she could do with a quiet afternoon – but the thought of Karen's little face at the bars of her cage stopped her. It would be more difficult to meet up and persuade him to take Karen while she was working. He was already a few days into his holiday, so the sooner he settled Karen in, the better.

Ok. See you then.

Grace took her seat at the café at five to four, but there was no sign of Will, which was unusual. Usually, he was the early bird. She'd wait for him before she ordered. Repeated honks of a boat horn a few feet away made her look up. She could see a man standing up in a small wooden boat. Why was he making all that noise on a Sunday afternoon?

The penny dropped as the man waved in her direction. Oh, no, not a boat. He'd surprised her with a motorbike, now a boat. How many toys did this man have? Was he going to land on the roof of the language school in a helicopter next? Boats were her least favourite thing. She'd better go over and explain that the afternoon was off.

'Grace! Over here.'

Grace made her way to where Will stood on the quay.

'Surprise!'

'Yes, and I wish you'd told me. I hate boats. I would have said no straightaway if you'd warned me.'

Boats had been Phil's thing. Not hers.

Will's face fell.

'Ah, I thought you'd be pleased.'

'Well, you thought wrong.'

Grace was aware she was being rude, but really Will couldn't have picked a worse idea.

He pointed seawards.

'If you're worried about the water, it's calm as a millpond out there this afternoon. There won't be any waves, and I'll stick close to the shoreline. I just thought it would be a nice idea to potter around the island, get away from the crowds and see the beaches from a completely different viewpoint.'

His face was that of a small boy's who'd been told that no, he couldn't go out to play with his friends, but still thought it was worth trying it on.

'I've got my captain's licence if that's what's worrying you. We'll be perfectly safe. Why don't you give it a go, and if you still hate it, I'll bring you straight back and we can go for lunch in town.'

His sales pitch was impressive, she had to give him that. And she had only been out on a boat once, in the middle of a roaring gale in the Channel, with the rain driving into her face like nails. She had no idea what it would be like to be out in a boat in the Greek sunshine on a calm sea. Maybe he had a point. And she mustn't forget the whole reason for seeing him was to persuade him to take Karen.

'OK, five minutes it is. And you promise to bring me back if I hate it?'

He did the sign of the cross on his chest.

'Cross my heart and hope to die.'

'Slightly dramatic.'

Will put out a hand to help her onto the boat. She sat down as directed on a polished wooden seat at the back of the vessel while Will manoeuvred out of the busy port. The boat was certainly well looked after. Everything gleamed. It reminded her of Will's shoes. It was like one of those boats you'd see in films from the sixties with Sophia Loren in a silk headscarf being piloted along the Riviera by a hunky Italian. Grace wished she'd brought a headscarf with her. Her hair would no doubt be a tangled mess by the time they'd finished.

Within minutes the craft was hugging the coast and Grace sat back and let the hot sun beat down on her. The occasional spray thrown up by the motion of the boat peppered her body with welcome droplets of water. She had to admit that so far it was nothing like her previous experience off the English coast on a grey Sunday in March.

The sound of the engine made it hard to talk, but Grace was quite content to sit and take in the scenery, as the familiar landmarks she saw on her walks punctuated their route. It was strange to see the little white churches with their blue domed roofs from another angle and to realise how tiny they looked from out at sea. They passed the town beach, which was packed, and she strained to try and see if Charlie and Sarah were there, playing with Buster, but they weren't close enough to make out individual people.

The little coves scattered all along the coastline looked inviting, and as they neared the top of the island, there were fewer and fewer people lying on the sand or swimming.

Grace remembered to look at her phone. They'd been going for twenty minutes. She'd been so absorbed, she hadn't even noticed.

Will turned back for a moment.

'Feeling OK? Happy to carry on?'

Grace couldn't pretend the trip was an ordeal. She did a thumbs-up and watched as Will stood firm at the wheel, making slight movements this way and that. His swim shorts and white T-shirt left plenty of opportunity to watch the muscles in his arms and legs as they worked to keep the boat on course. Grace forced herself to look away. It wasn't like she was studying for an anatomy exam any time soon.

The boat slowed down once they'd rounded the end of the island, and she could see that Will was heading for a tiny cove almost hidden in the rocks. A few metres from shore he killed the engine.

'We need to wade in from here. So, shoes off, and then I might need a bit of help pulling the boat onto the sand, please.'

'Wilco. Over and out.'

Why had she said that? As if she was one of his men on an exercise. But he was lucky he wasn't with Angeliki or Celine. They wouldn't be much use hauling a boat around. Not that he'd pick his girlfriends for their brute strength or ability to drag boats to shore. That would be a bit niche.

Once they were settled on the sand, on Will's trusty lightweight blanket again, he unpacked the picnic.

'I take it you're hungry?'

'Why do you always assume I'm hungry?'

'Aren't you?'

He went to put the stuff back into his rucksack.

'OK, yes. But you make me sound like I'm constantly desperate to stuff something down my gob.'

His smile reached all the way to his eyes.

'Charming thought. But having known women who don't appear to let more than a morsel pass their lips, I like the fact you've got a healthy appetite.'

Celine's stick-like arms came into Grace's mind. It probably was a refreshing change spending time with someone who ate like a horse. She must stop thinking about Celine though. It wasn't as if she was some sort of rival. Grace had no desire to even be in the contest.

Will pulled out a series of containers.

'A lot of this is stuff left over from the party. It needs to be eaten up or I'll have to chuck it out.'

'And I'm the human dustbin who's going to do it?' Grace smiled to let him know she wasn't serious.

'Exactly.'

There was a bottle of sauvignon blanc in the bottom of the rucksack, which Will opened and poured her a glass of, before helping himself to water.

'Are you not having one?'

'Not when I'm in charge of the boat.'

'So, you just keep plying me with drink...' Grace stopped before the words 'and have your wicked way with me' even thought about coming out of her mouth or lodging in his mind. She downed the wine instead and concentrated on the horizon.

The sound of a phone buzzing in his rucksack made her look round. Will delved inside and pulled it out.

'More people thanking me for the party. I'm going to turn the bloody thing off for a while. Enjoy the peace and quiet.'

'Me too.'

Grace switched hers to silent as well and stretched out her legs. The whole 'having to be permanently connected to the rest of the world' thing got to her sometimes.

'Do you remember the days when there was only one phone in the house?'

Will smiled. 'Yes. Ours was in the hall, and we were told not to use it without permission on pain of death.'

'Ours was in the front room. My dad used to go ballistic about the phone bills. With two girls at home who needed to speak to their mates a lot, they were high.'

'I can imagine.'

'But I found a way to outsmart him.'

She'd got Will's interest.

'How?'

'A boy at school's dad worked for BT and he gave me a special number that the engineers used to test the phone. It was something like 147. So, I used to sneak into the front room when no one was looking, ring the number and then run out again. Then I'd shout out "I'll get it!", rush back in, ring a friend's number and talk away for as long as I wanted, with my dad thinking they'd made the call. He couldn't work out why the bills weren't going down.'

Will stared at her for a moment.

'Wow. Very naughty. But also impressive. I bet you were a right handful as a teenager.'

'You could say that.'

Memories of staying out late and keeping her poor dad waiting up for her came back into her mind. He'd be sat in his pyjamas in the kitchen with a cup of tea and the paper when she got back from whatever party she'd been to, and the rows would start.

'I did give my dad the runaround, I will admit.'

'I feel for the guy.'

'So did I, once I grew up and had kids of my own that I worried about as teenagers, still worry about as adults. I loved my dad to bits, but at the time I didn't think where I was going and what I was doing were any of his business. It's funny how your mindset changes.'

'I think all teenagers like to keep a few secrets from their parents. Which is probably a good thing.' Will's smile had her wondering what sorts of secrets he was talking about. 'Every generation thinks they've discovered the wonder of sex, don't they?'

Ah, those sorts of secrets. She didn't want to start swapping stories of teenage fumbling.

'I feel sorry for kids these days,' she replied. 'We had so much more freedom. There wasn't all this tracking your loved ones with phone apps and knowing where they are every moment of the day and night.'

'No, you're right. In the holidays, my mum would chuck us out of the door in the morning and not expect us back until teatime. No one had a clue where we were or what we were doing. Usually, nothing much. Riding our bikes to the stream, smoking or trying to chat up girls was probably as far as it went.'

Grace had an inkling that Will hadn't had to try too hard. She accepted another glass of wine and a small piece of the moon-shaped birthday cake, then they both lay back on the blanket. There wasn't a lot of shade on the beach, and unless she did something fast, she was in imminent danger of dozing off.

The extra layer of her swimming costume under her clothes made her even hotter. She'd put in on before she left in case there wasn't anywhere easy to change. She hadn't fancied doing it under Will's eagle eye.

'How about a swim before we head back?'

Will had taken the words out of her mouth.

'Just what I was thinking.'

Grace stripped off and rushed into the sea before she could change her mind or be confronted with Will without his T-shirt.

He overtook her after just a few strokes, but she caught him again at the edge of the bay and shouted over. 'Last back to the picnic gets a prize.'

They raced neck and neck to the shore, but Grace just pipped him to the post as she flopped down on the blanket on her back.

'Yes! Winner!'

Will lay down beside her and leant over so his face was inches away. Grace thought for one crazy moment that he was going to kiss her, but she didn't have time to find out whether it was something she wanted, as he rolled away again.

'OK, you won fair and square. What do you demand as your prize?'

This was her moment. She propped herself up on one elbow.

'You know Karen, the kitten we rescued.'

'Yes…'

Will sat up.

'She's all grown-up now, and ready to leave home…'

'I think I know where this is going.'

'So, will you adopt her and have her at yours? Please?'

'That's quite a big prize for a very small swim. I don't know anything about looking after animals. I've never even had a pet.'

'What, never?'

'No. As I've told you, my dad was in the army and often away, and my mum had three of us boys to deal with. She said she couldn't cope with any more living creatures in the house that needed looking after.'

'Ah, that's sad. Every child should have a pet at some stage.'

'Except the ones who pull the legs off spiders for fun and then turn into serial killers, presumably.'

'Yes, except them… So, is that a yes?'

'You're a very persuasive woman, Grace. But you don't get off lightly either. I will expect you to come round regularly to help with … pet things.'

'You really don't have a clue, do you?'

'Do you want me to take the cat or not?'

'Yes, I do. Thank you, thank you.'

Grace reached over to hug Will at the same time as he lay back down on the blanket, and she landed bang on top of him.

Their eyes met for a moment before Grace unglued herself from his bare wet chest.

'Whoops.'

Will's eyes were full of laughter, and something else that Grace didn't want to think about. She leapt to her feet.

'Can we go and collect her now, please?'

'Now?'

'I'm sure Angeliki would open up for us. She only lives a minute away from the surgery. But of course'—Grace gave him the side eye—'you know that.'

'I do indeed.'

It was sensible to remind herself that Will had had several relationships on the island that hadn't worked out.

Angeliki was only too happy to get rid of Karen to a good home and was waiting for them at the surgery when they got back.

'I can give you some spare food and lend you this carrier for today, as long as you bring it back in the next couple of days, Will.'

'Scout's honour.'

Grace giggled, which earnt her a funny look from her friend. Two large glasses of wine in the afternoon could do that to her.

Karen purred away like a tiny motor when Grace transferred her from the cage to the carrier.

'See, she loves me.'

Angeliki looked between them.

'It's more important that she loves Will, unless you're planning to move in as well.'

Grace attempted a laugh, which had both of them staring at her.

'Ha-ha. Of course not. But I will be visiting regularly to make sure she's properly looked after.'

Will put his hands on his hips.

'How dare you suggest that I will fall short in any way!'

'Well, you certainly need a few lessons in pet care, from what you were saying earlier.'

Angeliki shut the cage door with a bang.

'Anyway, you two, I'm sure you've got things to be getting on with. I've got a date in...' Angeliki glanced at the clock. 'Fifteen minutes.'

Grace stroked the fabric of Angeliki's orange linen dress.

'I thought you were looking smarter than usual.'

'Charming. I come all this way to help you…'

Grace silenced her friend with a hug.

'Is it with Nick?'

'Yes.'

'Oooh, how exciting.'

'Well, if I don't get there, I'll never know.'

Will picked up the carrier and blew a kiss at Karen cowering inside.

'Thanks, Angeliki. Will she be OK on the boat? I've got to drive it back to the cove.'

'She won't break. As long as Grace can hold her steady.'

Grace waved her hand in the air. It would be a breeze compared to the rescue on the motorbike.

'No problem. So, coffee update in my lesson break tomorrow? Yes?'

'OK.' Angeliki directed a look at Will. 'It seems we have something to discuss.'

Grace gave her friend her best puzzled look and headed for the door.

The journey back was as gentle as the way there. Grace kept Karen entertained with little bits of a serviette she had in her bag and was rewarded with plenty of purring.

It really had been a glorious afternoon on the water. Consigning boats to being part of Phil's world and not hers had been shortsighted. And her world didn't need to be divided up like that anymore. It had taken her this long to realise it.

Chapter Twenty-Two

I t was just an ordinary Monday. Grace repeated that to herself over and over again. She couldn't let the fact that it was three years to the day since Phil had died overwhelm her. She refused to say she'd 'lost' Phil or that he'd 'passed'. They were such silly words to use. She hadn't 'lost' him – that sounded like he'd been mislaid in an aisle in Sainsbury's – and 'passed' always made her think of exams. One old neighbour had rung her the week after Phil's death to say she'd only just heard that Phil had 'passed'. Grace had had to summon up every ounce of her strength not to say, 'Yes, thankfully I don't have to drive him around anymore.'

It was up to other people how they described what had happened to their loved ones, but she just preferred to go straight in with 'died'. There was a lot of considering other people's feelings after a death, far more than she'd thought, and there'd been days when she'd been too exhausted to cope with anyone else's grief as well as her own. Her daughters or Sofia had gently turned people away from the door, saying that she was resting, which was a joke in itself. There'd been precious little rest in those first few weeks.

A vision of Phil's emaciated body in his raised bed at the hospice caused her to let out a tiny cry. This was no good. She had a lesson in twenty minutes, with Stelios's parents, the restaurant owners. Grace forced herself to think happy thoughts. She hadn't wanted to take the day off, or draw attention to the date, which held no significance for anyone else on the island. She hadn't even told Angeliki, although they were meeting for coffee later.

Grace had a quick look at her and Phil's wedding photo on her phone, both of them so young and full of hope, her in a white silk meringue of a dress with a bouquet of forget-me-nots and roses, and Phil in top hat, tails and embroidered waistcoat, flanked by three bridesmaids and a pageboy, coming out of the church.

Neither of them had wanted anything quite so flamboyant, but her mother had insisted. Parents had had a lot more say in those days, mused Grace, as she dressed. They were usually paying for everything and wanted their own friends and numerous elderly relatives present.

These days, as far as she could see, the happy couple paid for most of it themselves and had complete say over the guestlist. She thought back to Flo and Jilly's wedding, a ceremony in a barn, followed by an elegant vegetarian lunch for twenty, with their friends getting top billing, and none of her and Phil's cronies present at all. In many ways, it made a lot more sense.

Grace added a little more makeup than usual and put plenty of concealer under her eyes to try and cover up the dark circles that were all too visible. After the relaxing afternoon on the boat, she'd barely slept, haunted by dreams of her husband: Phil as a young man, Phil with the girls, Phil fighting for breath in the hospice. She had thirty-five years of memories to draw on. It wasn't like she was going to run out anytime soon.

A smiling Stelios opened the door to her when she arrived for his parents' lesson – a few minutes late, as she'd needed to carry out emergency repairs to her face after more crying. Grace made a big fuss of Mikey the dog before the boy took her out onto the large covered terrace where his parents were waiting.

'Grace. Welcome.'

Konstantina pulled her in for a hug, which almost set Grace off again. Was it a stupid idea to come to work today? It was people showing affection that undid all her good intentions, far more than indifference.

Grace held onto the woman for a few seconds longer than necessary and smiled in the direction of Apollo, her husband.

She managed to get through the lesson somehow, which she'd structured as role play: difficult restaurant customers and how to deal with them. Playing foreigners complaining about the table they'd been given, the wait for the food, and elements of the food itself was quite therapeutic, as was pretending to be annoyed by their responses to her gripes.

The couple worked calmly as a team to sort out the problems, and Grace was pleased with the progress she'd seen in their language skills in the few weeks she'd known them. They'd opted to take private lessons with her, and the investment was paying off.

'Well done, both of you. Your English really is improving fast.'

Apollo gathered his wife up in his arms and kissed her thoroughly before speaking.

'Thank you, Grace. You make it seem easy.'

The couple held hands all the way to the door to show her out again.

She mustn't fall into the trap of feeling sorry for herself, not today.

Angeliki was waiting at the café in the port near the surgery, two cappuccinos already on the table.

'You're late!'

'Yes, sorry. My lesson overran a bit.'

And she'd had to hide round the corner after leaving Stelios's house to have a little cry.

'Is everything OK?'

'Yes, fine.'

Angeliki didn't seem convinced. 'You look a little … tired.'

'Thanks.'

'I'm worried about you.'

'There's nothing to worry about, honestly.'

She hadn't been able to bring herself to tell her new friend about the significance of the date. It would all be over tomorrow, and then she could carry on as normal.

'Enough about me. What about you and Nick? How was the date?'

Angeliki's eyes turned dreamy.

'It was lovely. He took me to a rooftop bar and ordered champagne and strawberries with chocolate sauce.'

'Oooh, fancy. And did you feed them to each other?'

'No, we're not at that stage yet.'

'OK, didn't realise that was a stage.'

'But we're seeing each other again tomorrow night, for a proper dinner.'

'Sounds great.'

'I really like him, Grace. He's easy to talk to, he has minimal baggage for a man of his age and I think he's cute, like a cuddly teddy bear.'

'Yes, I bet he'd be very considerate in bed.'

'Grace!'

She wasn't sure where that had come from. Everything was out of kilter today. It was Sofia who came up with the raunchy comments, not her. At that moment a message came in on her phone. Will's name flashed up.

> Karen seems good today. But she's asking for you. Can you come over after work?

A picture of the cat with its paw raised, being held in Will's big hand, made her smile, but she couldn't possibly do what he asked, not today anyway.

Angeliki's eyes were on her as she took a sip of coffee.

'Who was that?'

'Oh, just Will. Asking me if I want to visit Karen today.'

'"Just Will"? What is going on between you two?'

'Nothing, I've told you before. We're friends but that's it.'

'Friends don't look at each other the way I saw you and Will looking at each other on the dancefloor at the party. He looked like he wanted to rip your clothes off on the spot, and you looked like you wanted to let him. You couldn't get a cigarette paper between you.'

'Rubbish. And anyway, why weren't you staring into Nick's eyes? You shouldn't have been spying on us.'

'I wasn't spying. It was hard to miss. Celine certainly thought so. She had me up against the fridge-freezer demanding I give her all the details.'

'Well, luckily there were none to give, because there is nothing going on.'

'OK, if you want to carry on saying that, it's up to you…'

'I do.'

Grace had to look away for a moment. If she told her friend about the significance of the day, Angeliki would probably feel awful about suggesting there was something going on with Will while Grace was mourning her dead husband. Angeliki knew that she was a widow, but obviously not what a big deal today was.

Grace rushed through the rest of her coffee under Angeliki's watchful eye.

'I'll have to leave a bit early. I forgot I'd booked in an extra lesson, and I've got to do some prep for it, sorry.'

'That's not like you, to forget.'

Nor was barefaced lying to your friends, but needs must.

'Can I make it up to you by taking you for a posh coffee at the Hotel Artemis tomorrow? Same time?'

Angeliki raised her eyebrows.

'Sure, see you there.'

Grace managed to get back to her room before she allowed herself a proper cry. She lay on the bed face down and wept into the pillow. When she raised her head, all the extra makeup she'd put on earlier was smeared across the pillowcase. She'd have to get it in the wash as soon as possible.

The computer in the corner sprang into life, and Sofia's icon appeared on screen. Her best friend was the only person she could bear to talk to. She'd messaged both her daughters earlier saying she was thinking of them today and put a picture of the four of them together on the WhatsApp group. They'd replied with kisses and hearts but, based on what had happened on the same day last year, they'd all agreed in advance that it would only be agony to try and speak. There was an added pressure not to get upset this year. Lottie needed to keep calm for the baby.

Sofia's smiling face appeared on screen but dimmed as soon as Grace appeared in vision.

'You look bloody awful.'

'Thanks. You're supposed to be my friend.'

'I am your friend. And I'm telling you that you can't go out looking like that.'

'I know. Thankfully, I've finished work for the day, and I'm not planning to leave my room again until after dark.'

'OK, that doesn't sound weird at all.' Sofia blew her a kiss. 'I'm not going to ask you how you're feeling, as I can see for myself.'

Grace let out a big sigh.

'Oh, Sof. I thought it would be better this year, that it would get easier, not harder.'

'The human mind is a strange thing. Its complexities can never truly be understood.'

'Crikey. Are you channelling Freud or something?'

'At least it's made you smile.'

'Seriously though, I don't know why everyone says that all the bad memories will go away quickly and be replaced by only good ones. That's bollocks.'

'Yeah, bollocks.'

'Some people seem to think that after a year, or two at the most, you should be over it and move on. That you're somehow'—Grace drew quotation marks in the air—'"wallowing" if you show any signs of still being heartbroken. That there's some strict grief timetable to follow that's written down somewhere, like the Bible.'

'But we don't care about the people who say that, do we?'

'No, we don't.'

A couple of serious-looking young women had appeared in her friend's office, and were standing waiting behind her.

'Really sorry, but I'm going to have to go into a—'

'Meeting?'

'Yes, I'll try you later. Chin up. Love you lots.'

'Love you too.'

Even the briefest chat with her friend had cheered Grace up a bit. She had a plan to get through the rest of the evening and night. It involved beer, crisps and a blanket.

A crime caper starring George Clooney took up a chunk of the afternoon, but Grace was relieved when dusk arrived at long last, and she could set out on Operation Phil. She walked to her special cove and set up camp between some big rocks on the beach. A night under the stars would do her the power of good. Phil had loved camping, so he'd approve. It would make her feel closer to him.

Everyone had left the beach for the night, and the little bar was closed, but she felt completely safe. The air was warm, and she had chilled beer and cheese and onion crisps in her bag. What more could a girl need? She could always get a taxi back if it all got too much.

Grace opened the first of the bottles and took a sip of the dry Greek beer. It slipped down easily. It never got completely dark on the island, as the canopy of stars above her head in the pollution-free sky gave out plenty of light. Tonight, by coincidence, there was a full moon as well, which left a shining strip of gold on the sea, like a pathway to another world.

She got out the scented candle she'd bought the previous day in town and a box of matches. Luckily there was no wind tonight, and the candle burned strong, giving out wafts of bergamot and jasmine. Not that Phil had been a big candle fan, but she'd always scattered them around the house when he'd been alive, so the smell reminded her of cosy nights in by the fire.

Grace lay back on the sand with her beer and let her album of Phil photos run through her mind on a loop. She was tempted to put on some of Phil's favourite music as well, but she'd forgotten her headphones and it probably wasn't fair on other people. Not that she was letting other people intrude into her thoughts tonight.

A sudden noise to the right made her sit up.

Will's face loomed up over the rock.

'Grace? What the hell are you doing here? Is everything OK?'

Oh, yes, it had to be him. Why was he skulking around the beach at night? He had a perfectly good house just a few yards away. Maybe it hadn't been such a brilliant idea to come here. Out of all the coves in all the world, she'd chosen this one.

He came round and knelt next to her. Again, his hair was wet and his chest was bare. He'd obviously just got out of the sea. Grace stared at the individual hairs on his chest until they blurred into one, unable to speak.

'Grace, what is it? Are you hurt?'

She managed to shake her head.

'Why are you here on the beach in the dark? I've been trying to get hold of you all day.'

It was true, he'd sent her several messages with different pictures of Karen, urging her to come over.

Will took her face in his hands.

'You don't want to talk. Is that it?'

Grace nodded.

'Have you ever been moonlight swimming?'

What was he on about?

'You swim along the line of the moon on the water. It's very special. I think it might help you with whatever you're struggling with.'

She had nothing to lose. The evening couldn't possibly get any worse. She'd put her costume on underneath her shorts and T-shirt anyway in case she managed a swim before night fell.

He held out his hand, and Grace got to her feet and stripped off her clothes. They walked together to the sea's edge, still holding hands. Will turned to face her.

'Do you trust me?'

Weirdly, and she'd probably regret it, but she did. She nodded.

They entered the water slowly, Grace acclimatising her body to the still warm water, but slightly disorientated by the dark.

Once her eyes focused, it was easy. They swam along the light path, and then floated on their backs for a while, staring up at the stars, in complete silence. The beauty of the moon on the water did lift her spirits a tiny bit.

Will seemed to know when she'd started to feel chilly and took her hand again to pull her towards the shore. They flopped down on the sand together and Grace took two beers out of the bag and passed one to him. He hadn't pushed her to say anything, for which she was grateful. It also helped that it was properly dark now. She didn't need to look at his face.

Halfway down her beer, Grace stopped drinking, unable to stop the tears.

His arm went around her shoulders.

'What is it, Grace? You can tell me anything.'

She probably could as well.

'Today is the third'—Grace paused for a gulp—'anniversary of Phil's death.'

'Oh, you poor love. I'm so sorry.'

He reached round and folded her into his arms. Grace gave in to the temptation to sob on his chest. The living, breathing man in front of her wanted to comfort her, and she needed that comfort.

Grace lifted her head for a moment and was able to see his eyes illuminated in the moonlight. There was a lot more than simple comfort there. And she was going to take what was on offer. Grace bent down and kissed him gently on the mouth.

Will's shock only lasted a second before he kissed her back, their tongues exploring each other's mouth, and their bodies entwining.

A fire had been lit inside her, and Grace knew there was no stopping it. It had been smouldering for weeks, but she'd been too scared to fan the flames.

Will turned his body, so that she was partly underneath him. He raised himself up on one elbow and stared into her eyes.

'Are you sure about this?'

It was like her body was making all the decisions rather than her mind. And her body had vetoed any objections that her mind could come up with.

Grace nodded and Will kept up eye contact all the time he spoke.

'It's what I've wanted for a long time … ever since the moment I saw you climbing over that wall, if I'm being completely honest, and more and more since I've got to know you. But I need to know that you want it too.'

Grace put her finger to his lips. There'd been enough talking.

'Shush. I want it.'

Will pulled down the straps of her swimming costume, exposing her breasts to the night air, and stopped to lick and suck them, making Grace arch her back like a cat. She reached down and touched him through his swimming trucks. He moaned softly.

He whipped off the rest of her costume and his own trunks in seconds and threw them on the sand. Grace pulled him down on top of her. As their bodies connected, she tried not to question whether it mattered who was making her feel like this. After so long without physical affection, could it have been any man she'd stumbled across on the beach or in the town? Did it need to be Will?

Grace let out a little cry as he entered her, his urgency matching her own. Will was the man bringing her body alive again. She needed to stay in the present. Grace deliberately emptied her mind and prayed for oblivion.

Salty skin met salty skin and the sound of the waves in her ears added to the rhythms in her body, as Will pressed into her over and over again. The waves built, crashing to shore faster and faster, until her mind and body hit overload and she screamed into the night air at the same time as Will let out a shout.

But the night was far from over. Will moved slowly down her body, kissing every inch of her skin on the way to his ultimate goal, and Grace cried out again at the touch of his tongue. Their bodies, hands and mouths met each other time and time again, changing shape but constantly connected.

It was a night like Grace had never known.

Finally, she lay naked and spent under the moonlight, Will breathing softly next to her. Her mind zoned back in and overpowered her body. What the hell had she done? The logical part of her brain told her they were both single, fully consenting adults who'd experienced something incredible together. So why did it feel like she'd been unfaithful to her husband? And why had she picked the anniversary of his death to do it when there were three hundred and sixty-four other days to choose from? What kind of person did that? A little voice in her head was asking her over and over again how she could betray Phil like this. Tonight of all nights.

Chapter Twenty-Three

The tears ran down the sides of her face and away onto the sand. There'd been so many tears today, but these were tears of shame, not sorrow. After pulling on his trunks, Will placed her T-shirt and shorts in her hand in the dark, and went to stand behind the rock he'd popped up from earlier that evening, so she could dress in private.

Luckily, he seemed to understand that she didn't want to be touched. There would be no repeat performance of whatever it was that had just happened. The horror of what she'd done, having sex on the anniversary of her husband's death, with a guy she'd only known for a couple of months, made her want to cover her eyes with her hands. No one could ever find out.

The fact that she'd never had sex like it wasn't somewhere she could let herself go. Sex with Phil had been good, very good at times, but nothing like that. That was an out-of-body experience, except her body had been very much present. It had been almost animalistic.

She dragged on her shorts and T-shirt and stuffed her bits

and pieces back into the bag. The night was well and truly over. It had ended in a way she'd never expected or planned. Will needn't think they were going back to his for another session. She took out her phone to call a cab, but he must have seen the light flare.

'I'll take you back, on the bike. I've only had one beer.'

It would mean touching his body again, but it was the quickest way to get back to her room and into the shower to wash away any trace of the evening. She might have to wait ages for a taxi at this time of night.

They made their way up to the house without speaking, and Will left her on the terrace for a moment while he dashed inside. He put on a T-shirt and some shoes but kept the swimming trunks. Probably worried that she'd change her mind and run off somewhere into the night. He might just be right.

The journey home in the dark was strangely intimate. The warm wind whistled past her ears and the crashing of the waves on the sand was the only sound she could hear above the engine. She tried not to wrap her arms around him too tightly, but it threw her off balance, so she had no option. It was only for a few minutes. His body was still damp against hers and the tang of salt in the air was something she knew she'd always associate with him from now on, whether she wanted to or not.

Outside the language school, he killed the engine and dismounted when she did, still not speaking, for which she was grateful. Once she'd put her key in the lock, she turned back and nodded her head at the man who'd followed her to her door.

'Thank you for taking me home.'
Will smiled briefly and walked away.

Grace stretched in the bed at the sound of her phone alarm. She'd slept like a log. Muscles that she'd forgotten she even had reminded her they'd been in full use recently. The night came back to her frame by frame. Her body felt like it had been put through some sort of assault course. The sheets were still a little damp from the shower she'd had the moment she'd got in. Unable to wait to dry herself properly, she'd been desperate to go to sleep and pretend that nothing had happened. At least she didn't need to worry about getting pregnant at her age, but she hoped she was the only woman that Will had slept with recently. A visit to an STD clinic didn't bear thinking about.

It was time to get on with the day. A lesson beckoned with an older Greek woman, Irene, another of Rose's castoffs that had been transferred to her timetable. Her pupil had an English pen pal and wanted to improve her letter writing. Irene was a sweet widow, who always pressed homemade cookies onto Grace when it was coffee time and wouldn't take no for an answer, like most of the Greeks she'd met. At least it wasn't Nick she was teaching, who might ask some awkward questions. She was sure she had scarlet woman written all over her face. The lesson was in half an hour, and she still had to dress and go to Irene's house. She'd better get a move on. Meeting Angeliki afterwards wasn't something she could even think about now. One step at a time.

Seated on the terrace of the Hotel Artemis two hours later,

Grace was beginning to feel a little better. The anniversary of Phil's death was over and done with, and no one need ever know what had happened last night. She was confident of Will's discretion, if nothing else. He hated gossip. If the two of them could get back to being friends again, with none of the sex stuff thrown in, that would suit her.

But if she'd helped ruin that idea for good, she only had another two and a half weeks to get through, and then she'd be back home in Oxfordshire. She wouldn't dwell on why the thought didn't bring her a whole lot of joy.

Angeliki took her seat at the table and raised her hand for the waiter.

'Cappuccino?'

'Yes, please, the usual.'

Angeliki had a strange air of suppressed excitement about her. It was just a simple coffee before she went back to work. The vet wasn't quite as busy these days as many of her regular customers had taken their pets on holiday with them and she was up for drinking her coffee out of the surgery. But she was definitely twitchy. What was going on? And why was she looking at her like that?

'Are you OK, Grace?'

'Yes, I'm fine. Why wouldn't I be?'

Grace reassured herself that Angeliki couldn't possibly know what had happened between her and Will. The island jungle drums weren't that good.

A message came in on her friend's phone and Angeliki glanced down briefly. There it was, that secretive look again.

Seconds later, there was a rustling behind the nearest olive tree on the terrace, and Sofia leapt out from behind it.

'Surprise!'

Grace rose to her feet to hug her friend.

'My God. What are you doing here?'

'You seemed so down yesterday that I took a few lieu days and jumped on a plane.'

'And … how did you know where I was this morning?'

Grace had had enough surprises in the last twenty-four hours. It was lovely to see her friend, but the whole thing was mighty confusing. Sofia and Angeliki were smiling at each other now.

'Ah, that's the clever bit. I'd heard you talk a lot about your new friend, Angeliki the vet, so it wasn't exactly hard to track her down and ask her a few questions. She was also worried about you, so we hatched a plan.'

'You sneaky little…'

Angeliki pulled up another chair for Sofia.

'What you mean to say is how lovely it is to have us both here with you, worrying about you.'

Grace had to smile. They'd gone to a lot of trouble to show they cared about her. She held out a hand to each of them.

'Thank you, Angeliki, for helping Sofia to keep this a secret. And thank you, Sofia, for dropping everything to come and see me. Is that better?'

Sofia summoned a waiter with the flick of a hand.

'Much better. Another cappuccino here, please.'

There was some chat about Sofia's flight and Angeliki's problem cases, which Grace tuned out of. She waited for Sofia to focus on her. It didn't take long.

'So, now it's not yesterday anymore, have things improved at all?'

Grace noticed the puzzled look on Angeliki's face, but so, unfortunately, did Sofia.

'She didn't tell you, did she?'

Angeliki leant in.

'Tell me what?'

'That yesterday was the third anniversary of her husband Phil's death?'

Angeliki did the sign of the cross on her navy linen shirt.

'No! Grace, how could you keep it from me? If I had known, I would have been at your side all day.'

Grace put her hand on her friend's arm.

'I'm sorry, but I was desperately trying to keep things upbeat. To kid myself that it was just a normal day.'

Just how abnormal it had turned out to be wasn't something she wanted to reveal at this point.

'But it was obvious that something was wrong. You looked so sad. And I could tell you had been crying.'

Grace gave Sofia a 'do you think this is helping?' look.

'Again, I apologise for keeping it to myself.'

She had told only one person on the island the truth but look at what that had led to.

Angeliki put down her coffee.

'Oh, no, I've just remembered that I was pushing you to talk about what was going on with Will! And all the time you were grieving for your dead husband. How could I have been so insensitive?'

'Don't upset yourself. You didn't know, and, as I said at the time, there's nothing going on with Will.'

Grace didn't want to catch Sofia's eye. Her friend had a nose for gossip that was more refined than any bloodhound.

'Will?'

'Sorry?' Grace tried to pretend for a moment she had no idea what Angeliki was talking about.

'She clearly said Will. That hot guy we saw in the street you told me was gay?'

Angeliki snorted so hard that some of her coffee went on the table.

'Will's not gay. Far from it.'

Grace looked up to see both pairs of eyes firmly trained on her.

'In my defence, when I said that, I genuinely believed it to be the case.'

Sofia turned to Angeliki.

'And do you know for sure that this Will is straight?'

Angeliki tried not to smile.

'I do, because he was my boyfriend for two years.'

Sofia slapped her hand on the table.

'Wow, this is a small island, isn't it?'

Grace started laughing at the same time as her two friends. Proper tears in your eyes and a pain in your stomach laughing. People from other tables looked their way as the three of them linked hands.

Her friends had inadvertently revealed two big secrets to each other, but her biggest and most shameful secret was still safe. She couldn't believe Sofia would leave it there though. They hadn't kept anything this big from each other in forty years. Grace let the laughter die away and waited for Sofia to carry on the inquisition.

'But why were you talking about Grace and Will? The only man I've heard her talk about is someone called Nick.'

Angeliki gave Grace a hard stare.

Oh, great, now Angeliki was going to think she had a thing for Nick. She'd better nip this in the bud. It was like some terrible stage farce with people rushing in and out of each other's bedrooms and lots of mistaken identities.

'Sofia's got the wrong end of the stick. I only mentioned Nick because he's one of my new students. He's a lovely guy.'

She gave Sofia their 'shut up now or I'll kill you' look.

'In fact … Angeliki has just started dating him. They met at Will's party.'

Sofia winked at her out of Angeliki's eyeline.

'Aaah, I love new romances. You'll have to tell me more. But I'd still like to hear all about Will's party.'

Grace stirred the froth on her cappuccino and put a spoonful in her mouth.

'There's nothing to tell.'

'Angeliki? What's your version? What was it that had you thinking there was something between our Grace and this Will?'

Grace knew that look. It spelled danger. Sofia was obviously furious at being left out of the loop.

Angeliki paused a moment.

'All I can say is that Will never looked at me like that when we were dancing. Talk about steamy.'

'That's so not true, Angeliki.'

Grace tried to hide her irritation at the way the conversation was going. Sofia wouldn't let it drop now, for sure.

Her phone buzzed with another message. It was the fourth that day from Will.

We really need to talk about last night.

He might do, but she certainly didn't. She wanted to forget last night ever happened.

Sofia moved her chair nearer to Grace's.

'Is that Will?'

'No. Why are you saying that?'

Her friends exchanged a look. Great, now they were ganging up on her. It was like being back in high school. She expected them to start singing 'Grace and Will, sitting in a tree' any moment.

Sofia bumped shoulders with her.

'Because you've gone bright red. It's soooo cute.'

'Shut it, now.'

Angeliki stood up.

'As much fun as this has been, I have to get back to some sick animals. Thanks for the coffee, Grace, and let's the three of us go out one night. It's been lovely to meet you, Sofia.'

'You too, Angeliki. Very illuminating.'

The two of them exchanged a smile.

As soon as the vet had left the terrace, Sofia threw down the last of her coffee.

'My hotel room, now.'

At least it wasn't far to walk was Grace's first thought, as they stepped into the lift to go down.

Sofia pressed the button for her floor.

'You look like you're being taken to the tower to be executed.'

'That's a bit how it feels.'

'Don't be ridiculous. We're just going for a girly chat.'

Grace resigned herself to her fate. The best in the business couldn't compete with Sofia when she wanted to pull something out of you. Her friend wasn't a highly paid lawyer for nothing.

The opulence of Sofia's hotel room startled Grace. Five-star luxury had never been her thing, personally or financially, but she could get used to this for a night or two.

The wooden ceiling high above them was divided into panels, each painted with a different scene, and the four-poster bed had a pleated white silk canopy above it like something she'd seen in a stately home. Antique furniture was dotted about, and the highly polished wooden floor was adorned with Persian rugs. The light lavender-coloured walls had a darker band of the shade at the bottom and on the woodwork, and instead of a boring pendant light, there was an intricate glass chandelier with flower-shaped bulb holders, delicately fluted in the same lavender as the walls.

'This is seriously beautiful, and, I should imagine, cripplingly expensive.'

Sofia led her over to the purple velvet sofa which faced the floor-to-ceiling windows and the view out across the bay.

'It is. But remember, I get a staff discount.'

Sofia winked.

'Oh, yes, the boy Adonis. Is that still going on?'

'He's not a boy, he's a fully grown man. And yes, it is. You make it sound like I use men up like tissues and then just discard them.'

Grace raised her eyebrows.

'So, it's not just me you're back for.'

'Don't be silly. I would have come back to the island at some point anyway, but this has just brought it forward a bit.'

'I bet Adonis is pleased. He's arranged the best suite, and we're still in tourist season. He must like you.'

Sofia patted the space next to her on the sofa.

'We're not here to talk about me.'

Well, it had been worth a try.

As soon as Grace sat down, Sofia grabbed both her hands so that she had no choice but to face her friend.

'This Will… Have you slept with him?'

Grace's heart beat a tattoo in her chest.

'No, of course not.'

Sofia's eyes were full of understanding.

'OK, that's a truly pathetic attempt at lying.'

Grace's eyes refused to obey her yet again, and the tears fell thick and fast.

Sofia took her in her arms and stroked her hair.

'Did it happen last night, the night of Phil's anniversary?'

It was like the woman was psychic. Grace nodded miserably.

'OK, not ideal timing, I'll admit. But never mind.'

Grace took the tissue that Sofia offered.

'One last question, and then you are free, little one.'

Grace mentally adopted the brace position.

'What?'

'What was it like?'

She looked her friend in the eye.

'It was amazing. Scary, but amazing.'

It felt good to say it.

Sofia stood up and punched the air.

'Yes! At last! Go Will.'

'OK, calm down.'

Having admitted that no, she didn't have any more lessons that day, and yes, she could go shopping and out to dinner, Grace was again witness to Sofia's desire to spend money.

They'd been in nearly every shop in town and had the embossed bags to prove it. Grace was more than ready to call it a day, but Sofia's eye had been caught by a tiny boutique whose window was stuffed with no doubt extremely expensive things.

'Let's go in here. Last one, honest. Then I'll treat you to a fabulous dinner at the hotel. Please.'

'OK. I suppose so.'

Her friend had come all this way to see her, and she never had much free time to shop in London. Grace watched Sofia stroke a watered silk dress with a reverence usually reserved for a firstborn.

'I want to try this.' Sofia rifled through the rails. 'And this, and this. So many lovely things that want to come and live in my wardrobe.'

'I'm surprised there's any room.'

Sofia stuck out her tongue and disappeared into the changing rooms with her booty.

Grace took the pink velvet stool outside and waited. A movement at the back of the shop distracted her from totting up Sofia's spending. A door opened, and Celine walked through it. That was all she needed. She should have thought when she saw the enormous gold C outside the shop. It was the sort of place she'd normally never venture into in a million years.

She spotted the Frenchwoman a fraction before Celine saw her, so she was able to observe the way she put on her professional smile.

'Grace, *kalispera*.'

'*Kalispera*, Celine.'

'Are you waiting to try on some of our clothes?'

Celine didn't bother to temper the astonishment in her voice. It was almost comical.

'Out of my price range, I'm afraid. I'm waiting for my friend.'

'Ah, I see. I was worried that we might not have your size.'

Grace contented herself with a tight smile. It was either that or punch her.

Celine fiddled with a dress on the 'not wanted' rail.

'You left Will's party early. Strange, as you seemed to be enjoying yourself so much.'

'I wouldn't say early.'

Celine leant over and lowered her voice to a whisper. Her cloying perfume got right up Grace's nose, in more ways than one.

'I stayed right to the end, and I mean right to the end. I spent the night in Will's bed.'

Grace's heart squeezed in her chest. She mustn't let Celine see her shock. She was probably lying anyway.

'Good for you.'

The curtains opened with a flourish and Sofia stepped out. Grace wasn't sure how much of the conversation she'd heard.

'There's nothing here that I want.'

Celine looked past Sofia at the selection of clothes left hanging up in the cubicle.

'That is a shame. There are some stunning pieces.'

Sofia linked arms with Grace and walked towards the exit.

'Some of the quality is not what I would expect' was loud enough for another two women browsing the rails to turn round.

Grace snuck a look at Celine, who had a face like thunder. As soon as they were out of earshot, Sofia halted her stride.

'Who the hell was that? What a bitch. She sounded as if she hated you.'

Grace was confident that Sofia hadn't heard Celine's final words to her, otherwise she'd have been straight in with that. She wouldn't be repeating them to anyone.

'She's another of Will's exes. A very recent one.'

'Shit. Has he slept with every female on the island?'

The thought made her dizzy for a moment, but she needed to keep it light. The way to get through this was to make out that her night with Will had just been a bit of fun. Treat men like Sofia did, take what she wanted and move on. Will had broken her duck, admittedly in the most spectacular way possible, but he wasn't the only man out there.

'It's just the three of us, as far as I'm aware.'

She had no real idea if that was true.

'I'd like to meet this Will.'

Not if she could help it. She didn't want Will to know that she'd confessed all to Sofia. What had happened between them was private. But what Celine said had unnerved her. What if she was telling the truth? Last night had felt like something special. But maybe it was all in a day's work for Will. The sooner they got back to being friends and put the whole thing behind them the better.

'Maybe… But I don't think we'll manage it before you go. He's not around much.'

'He seems to be around you a lot.'

Grace hoped her frown was fierce enough to shut Sofia up.

Her friend threw up her hands.

'OK! I've got the message. Shame that woman in the shop was such a cow. The clothes were amazing. I'd have bought everything I tried on.'

Grace was just relieved they were off the subject of Will.

Chapter Twenty-Four

Grace had managed to avoid Will for almost three whole days, despite the numerous messages he'd sent, asking her to come over and visit Karen. He'd also supplied her with plenty of videos of the cat and she was pleased to see that his animal husbandry skills seemed sufficient to at least keep Karen alive. His hands appeared in most of the videos, stroking Karen, picking her up or teasing her with a toy, but she blanked those bits out, expanding the moving pictures so that she could only see the cat. Thinking about his hands and what they could do wouldn't help her at all.

His frantic texts after their night at the beach had finally forced her to send a short reply letting him know she was OK but very busy. He knew where she lived, and she didn't want him turning up on her doorstep. A bit of distance would do them both good.

Work and entertaining Sofia had genuinely kept Grace at full stretch, plus they'd had their promised night out with Angeliki, which included plenty of drink and laughter. Sofia had clearly made the most of her time in the four-poster with Adonis and was planning a rematch in September. Not that Grace would be around then to hear about it first-hand. But she'd made Sofia promise not to let on to Angeliki, or anyone, about what had happened with Will, and, as far as she could tell, her friend had kept her word.

Sofia had flown out this afternoon, and Grace was now ready to face Will at last and try and put their relationship firmly back in the friend zone. His holiday would be over soon, and he'd be working at the villa during the day, so Karen would need someone to pop in and keep an eye on her. Grace planned to offer her services. Will being out at work was greatly preferable to Will being there all the time, and she was genuinely keen to spend some time with the cat before she left.

The fact that she only had just over a fortnight more on the island wasn't something she could even think about.

Will's house came into view as she dropped down from the headland onto the familiar path to the cove. She hadn't ventured this way since the fateful night; she'd taken Sofia to a beach much nearer town. Sea grasses crunched underfoot on the sand path, filling her nostrils with the all too familiar salt tang. The smell of Will. It was vital that she kept her eyes fixed straight ahead, no looking down at the beach. She could do this.

There he was, larger than life, waving from the terrace. She tried out a jaunty 'we're just friends, nothing to see here' wave back.

'Grace!'

'Hi.'

He was holding Karen in his arms, looking like some sort of

adoption ad where they were deliberately trying to move away from the image of middle-aged women and cats and going instead for shots of a hunky guy cradling a tiny, vulnerable kitten. It wasn't going to work on her. She couldn't let it.

Grace focused on Karen, so she didn't have to look at him.

'She's grown again, in less than a week.'

'Yes, she has. Even I can see it.'

Will indicated the sun lounger by his side.

'Coffee?'

'Yes, please.'

'While I make it, can you hold Karen? I'm still a bit wary of letting her run around outside on her own.'

Grace nodded. It was like they were talking about a toddler they were looking after, maybe a grandchild. She had a sudden vision of them watching a little boy with dark unruly hair running around the terrace and blinked hard to get rid of it. She settled herself on the chair and waited for Will to put the kitten in her lap. Their fingers touched as he transferred his little bundle of fur to her, but she still didn't look up.

Karen stared at her with solemn green eyes, and Grace tentatively stroked the top of her head and down her back all the way to her tail. The cat was silent for a few moments, but Grace's heart leapt when she heard the telltale purr.

'Yes, sweetheart, you haven't forgotten me, have you? Sorry I haven't seen you for a few days, but I've had a lot on, and I haven't been able to come over here, much as I wanted to. But I'll make it up to you, I promise.'

When she looked up, Will was stood with two cups of coffee in his hands, a plate of biscuits balanced on top of one of them, and a big grin on his face. How had he snuck up on her like that? Did he have some sort of special shoes from his army days that made no noise?

'Are you going to make it up to me, too? I've got a few ideas on how.'

Grace pretended she hadn't heard him speak and reached for one of the coffees that Will seemed reluctant to hand over. He pulled it out of her reach.

'Can you drink this and hang onto Karen at the same time, or shall I put her inside for a minute?'

'I'm perfectly capable of doing two things at once, and not covering the cat with boiling coffee, honest.'

'I'm sure you are. You're a very versatile woman.'

The way he said 'versatile' with a tiny lift of the eyebrows made her squirm in her seat. She'd have to get the 'we're only ever going to be friends' conversation on track as soon as possible.

Grace settled Karen at her side and took a long slurp of freshly ground coffee. Will proffered the plate.

'Biscuit? They're homemade.'

She'd never had Will down as a baker, so it was probably one of his many women friends who'd brought them over.

'And before you ask, yes, I did make them myself. There's not been much else to do these past few days. All the books say you should spend as much time as you can with an animal in the period straight after you adopt them. So apart from the odd swim'—Will looked ahead to the beach, while Grace kept her eyes firmly on Karen—'cooking and reading have been my only distractions.'

'Couldn't you ask a friend to come over and keep you company?'

As soon as she'd said it, Grace wished she hadn't. She'd stressed the word 'friend' a little too heavily.

Will's eyes crinkled into a smile.

'I did, but she was far too busy to spare any time for little old me or our cat.'

'I did explain how busy I was... My best friend arrived without warning, and I'm still teaching private lessons.'

Will reached across from his seat. Grace thought he was about to touch her, but instead he stroked the cat, who purred instantly under his fingers. *Lucky cat* was Grace's first thought, which she pushed to the back of her mind.

'It's just that we missed her, this friend, didn't we, little one?'

They really needed to get this on a different footing. Will was straight out flirting with her. She couldn't afford to respond. There was no future in it. She was probably one of many women he flirted with. The night on the beach had been a one-off, to be treasured, taken out of her memory trunk and pored over like a family heirloom now and then, but never repeated.

The thought of Celine's over-tanned body entwined with Will's in his big bed a few feet away stiffened her resolve. She wasn't going to lower herself to ask him if what the woman had said was true. It was none of her business.

'You're back at work next week, aren't you?'

'Yes, why?'

'I was going to offer to look after Karen during the day in my breaks, so she had someone with her. My busy period's over, and I don't have many lessons in the fortnight before I go back to England. Most of them are in the evenings anyway, so I can be here when you're not.'

His brown eyes bored into hers.

'You're only on the island for another two weeks? I didn't realise you were leaving so soon.'

Was that all he'd taken away from what she'd just said? He hadn't even responded to her suggestion that she come and see Karen.

'I'm sure I mentioned it, but yes, my contract will be up then.'

Will's hand on hers forced her to look at him.

'Grace… We really need to talk about the other night.'

She couldn't do this. Not now.

'No, we really don't. It was fun, but we're both adults who've been around the block a few times.'

Why was she talking in terrible clichés?

'Fun? That's what you're calling it?'

Will tore his hand away from hers.

'It was a hell of a lot more than that, and you know it. You're just too scared to admit it.'

She'd certainly got him rattled. His hands were clenched into fists at his sides.

'I'm not in any position…'

Wrong word to use. It brought back a memory of them locking eyes while he was still inside her. Having him so close again had her rattled too. It was tempting to throw caution to the wind and suggest they went upstairs and bonked each other's brains out. It might get him out of her system. But she wasn't Sophia. For better or worse, Grace Foreman didn't behave like that. Or not more than once. Her Oxfordshire cottage and the single life she'd carefully created there beckoned.

Will was part of her Greek adventure, a moment out of time. He wasn't her reality. She needed to make the situation clear.

'I'm really not able to be anything other than friends with you.'

Will stood and gathered up the cups.

'OK, Grace, have it your own way.'

Before he went back into the house, he bent low over her head and whispered in her ear.

'Don't think that night on the beach was a typical night for me. I swear I've never experienced anything like that before in my life.'

Grace lay stock still for a moment on the sun lounger. She reached down to give Karen a stroke and tried to regulate her breathing.

When Will returned, he'd lost the promise in his eyes, which Grace convinced herself was a good thing.

'Do you want to come and check out where Karen sleeps and talk about where everything is? I can show you where I keep the spare key to let yourself in when I'm working.'

He could have been talking to the cat sitter. So that was how it was going to be. Well, she'd insisted on the 'let's just be friends' vibe. He was a proud man, and she couldn't have it both ways, but it was a hollow victory.

'Great.'

After some intense discussion on where and when Karen should be fed, and a look at her new cat bowls and bed, Grace couldn't bear much more. It was like a veil had come down over Will's eyes. The friendly banter they'd shared, let alone the private things they'd told each other, seemed way out of reach. Hopefully they could get back some of the friendship she valued so much before she left for good. She accepted a small glass of wine on the terrace, and a chance to play with Karen, but there was precious little talking.

Dusk would fall soon; way earlier than it had when Grace first arrived on the island. The seasons were nowhere near as distinct as they were in Britain, but she'd heard from Angeliki that autumn was one of the best times on the island. The tourists were mainly gone, the sea still warm and the beaches empty. It was time for the locals to relax and let their hair down. It sounded lovely. Maybe she could come back for a holiday in October.

Grace looked up at the darkening sky. If she was walking back, she needed to go now. A walk would clear her head as well. The afternoon hadn't exactly been what she'd describe as a success. She stood up and passed the kitten to Will.

'I'd better be off then.'

'Right.'

Will held Karen up towards the sky, brought her down again and kissed her on the nose.

'Hang on…'

Grace was surprised to see him carefully put the cat inside the house and lock the door behind him. In the last couple of hours, he'd given her the impression she was the last person he'd want to spend time with.

'I'll come with you. I fancy a walk. And I always have a little scout around the villa before I turn in for the night.'

'But you're on holiday.'

'What can I say? Old habits die hard. My employers are back from holiday at the weekend, so I like to make sure they're coming back to the same place they left behind. I trust Maria the housekeeper totally, but the gardener needs keeping an eye on. He has a tendency to do a sketchy job and bugger off early.'

'Very…'

'You want to say "control freaky", don't you?'

She'd almost got a smile out of him. The first genuine one since she'd mentioned just being friends.

'Not at all. I was going to say dedicated.'

'I believe you. Thousands wouldn't.'

It was something that Phil used to say regularly. She mustn't get flustered. It was a common saying.

'Isn't your deputy in charge of things while you're away?'

'He's still with the family at their holiday home. But we've got Achilles and Andreas, the night security guards, keeping watch in turn at the villa.'

Grace laughed into the cooling air.

'They sound like a puppet act, or a pop duo. Coming to you all the way from Greece… Give it up for Achilles and Andreas.'

'Amusing.'

At least their conversation was getting back to something approaching normal. It would take a while, but she was determined to get there.

Will gestured for her to go ahead of him.

'After you, madam. Remember we're going via the villa. I'll come all the way back with you to yours afterwards.'

'Aye, aye, captain.'

They walked in single file until they reached the path for the town beach and further on until the whitewashed villa loomed large in front of them. The thick brick walls around the property reminded Grace of the day she'd met Will, trying to clamber over the top to get to the beach. They'd been through a lot since then. They'd told each other things that no one else knew, and they'd faced up to grief and found joy together. Grace stopped herself thinking about the joy. Will was staring up at the windows.

'That's odd.'

'What?'

'There's a light on up there. Maria would have gone home hours ago. Maybe she forgot to switch it off, but it's unlike her.'

He took a bunch of keys out of his pocket.

'Mind if I have a quick look? You wait here just in case there's a problem.'

'Go ahead.'

Will unlocked the gate and disappeared into the garden. There was no way she was going to wait where she was told if there was a problem. She might be able to help.

Chapter Twenty-Five

Grace crept into the garden a few seconds later. As her eyes became accustomed to the gloom, she had to stifle a scream. Will was stood over a man whose arms and legs were tied with ropes and there was some sort of gag over his mouth. Will ripped off the tape and there was a rapid conversation in Greek.

Before she could move towards them, two masked men dressed in black came out of the front door of the villa, carrying holdalls. Grace clearly saw a knife glint in the low light.

'Will! Behind you.'

Her heart was in her mouth.

Will spun round and tackled the man with the knife, wrestling him to the ground. They rolled around on the earth together while the other guy dropped his bag and ran off towards the beach.

Grace darted forward and started to untie the security

guard's ropes, Achilles or Andreas, she didn't care which, while glancing back at Will's struggle every few seconds. It was a close contest, but he appeared to be winning against the masked man and was managing to hold the knife away from his own body.

His eyes met hers for a moment.

'Grace, stay back!'

She ignored Will's shout. The security guard's wrists were nearly clear of the ropes. He worked with her to free his feet and leapt up to help Will tackle the knife-wielding intruder.

The two of them held the man down and turned him onto his front. Grace saw Will rip the knife from the raider's hand and throw it across the terrace.

She had an idea.

'Catch!'

Grace lobbed the discarded rope their way and Will bound the man's arms and legs tightly, while the security guard knelt on his back.

'Call 112, please, Grace.'

It was the international emergency number, which Grace had installed on her phone when she arrived, never thinking she might need it. She pressed the contact.

Will sat back on the path and in the dim light Grace gasped as she caught sight of the bloodstain on his white T-shirt. It was getting bigger by the second. He must have been stabbed in the fight.

The security guard shouted over to her as the operator answered her call.

'He's hurt. Ask for an ambulance as well as police.'

Grace gave the operator the details and rushed to Will's side. She'd been one of the trained first-aiders at her school. She knew what to do. The ambulance would take a while to get to them on the cliff path.

The security guard looked like he was about to lose it. He was probably in shock, but she needed to keep him calm. He was no use to her as a quivering wreck.

'What's your name?'

'Achilles.'

He got a phone out of his pocket.

'I must ring the boss, to tell him what's happened. It's all my fault.'

'Not yet… Listen to me carefully.'

The man managed to focus his wild eyes on her, rather than staring all round him. Will was slumped forward now, and his eyes were already shut, which made Grace's heart miss a beat.

'Take off your T-shirt.'

Achilles looked at her as if she was mad.

'We need it to staunch the blood. Now!'

The man ripped off his top and Grace showed him where to hold it against Will's body. His arms would be stronger than hers, and it would free her to direct the ambulance.

'Don't move. Keep up the pressure.'

Grace put her phone in torch mode and tried to examine the wound from above. It was on Will's right side, but she had no way of knowing if it had pierced any of his vital organs. Blood loss was the most immediate worry.

She moved round to stroke his head and face.

'Can you hear me, Will?'

There was a soft grunt.

'Try and open your eyes. It's important that you stay awake.'

Very slowly the brown eyes she knew so well opened and fixed on her. Will attempted to speak but Grace put a finger to his lips.

'Don't worry about talking. An ambulance is on its way. You're going to be OK.'

She had no idea if it was the case, but positive thinking could work, couldn't it? It had to work. She couldn't cope with the alternative. The wail of screaming sirens cut through the night air and became louder and louder. Before she raced up the path to show them exactly where to go, Grace leant over and kissed Will full on the lips.

She turned again to a shaking Achilles.

'Keep talking to him until I get back. Don't let him go to sleep.'

As she crossed the terrace, Grace aimed a kick at the guy lying on the ground, the knife well out of his reach a few feet away. It was covered in blood, Will's blood. She knew better than to touch it. It would be needed as evidence.

The ambulance screeched to a halt at the edge of the path just as she reached it herself, followed by three police cars, blue lights flashing.

Two paramedics, a man and a woman, jumped out of the ambulance and ran towards her.

'This way!' Grace shouted into the wind. 'Please hurry.'

She led the paramedics down the path to Will. While running, she shouted back to the police that she'd seen a man run towards the beach. One of the teams peeled off in the direction of the escaped burglar, while the other two headed for the house. Not that she cared where they were going.

All Grace could think about was Will. The paramedics knelt and took over from Achilles, who had to be pulled away from the older man's body.

The security guard got straight on the phone, presumably to their boss at his holiday home, but Grace couldn't understand any of the shouted Greek conversation.

Not that it mattered what he was saying; all that mattered now was that Will received the right treatment and survived the stabbing.

Achilles got it together enough to help the medics carry the stretcher up the path and into the back of the ambulance. While she waited for the paramedics to stabilise Will for the journey, with a drip and an oxygen mask, Grace witnessed the police tear off the assailant's balaclava and put him in the back of the police car. He was barely more than a boy.

She climbed into the ambulance after Achilles, who sat rocking in the corner. She positioned herself firmly at Will's side, as close as the paramedics would allow her. Will's face took on a grey tinge as they tore along the coast road, and Grace held on fast to his hand.

The speed of the vehicle made every streetlight illuminate the gory scene in the back of the ambulance like a freezeframe from a film. There was blood everywhere, on the floor, on the hands of the paramedics and all down Achilles's front, besides what was still coming out of Will.

When the lights of the town concertinaed up together,

Grace breathed a sigh of relief. It could only be moments until they reached the island's tiny hospital.

But the ambulance turned the opposite way, away from the town, which struck fear into Grace's heart.

'Where are you going? The hospital's the other way. We need to go there, now!'

The female paramedic turned round.

'Don't worry. This injury is too serious to be dealt with on the island. This man, your … friend, will need an operation. He is being taken to a private hospital in Athens, where he will have a much better chance of survival.'

So, there was a chance he wouldn't make it. It was all she heard. Grace choked back the tears.

'But that will take too long.'

'There's an air ambulance helicopter waiting for us at the airfield, with fully trained paramedics on board. It's all been arranged and it's only a short flight, twenty minutes at the most.'

'But it's dark. Helicopters don't fly at night!'

The paramedic put her hand on top of Grace's for a moment.

'They do in emergencies and with a skilled pilot. Please don't upset yourself.' The woman nodded her head at Will. 'Things will be smoother if you are calm.'

That was her told, then. *You try being calm when someone you care so much about is hovering between life and death* was what Grace wanted to say, but the paramedic was only doing her job. The patient came first, and the hysterical Englishwoman on board wasn't helping.

Grace concentrated on stroking Will's hand as the ambulance climbed up the road to the airfield. His hand was all she could reach, as the oxygen mask covered most of his face.

In front of them, as promised, was a helicopter waiting with its lights on, ready for take-off.

The rest of the airfield was deserted, with a single light in the tower. They must have pulled someone in to man air traffic control. Will's boss was obviously a powerful man. It gave her a little hope.

The back doors of the ambulance sprang open as soon as they came to a halt, and a second paramedic crew worked seamlessly with the first to transfer Will onto a trolley, with all his equipment attached.

Achilles was still curled up in the corner, and Grace saw for the first time in the bright overhead light that he had huge purple weals on his wrists. He'd need some attention too, but hopefully it was something they could deal with at the island hospital.

While they prepared Will, Karen's little face leapt into Grace's mind. They'd left her there all alone.

'Achilles.'

The man looked up with hollow eyes.

'There's a cat locked in Will's house. She needs to be fed. There's a key under one of the pot plants. Please can you sort it. Or ask Angeliki, the vet in town to help you. Do you understand?'

The man nodded slowly.

The paramedics had finished their work. There couldn't be any more delays. Will had to come first.

Grace climbed out of the back of the ambulance and followed the trolley with the stretcher across the airstrip.

One of the new team of paramedics turned back to speak to her.

'What are you doing?'

'I'm coming with you. On the helicopter. I can't leave him now.'

The man shook his head.

'We have limited space. It's strictly family only.'

There was no way Grace was going to let Will go off on the most important journey of his life without her.

'I'm his sister.'

Will made a small sound from the trolley.

The paramedic looked from her to Will and back at his colleague, who shrugged.

Grace put her hands together in prayer.

'Please.'

The man obviously had bigger things to worry about than arguing with her.

'OK, you'll have to wait till we've loaded him on, and do exactly what we say.'

'Thank you.'

Grace watched Will being taken on board and winced every time there was a tiny adjustment of the stretcher. They were being as careful as they could be, but she experienced every movement along with him. His soft moans were agony to her ears.

It seemed ages but it was probably less than a minute before the first paramedic beckoned her up the stairs and showed her to a seat near the back.

'Strap yourself in, and don't try and get up at any point during the flight.'

Grace nodded and smiled to herself. She'd made it onto the helicopter. At any other place and time, she'd have been excited by the prospect. She'd always wanted to go on one. But this was no joyride over the sights of Athens.

Will was up the front of the helicopter being worked on by the team. She hadn't wanted to leave his side, but the guy had made it pretty clear he was doing her a favour by even allowing her on board.

'Clear for take-off.'

The pilot's voice over the tannoy was loud. But it was nothing to the noise of the rotor blades as the metal machine rose up and swooped low over the tip of the island, along with Grace's stomach.

She looked through into the cockpit to see the pilot and co-pilot wearing ear defenders. They needed them. She wouldn't have been able to speak to Will anyway over the noise. Once they'd stabilised, Grace stared out of the window at the blackness all around. There was one fishing boat out there below them, throwing out a tiny shaft of light, but otherwise it was a sea of darkness. Grace strained to see the mainland ahead.

Pinpricks of light told her they'd reached the Athens coast and gradually the lights arranged themselves into strings, then clusters, and finally whole baskets full of diamonds, twinkling away.

The helicopter dipped in the sky, and the pilot came on for the last time.

'Prepare for landing.'

Anonymous shapes turned into definite structures. Grace was puzzled that they appeared to be above central Athens and not coming into the airport, which was to one side of the city.

A large, illuminated building came into view, with blue-lit ambulances pulling up to its entrance far below them.

They were going to land on the roof of the hospital! She'd seen it done in movies, and in any other circumstance she'd have been excited.

A steep drop knocked the breath out of her, but the touchdown on the tarmac was soft. The paramedics were up and headed for the exit with Will in moments. The man who'd allowed her on leant in as he passed.

'Stay put until we've got him on the ground.'

Grace managed to touch Will's hand as the trolley passed.

She rushed down the metal stairs as soon as she could and followed the others into the lift that opened its doors onto the roof.

It was a tight squeeze, but she wasn't waiting for the next one.

When it stopped a few floors down she kept within touching distance as they raced the trolley along the passageway. At the end of the corridor, a big sign said OPERATING THEATRE in both Greek and English.

The doors swung open, and Grace saw a gowned-up team waiting on the other side. The paramedic who'd been kind to her put his hand on her arm.

'This is as far as you go.'

Grace reached forward to give Will's hand one last stroke before the doors slammed shut in front of her.

How could she ever have thought they could be friends? Who was she kidding?

She was falling in love with him. Pure and simple.

It had taken something truly horrific to shake the truth out of her. She'd already had one man she loved torn from her. She couldn't go through it again. Grace bowed her head and prayed.

Chapter Twenty-Six

A hand on her arm brought Grace out of a daze. For a moment she struggled to remember where she was. She looked up at a woman wearing a blue uniform. A nurse's uniform. She was in a hospital, the place she hated most in the world.

For a moment she thought it was Phil she was waiting for, waiting to hear whether his latest operation had finally got rid of the cancer that was taking over his body.

But of course it wasn't Phil. Her husband was long dead. The events of the evening came back to her in a rush. It was Will in there. Will was being operated on at this very moment. There were people behind those doors trying to save his life.

'I'm sorry, but you can't stay here.'

It was like the woman was talking to her through a glass barrier.

As soon as she finished speaking, a trolley with another patient lying flat on their back was rushed past them and through the magic doors.

The nurse held out a hand and Grace took it and staggered to her feet.

'I'm Eva, and I will take you to our reception area, where you can wait for news.'

Grace looked back at the metal doors that had swallowed up the next patient and slammed shut in her face again.

'But I want to go in there.'

Eva pulled on her hand.

'It's not possible. Please come with me.'

Grace let herself be led away, away from the man she'd only just admitted to herself how much she cared about. As she walked down the corridor hand in hand with Eva, yet more medical staff rushed past in the opposite direction. Grace tried not to think about where they were going and what emergencies they'd have to deal with when they got there.

After Phil's last spell in hospital, when they'd sat her down and told her that a hospice was the next and final step for her husband, she'd vowed never to set foot inside a hospital again if she could help it.

But she couldn't help it now. She could no more walk away from Will than she could one of her own children.

She put up her fingers to pinch her nose shut. This was obviously a luxury hospital; the neutral decor was immaculate and there were staff everywhere you looked. From the corridor she glimpsed smart offices and rest rooms with pastel furniture and rugs. A bit different from the hospitals she'd been in with Phil. They'd had scruffy eau-de-nil walls and broken chairs, though admittedly the same incredibly dedicated staff, just far fewer of them. But however much money they'd lavished on this hospital, underneath the citrus air freshener being pumped out, it was the same smell. A smell she could never forget. Disinfectant mixed with a myriad other notes. The smell of despair.

The nurse took her to a brightly lit reception area and sat her down in a pale green upholstered armchair.

'Would you like a coffee? Or a water?'

Grace shook her head.

'I think you should try to drink something. You have a long wait ahead. Mr'—the woman looked at the electronic tablet she was holding—'Lancing will be in surgery for several hours yet.'

So, Will's second name was Lancing. He was Will Lancing. She hadn't known. How could she feel so much for the man, a man she'd had glorious sex with, when she didn't even know his second name?

'Several hours? So there is no news yet?'

'No, and there won't be for a while. Please accept a coffee.'

Grace nodded this time. The Greeks thought coffee was an answer to many a problem. It couldn't solve everything, but it was a good starting point.

The nurse went off to fetch her drink, and Grace caught sight of the front of her own T-shirt. The pale pink cotton was splattered with blood, Will's blood.

A man sitting on the other side of the room gave her a confused stare.

Grace waved.

'It's OK, don't worry. It's not mine. None of it's mine. It's all Will's.'

The man looked away again. He obviously thought she was insane.

Eva had added sugar to Grace's coffee. She almost spat it out, but the nurse encouraged her to drink it.

'The sugar is good for shock. Please try.'

Grace swallowed the hot sweet liquid and drank most of the bottle of water the nurse gave her as well. Her head did feel clearer.

Eva pointed at her T-shirt.

'We have a lost property section here. I could find you something to put on if you like.'

Grace held onto a fold of the T-shirt. She was ready in case the woman tried to bodily take it off her. It might be all she had left of Will. Some drops of his blood.

'No!'

'OK, that's fine. Don't worry.'

The woman was looking around her as if she didn't want to alarm the other relatives waiting for news. The room had filled up a bit since she'd first arrived.

'Sorry, but I'd like to keep it on.'

'I understand.'

She obviously didn't but had been trained in dealing with difficult customers.

'There is a hotel around the corner where we send our relatives in these circumstances. It's only a two-minute walk, so would you like me to arrange that? It's all paid for by Mr Lancing's employers. We will ring you the second there is any news.'

'No, thank you. I want to stay here until Will comes out of surgery.'

Eva gave her a look which told Grace she'd been hoping to get rid of her.

'I understand.'

She wished the woman would stop saying that. She didn't understand anything. When she'd walked out of the hospice for the last time, she'd had to leave her husband in there. Or what was left of him. She wasn't going anywhere.

'There is a cafeteria at the end of this corridor'—the woman pointed in the opposite direction to the operating theatre—'where you can buy meals. And the machines with coffees and snacks are behind me. They are free.'

'OK.'

'Please don't ask reception for updates. They won't have that information. I will be on shift all night, and I will come and tell you as soon as we have any news.'

Grace nodded.

'I'll get you a blanket, and then I suggest you get some sleep. You can use one of the sofas if you like.'

Sleep was the farthest thing from her mind.

The woman came back with a pale green fluffy throw, which matched the furniture, of course, and a clear plastic bag with a phone, some keys and a wallet inside.

'These are your … brother's things. I'm passing them to you for safekeeping.'

Grace dimly remembered saying she was his sister, to be allowed on the helicopter. That seemed like many hours ago. It had obviously gone down on the official form. She stuffed the sealed bag inside her rucksack. Then she quickly checked to see if there was anything useful already in the rucksack. She couldn't for the life of her remember packing it. All it had in it was a bottle of water, her phone, keys, sunglasses and a cat toy she'd forgotten to give to Karen. Nothing remotely useful. Not even a spare T-shirt. It was only supposed to have been a quick walk to Will's and back along the coast path.

'Thank you.'

'Could you sign here, please, to say you've received them.'

She scribbled her name, Grace Foreman, on the tablet with the plastic pencil, under the eagle eye of the nurse.

'I take it that's your married name?'

'Yes, that's right.'

That at least was true. Or it had been. She wasn't about to sign it as Grace Lancing – that was edging into fraud territory. She might be dazed, but she wasn't stupid.

Eva was staring at her bloodied T-shirt again, obviously desperate to wrench it off her.

'As I said earlier, it would be a good idea for you to get some sleep.'

'I'll try.'

Grace was convinced it was code for 'Be quiet and don't make any more trouble.' She checked the time on her phone. It was two o'clock in the morning. A sudden pang of hunger made her stomach growl. She'd had nothing to eat since a couple of biscuits at Will's about ten hours before. The woman had told her it would be ages yet before they heard anything, so she might as well grab something.

Since it was a cafeteria in a Greek hospital, there was plenty of food on offer, even at this hour of the morning. Grace chose a portion of what looked like homemade moussaka with greens, or horta as they called them, and poured herself a glass of water from a jug. Will wouldn't want her to starve. He constantly made comments about her 'healthy appetite'.

Various medical staff were seated at the tables, talking

animatedly in Greek. Perhaps they were discussing cases, but for all she knew they could be chatting about nightclubs and cocktails. She picked a seat at the only unoccupied table, in a corner. As soon as she sat down, a middle-aged man with faded blond hair appeared with his tray and gave her a sad smile.

'Are you English?'

'Yes.'

'Ah, I guessed right. Do you mind if I share your table?'

It wasn't really what she wanted, but she could hardly say no.

'Please … go ahead.'

He sat down opposite her.

'I'm Hendrik. I'm just visiting. We live in The Hague.'

Grace forced a smile.

'Grace.'

She looked down at his tray. It boasted a very strange selection of things. A yoghurt, three chocolate bars and a child's drink, bright orange, in a see-through plastic bottle. It was like he'd chosen his food in the dark.

Hendrik tore open the straw and started on the drink. Grace forked up a mouthful of moussaka and realised just how hungry she was. She ate her way through the plateful while she watched Hendrik eat two of the chocolate bars in quick succession, cramming them into his mouth.

When he started on the third one, she realised his eyes were full of tears.

She reached over and held his hand.

'What is it?'

'It's my wife, Johanna. She collapsed in the street.'

'Oh, no, that's awful.'

'She has always wanted to see the Acropolis…'

The man took a deep breath.

'The doctors told us last month that her cancer had returned.'

He wiped his eyes with a serviette.

'They said that if there was anything she wanted to do, she should do it now.'

Grace felt the room spin. She'd forgotten for a moment that she was in a hospital full of sick people and their relatives. It wasn't just her and Will. She'd had so many chats with random strangers in hospital cafeterias just like this one when her husband was alive. They'd pour out their stories and she would tell them hers. Phil would be somewhere out of sight, being operated on, or receiving treatment in some far-flung corner of the hospital. It didn't matter whether it was night or day, there was always someone waiting and willing to talk in the cafeteria. It was the same grey light above them, fluorescent panels that created a strange twilight world she wouldn't wish on anyone.

She had to get out of there before she fainted.

Grace pushed back her chair and picked up her rucksack. She gave the man's shoulder a squeeze as she passed.

'I really hope your wife improves. I'm sorry, but I've got to go.'

Outside in the corridor, Grace bent double and took in great gulps of air. Would she ever be able to separate Will from the memory of her husband and truly move forward? What if Will survived but was permanently disabled and needed round-the-clock care? Could she really take that on?

Just a few minutes back in a hospital and she was already losing it.

Grace sank to the floor with her back against the wall for a moment and closed her eyes. When she opened them again, it came to her, clear as a bell.

It was time to fight for the living, not dwell among the ghosts of the past. There was a man just a few feet away who needed her to believe he was going to make it. Will and her husband weren't rivals for her affection; they never had been. She'd got it all wrong and mixed everything up in her mind. Her love for Phil had been all too real, but that part of her life was well and truly over. The girls were grown and gone too, focused on their own lives, as it should be.

But she hadn't died along with Phil. It had sometimes felt like that, but life was a precious gift, and she was going to grab it with both hands.

If Will pulled through this, she was ready, at last, to see where it took them. But even if it didn't take them very far, her time in Greece had helped her realise that she could cope on her own and still enjoy life. She'd achieved more in the past three months than the previous three years.

Her new experiences had given her renewed strength, and it was time now to use that strength to help Will as much as she possibly could.

Grace made her way back to reception and checked her phone yet again. People always said that no news was good news. She had to believe that was true.

The nearest sofa beckoned, so she took off her shoes and cuddled up under the blanket, although sleep was out of the question.

Someone shaking her arm pulled her out of a dream where she had to choose who to save in a ferocious storm at sea – Will or her husband? The waves were overwhelming the boat. She had to know the answer. She tried to stay on board, but the picture was dissolving in front of her eyes. Eva was stood in front of her.

She studied the nurse's face for a sign of what was to come, but the woman gave nothing away. Had she perfected the blank expression on some sort of course? Grace looked her in the eye.

'Tell me. Please.'

If it was bad news, she wanted to know immediately. No beating around the bush. She'd had enough of that.

'Your brother has come through his surgery successfully.'

Grace punched the air.

'Yo!'

'He is weak, but he was lucky.'

She'd hardly call him that, but she let it pass.

'The knife did not damage any vital organs. He has lost a lot of blood, and he needs another transfusion, but the doctors are hopeful he will make a full recovery.

'Yes!'

Grace did a little dance around the waiting area, but the thought that other people might not receive such good news stopped her in her tracks. She'd been on the other side of the fence too.

'Can I see him?'

'We don't usually let relatives in at this point. Mr Lancing's still in the intensive care unit.'

Eva pursed her lips.

'But you do seem very devoted to your brother. I'll have a word with the surgeon.'

Grace crossed her fingers on both hands until Eva came back and beckoned her forward.

'Just a couple of minutes. He really needs to rest.'

The sound of machines whirring, doing their vital jobs, hit Grace as she entered the room. She'd been asked to mask up, and the sight of doctors and nurses in green scrubs attending to patients made her halt briefly at the door. The inside of an intensive care unit was something she'd hoped never to see again. But this wasn't about her. She was here for Will.

There was a patient in a bed in each corner of the room, and from where she stood it was hard to tell which was Will. They were all in white hospital gowns and covered in wires and tubes.

Grace forced her feet to move and passed the first two people, trying not to stare too hard. They had enough to deal with without her gawping at them. She spotted Will's muscular hairy legs first, sticking out of his gown. He was at the end on the right. The gown stopped above his knees; they obviously didn't have one quite long enough.

When she reached his side, she stopped for a moment to take in the face that had become so dear to her.

Will's eyes were firmly closed, but the nurse at his side motioned for her to come closer.

Grace leant in and stroked his face.

'Will…'

He opened his eyes as if it was a huge effort, but when he saw her, Grace was rewarded with a big grin.

'Hello, sis.'

Chapter Twenty-Seven

The laughter in his eyes encouraged her more than any medical update.

'Ah, so you did hear that.'

'Sure did. I've always wanted a sister.'

Grace put her finger to her lips in case any of the staff were listening. Although she was fairly sure they had more important things to concentrate on.

'Shhhh. You don't want to get me chucked out, do you?'

Will reached for her hand.

'Thank you … for being there and for not doing what you were told.'

'I don't usually get thanked for that, but I'll take it.'

'Your help was invaluable. If you hadn't untied Achilles when you did, things could have got a lot worse.'

'Did a lot of knot work in the Brownies.'

Will attempted to laugh, which turned into a cough and attracted the attention of one of the staff, who looked over and frowned.

Grace grabbed a water beaker with a spout from the side.

'Here, drink this.'

'Yes, nurse.'

The word sent a shiver down Grace's spine.

'I think they genuinely are about to chuck me out. I've got your things, phone, keys and wallet, safe.'

'OK, thanks. Hang onto the wallet and feel free to spend the money if you need it, but please can you bring my phone in later.'

'Will do.'

She wouldn't spend his money – she had some of her own in the rucksack – but it was nice of him to offer. She couldn't abide a mean man. A mean anyone really.

A sudden grimace had Grace worried that Will was in severe pain. He pulled her close.

'What about Karen? We left her there. She's all on her own in the house.'

The idea that he was more worried about the cat than himself made her go all gooey inside. But this wasn't the time to start examining their relationship. He needed to focus on getting better first.

'Shhhh. Don't worry, I told Achilles where the spare key was and he's going to sort it. I'll check with him later.'

'Good thinking, Batman.'

The nurse who had looked her way was doing a cutthroat sign to tell her it was time to leave.

Grace patted Will's hand and put on her best Arnold Schwarzenegger voice.

'I'll be back.'

No one blinked an eyelid when she walked into the hotel reception in a bloodstained T-shirt. She assumed they were used to it.

'Here is your room key and your complimentary robe, madam.'

Grace nodded at the female receptionist.

'Thank you.'

'And we have a selection of clothes here that are available to buy if that's of any use to you.'

Grace flicked through the catalogue placed in front of her. It was all pretty pricey. She wasn't sure if Will's bosses would be covering the cost of replacement clothing, so she opted for a plain white T-shirt. Her shorts were fine, and she could rinse her knickers in the sink.

'We'll have that sent up to you, madam.'

Her room offered yet another view of the Acropolis. Grace stared down at the people in the street going about their business as usual. Cafés were opening up, flower stalls were setting out their wares, and dogs were being walked. It was an ordinary Friday morning in Athens. How could that possibly be, after what she'd just been through? Pictures of Will slumped on the ground covered in blood flooded her mind.

A knock at the door jolted her back to the present. Outside was a cellophane-wrapped T-shirt. Running the powerful walk-in shower as hot as she could bear it, Grace closed her eyes and tried to wash away the memories as easily as the dirt. Wrapped in her robe, she checked the time again on her phone.

She was supposed to have a lesson with Nick in an hour. She had to let him know.

'Angeliki?'

'Grace?'

Just the sound of her friend's voice set her off. She gulped back the tears.

'What is it? What's wrong?'

'I can't teach Nick today.'

'Why? What's happened? You're not making any sense.'

'It's Will. He's been stabbed.'

Angeliki's sharp cry at the other end forced her to focus.

'Sorry, don't freak, he's OK. We're in hospital in Athens. He's been operated on, and he's come through it well. I'm going back there later. I'll update you.'

'But…'

'Also, can you please check that Achilles is looking after Karen. The spare key's under the second plant pot to the left.'

'Wait…'

'Sorry, I have to go.'

Grace threw the phone down on the bed. She could barely keep her eyes open. Tiredness had seeped into her bones. She needed sleep, but first she'd better set an alarm to make sure she'd wake up in time for visiting hours.

Her rucksack lay open where she'd left it on the floor. Will's belongings stared up at her. He'd asked her to bring his phone in, hadn't he? She'd better check if it had any battery first.

The phone flickered into life. He hadn't password protected it, silly man.

She daren't, dare she?

Grace scrolled down to J for Jack. There was only one of

them. It must be him. Will had praised her earlier for not doing what she was told. It was a big risk, but one worth taking, in her opinion. Her heart was in her mouth as she pressed the number.

'Hello. Is that Jack Lancing, Will Lancing's son?'

'Yes, and who are you?'

'It's a long story, and please don't panic, but I have some news about your father.'

Five minutes later, she'd filled Jack in, and he'd vowed to get on the next flight from Heathrow to Athens. What Will would make of her actions, she wasn't sure, but the guy sounded genuinely concerned. They'd exchanged numbers and he was going to let her know when he got to the hospital. She'd vowed to help Will get better in any way she could. Surely seeing his son would be a boost?

Grace lay back on the bed and let her mind drift away.

After a few snatched hours of sleep and a call to Sofia, she was back at the hospital reception in her box-fresh white T-shirt with pressed creases down the front. Eva would have gone off shift by now, but they must have her details on file.

'I'm here to visit Will Lancing in the intensive care unit.' She added, 'I'm his sister,' before the man behind the desk could raise any objections.

He looked down at his computer and up again.

'I'm sorry, we have no record of a Will Lancing in the ICU.'

Grace fought for breath.

'What do you mean?'

Surely someone would have rung her if anything catastrophic had happened?

CLAIRE CARVER

'Ah, OK, I've found him. He's been moved to a private room, Omega 3, second floor.'

Grace breathed in and out again slowly.

'Not full of fish oil, is it?'

'Sorry?'

The joke obviously didn't translate.

Grace knocked in case Will was having anything done he wouldn't want her to see.

'Come in.'

The voice was female. Grace brushed off her irritation at seeing an attractive young nurse bent over Will, taking his blood pressure. That would suit him down to the ground.

'I'll leave you with your visitor now, Mr Lancing.'

'Call me Will, please.'

The nurse gave him a big smile.

'Will it is. I'll check in on you later.'

Grace took the seat next to the bed. Now that his upper left arm wasn't hidden by his shirtsleeves, or the dark of the beach, she could clearly see that in the middle of Will's tattoo was the name Jack. It boded well. She took Will's phone out of her bag and handed it to him.

'There you go.'

'Thanks.'

Will's eyes were trained on her.

'New T-shirt?'

'Yes. The old one got a bit too Jackson Pollock for my liking.'

'Sorry about that.'

'Well, you couldn't help it. How are you feeling?'

Will reached for her hand.

'Better now you're here. But like I've been run over by a steamroller. I ache all over.'

'You poor thing.'

The next moment he'd drifted off again, and Grace spent a peaceful couple of hours reading the latest blockbuster she'd picked up in the hotel reception.

When he came to, she handed him the phone. It had been beeping away while he slept.

'You'd better check as there seem to be lots of new messages.'

She'd asked Jack not to call or message. He'd let her know half an hour ago that his plane had touched down in Greece. He'd be with them soon.

Will peered at the screen.

'You don't have any reading glasses, do you? Mine are at the house.'

'Yes, here.'

Grace thought her shocking pink glasses rather suited Will. She'd bet that young nurse wouldn't be able to produce some glasses at the drop of a hat. After reading the messages, Will held the phone to his ear. Grace strained to hear the content of the voicemail. It sounded like a male voice. Not that she was bothered what sex the caller was. Will put the phone down on the bedside table with a smile.

'Ah, that's good. They caught the guy that ran off. They've both been charged, and all the property recovered.'

'Wonderful.'

'They were just a couple of youngsters who obviously thought they'd give it a go. Probably the same two I'd seen hanging around the villa the day before I met you.'

The warmth in his eyes took Grace right back to the night on the beach. She'd need to open a window soon.

'Ah yes, when you accused me of being some sort of female Fagin, running my little gang of criminals.'

'That's not quite what I said.'

'And remember, they weren't quite hapless innocents. One of them was carrying a knife. A knife that could have…'

Grace swallowed hard.

Will reached for her hand and stroked it.

'Don't get upset. It's all over now. I'm going to be OK, thanks to you.'

Grace turned away so he couldn't see her eyes water. When she turned back, she was pleased for once to see Will's smirk make a comeback.

'And my employers sincerely hope that having my sister nearby will aid my recovery no end.'

Grace looked out of the window. They must have had notification from the hospital that she was with him.

'You're not going to let me forget that, are you?'

'Nope.'

The text that she'd been waiting for came in on her phone. Jack was in reception. Grace debated keeping it a total surprise for a moment. But maybe that wouldn't be good for someone in Will's condition. She'd have to tell him.

'There's something else you need to know.'

Will's face creased into a frown.

'Yes…'

It was best just to rip the plaster off.

'Your son's here to see you.'

Will tried to sit up straighter.

'What? How the hell…?'

'I rang him. I figured if it was me lying in a foreign hospital, I'd want my daughters to know.'

The frown got deeper.

'But I'm not you.'

Grumpy Will was in danger of making an appearance.

'I would never have bothered my son with this. And you shouldn't have either.'

Grace held her head high.

'He's come all this way now. You're not going to turn him away, are you?'

Will shook his head in mock despair and turned away. But Grace had seen the glimmer of a smile.

'Are you?'

'Grace, you go too far sometimes.'

She decided to leave while she was on a roll and headed for reception. Will's son was easy to spot. He had the same tall frame, but his hair was a dark blond.

'Jack!'

He held out his hand.

'Hi, you must be Grace.'

He had a nice firm grip, like his father. And big strong hands. Well, not quite like his father … but that way madness lay.

'Grace?'

'Sorry, yes, that's me.'

She took him to one side and spoke quietly.

'Can you just go along with whatever I say to reception, please. I'll explain later.'

'Okaay.'

Grace approached the desk.

'This is Will Lancing's son, my nephew. I'm taking him in to see Will, if you could give him a visitor's badge.'

'Certainly.'

Jack's face was a picture. But he kept his cool. Definitely his father's son. Grace explained in the lift, which elicited a smile. She left him at the door to Will's room. Jack planned to stay in Athens for the weekend, and the two of them needed to have bonding time without her.

'Can you please tell your father I'll be back in tomorrow? We can liaise on timings, so we don't both go in at once.'

Jack leant in to give her a peck on the cheek.

'Of course, auntie.'

Yes, those two would get on very well, thought Grace, however long it had been since they'd seen each other.

Will looked miles better when she saw him the next afternoon, and even healthier the one after that. The colour had come back into his cheeks, and the hospital gown had been replaced with a navy T-shirt and shorts, which she presumed his son had sorted out for him. Grace herself had caved in and bought another T-shirt from the hotel reception, green this time, and a pack of extremely fancy lace pants that were practically see-through – the only underwear for sale. They were a bit of a cliché, and she wondered if the ordering had been done by a man.

When Grace reached Will's room, the same nurse had his T-shirt halfway up his chest and was doing something with his dressing. Surely she had other patients to see? But at least Will's smile held no trace of the pain of the first day. He beckoned her in.

'Sis, welcome. Your nephew has just left to go back to England. He was sorry to miss you.'

She was getting a bit sick of this one. The nurse gave Will a final sunny smile and closed the door behind her. Grace took the seat next to his bed and he reached for her hand.

'Seriously, though, I want to thank you again for contacting Jack. It could have backfired spectacularly.'

She had to stop him there.

'But it didn't.'

'No, and let me finish. As I was saying, I am genuinely grateful. It was a lovely thing to do. Sometimes taking a chance is the only way forward.'

There was a lot more riding on his words than thanking her for contacting Jack, and they both knew it, but now wasn't the time.

'I'm just pleased there's someone else in the world with the same sense of humour as you.'

Will fiddled with the edge of the bedsheet.

'But there is something huge I need to ask you.'

He looked so serious that Grace was worried he'd had some bad news about his test results. Phil had always been hesitant to give her more bad news.

'You know how much I hate being cooped up in here...'

'Yes...'

Was he about to suggest she sprung him from the hospital?

'The doctor told me today that there was a possibility I could go home, if...'

Grace thought she knew what was coming.

'There was someone there who could keep an eye on me.'

Grace swallowed hard. She'd nursed Phil on and off for

three years, and during the last six months of his life more or less constantly. She'd taken early retirement from the job she loved, so as to be at his side, because she knew there'd be no second chances.

Will took her hand and lifted it to his lips, sending shockwaves through her body.

'I know what I'm asking you, and what you must have been through with your husband. My employers have hired a nurse who will do all the medical stuff and change the wound dressing. But I couldn't bear a stranger in the house with me twenty-four hours a day.'

He gave her one of his superstar smiles.

'The only person I could bear being with is you. Will you at least think about it, please?'

Chapter Twenty-Eight

G race sat in silence for a moment and closed her eyes. She couldn't look at Will. Could she really do it? It would be way worse if she said yes now and then flaked out halfway through. Not managing to complete something she'd agreed to was a pet hate of hers. She'd rather say no early on than fail. She opened her eyes again and caught sight of his worried face. His smile had melted away and he'd let go of her hand. It was wrong to keep him waiting. Grace clenched her fists at her sides.

Why was she even hesitating? This would be a very different experience from the one she'd had with Phil. This time round she'd be with a man who'd get better and stronger day by day, instead of one getting weaker and closer to the end. She still didn't know if her relationship with Will had a long-term future, but this was the perfect opportunity to at least try and find out. They'd be basically living together for the next fortnight.

'Grace? Are you OK? You've helped me so much already. I totally understand if this is one step too far. I can always hire someone.'

Grace picked up his hand and stroked it. She couldn't let him be helped by a stranger when she was right in front of him.

'No, it's fine. I'll do it.'

Will grinned from ear to ear.

'Fantastic. That means we can get out of here tomorrow.'

'Will we be going back home in the helicopter?'

'You bet.'

'Yay!' Grace waved her arms in the air.

'That's what it's really about isn't it? A free 'copter ride.'

'Well, it will be lot more fun than the way here, worrying about whether you were going to make it through the night, that's for sure.'

There was no going back now. She was in it for the long haul, or at least until Will was back on his feet.

———————

Grace rang Elena from the hotel just before she set off to walk to the hospital for the last time. She started to tell her what had happened, but she only got a few words out before her boss interrupted.

'Oh, yes, it's terrible. We know Will, he's a lovely man, and his employers, Panos and Daphne, are friends of ours. We heard all about the burglary and the stabbing. Such a shock for our island. We will have to increase the security at our place too.'

Grace should have guessed they'd all be mates.

'But I wasn't aware of your connection with Will. How do you know him?'

Grace really didn't have the time to be interrogated by Elena.

'Oh, we're friends from way back. Anyway, I'm asking to be released from the last two weeks of my contract, so I can help Will at his house. I only have a few lessons, so maybe someone else can take them on?'

'Yes, of course. Don't worry about that. You concentrate on Will.'

'Thank you. I will move my stuff out of my room as soon as possible.'

'Oh, there's no hurry. There are no new teachers starting until September.'

'Thank you again.'

'It's my pleasure.'

The helicopter journey back to the island in the late afternoon light was a delight for Grace, as she homed in on all the little landmarks that she'd missed in the dark.

But her joy was tempered by her concern that Will looked way worse again. He'd graduated from a stretcher to a wheelchair, but by the time they'd got back to the house, and she'd settled him into bed with the help of a paramedic, she didn't want to leave him again and get a taxi to fetch her stuff from the language school. The journey had seriously taken it out of him.

She'd been expecting it. Phil had always gone downhill straight after leaving the security of a hospital, and being bounced in and out of an ambulance wouldn't have helped.

Will was an unbecoming shade of grey under his tan and his eyes were unaccustomedly dull. But this was the last time she'd compare her experiences. Will was going to get better under her loving care. She'd make damn sure of it.

One bright spot was how overjoyed Karen had been to see them both. Someone had obviously been feeding her as instructed but the poor little thing wanted company. She'd taken the kitten up to Will's bedroom so he could say goodnight to her, but he could barely keep his eyes open. Sleep was what he needed, and sleep was what he'd get.

There'd been no discussion about the bedroom arrangements, but Grace put herself in the spare room. They were firmly back on track as friends, and for the moment she couldn't think about anything more than that. All her clothes were filthy, so after a shower she'd borrowed one of Will's shirts from the wardrobe in her room and put on the last pair of the skimpy lace pants. She'd get the washing done tomorrow.

She peeped into Will's bedroom, but he was out for the count. The nurse would arrive at lunchtime tomorrow, so she'd better try and get some sleep too.

The sun streaming through the window and straight into her eyes woke her. She'd forgotten to draw the curtains, and a glance at her phone told her it was already nine o'clock. She could hear movement in the other room. Will probably needed help. She should have set an alarm. She wouldn't get her Brownie nursing badge at this rate.

Will was half sitting up in bed, but his pillows had fallen off. He was about to put his feet down on the floor so he could pick the pillows up.

'Stay there. I'll do it.'

Grace bent over and retrieved the pillows. When she straightened up again, Will seemed to be having some trouble with the sheet.

She put on a bright smile.

'Good morning. Is there anything you fancy for breakfast?'

Will's eyes went to her bare legs.

'Do you seriously want me to answer that?'

It dawned on Grace that she'd been giving him a bird's eye view of the see-through lace knickers. And she was wearing one of his shirts which barely covered her bum. Men were so basic sometimes. She didn't want him to think that she was deliberately trying to turn him on, bending over just inches from his face. All that blood rushing around his body wouldn't do him any good in his state.

'I haven't got my stuff yet...' Her face was already on fire. 'And these were the only pants on sale at the hotel.'

There was that smile again.

'I'm not complaining.'

'Was there an answer on breakfast? Not that I've had a chance to look in the kitchen.'

'I think the bread's still OK, and the milk might be in date, so toast and butter with a coffee would be lovely, thank you.'

At least there was some colour in his cheeks this morning.

Three days in, and they were getting into a routine. Will was still weak, and needed plenty of help, but she could already see improvements, which cheered her heart. Angeliki and Nick had ferried Grace's stuff from her room at the language school, so at least she had sensible clothes and decent underwear. The couple had spent quite a while chatting to her charge, but Grace had had to shoo them out after an hour, as she could see that Will was fading.

He mainly slept in the mornings, and, after the nurse had been, would sit out on his balcony all afternoon and early evening before turning in again. He liked her to sit with him, and they'd talk about everything and nothing, while watching the people on the beach. Will had a set of binoculars, which they'd pass between them.

Grace had finally shown him the video of her DJing debut, and he'd been suitably impressed. Will had confessed to a fondness for country music, so they'd spent several afternoons just playing each other their favourite tracks and comparing notes, between dozing off in the August heat. Grace wasn't sure she'd ever be a fan of country, but it would be weird if they liked exactly the same things. As a music lover, at least she could appreciate the skill of the musicians. She just tried her hardest not to wince every time she heard the whining notes of a harmonica.

Being together twenty-four hours a day, albeit in separate bedrooms, had shown Grace it was possible to be comfortable with Will while doing nothing, which was one of the hardest things of all for any potential couple. Now that they had seen each other at their best and at their most vulnerable over the past couple of weeks, most boundaries were down, and they were at ease in each other's company. Their bodies were another matter. The scent of expectation was in the air, but neither of them was willing to tackle the next step, and she had severe doubts that Will was up to doing anything even if he wanted to. The little flatmate bubble they'd created would do for the time being. No point rushing ahead.

Grace had just settled them both in the wicker armchairs with a coffee each when a familiar face loomed in the lens of the binoculars. It was only bloody Celine walking up the path. That was all Will needed. It was all *she* needed. She wouldn't let the Frenchwoman exhaust him or spoil their peaceful time out. The next thing she heard was the woman calling out Will's name from the kitchen. Had she never heard of knocking?

'Will, are you there?'

Grace sighed.

'Shall I send her away?'

Will shrugged. 'She'll only come back again. I know what she's like. Better just get it over with.'

'OK, she can have ten minutes and then I'll be back in.'

Grace was quite enjoying her gatekeeper role. Will gave her a wry smile.

'Agreed.'

Celine managed to keep the shock off her face when Grace greeted her at the bottom of the stairs. She'd heard about Will – Grace was sure it was all over the island by now – but the woman obviously had no idea who was staying there, looking after him.

'He's up on the bedroom balcony. I think you know the way.'

Grace hadn't meant to emphasise the word bedroom. It was funny what the subconscious could do.

Celine brushed past her without a word.

Just the thought of them in the bedroom together, let alone in the bed, had Grace glancing up at the clock every few seconds. Will wouldn't be up to much in his state, but she was sure that Celine was the mistress of invention, given half a chance.

When the woman came back down only a satisfying six minutes later, there were tears in her eyes.

This time, she looked Grace full in the face.

'Look after him, won't you. He is very special.'

Grace repeated 'He is very special' in a French accent to herself after Celine had walked out the door.

It was no good. She couldn't let this one fester. She had to know what had happened on the night of the party. She couldn't even think of committing herself to Will if she thought he was still planning to see Celine on the side. She could never be one of several women he had on the go, however good the sex had been. Celine's disappointed face a moment ago had led her to believe that Will wasn't going anywhere with the Frenchwoman, but she had to hear it from his own mouth.

She rushed up the stairs and stood behind Will's chair.

'I need to ask you something.'

Will's brow creased into a frown.

'OK.'

'Last week Celine informed me that she'd spent the night of the party in your bed. Is she lying?'

Will turned his head to look up at her and reached for her hand.

'Grace, we need to be honest with each other now...'

Her heart was in her mouth.

'Celine is telling the truth.'

Chapter Twenty-Nine

Grace pulled her hand away and backed out of the bedroom through the open door. She made it to the top of the stairs before he called out to her.

'Grace. Please let me explain.'

There didn't seem to be a lot to explain. He'd obviously slept with Celine just two days before their night on the beach. The night she'd believed was so special. The night Will had told her was like no other. But for him, it looked like a case of any port in a storm. If it was on offer, he'd grab it with both hands, literally. She mustn't let him see how hurt she was.

'Grace. I beg you. Just give me two minutes. Please. I'd get up and come after you if I could.'

She was torn between running down the stairs and out of the door to the beach, and considering the welfare of the man she'd agreed to look after. If he tried to follow her, he could fall down the steep stone stairs. He'd not gone further than his room, his en suite and the balcony yet. They might not be going anywhere romantically, especially if Celine had anything to do with it, but she'd promised to look after him. She owed it to him to hear him out.

As soon as she hesitated, she was lost. She'd listen to what Will had to say, but anything else was firmly on hold.

Grace took her usual chair next to him. Will tried to hide a smile.

'You look like a sulky teenager.'

Grace shot up out of the chair.

'Right, that's it, I'm going for a swim.'

'No, I'm sorry, please wait. Give me a moment.'

Grace rearranged her features.

'I'm listening.'

'What I was about to say, before you rushed off, is that I got so drunk after you left the party in a hurry…'

'Ah, you're blaming it on drink, the easy way out.'

'No … if you'll let me finish. I was so drunk that at some point I must have crawled upstairs to bed. When I woke up, Celine was in the bed with me.'

Grace gave him an 'I've heard this one before' look.

'Oh, poor little you, having an attractive Frenchwoman in the bed beside you, all primed and ready to go.'

Why had her voice gone up two octaves in the space of a sentence?

'Look, I didn't invite her into my bed, I didn't want her there, and absolutely nothing happened as I called her a cab and asked her to leave.'

Will's voice now held a touch of anger.

'Absolutely nothing? Not even some snogging?'

She not only apparently looked like a teenager but sounded like one now.

'No, not even some "snogging".'

That grin needed to be wiped off Will's face somehow. But before she could fire back, he took her hands in his, so she was forced to face him.

'The only person I wanted in my bed that night was you…' Will gave her a look that travelled all the way through her body, 'But you weren't available. Now do you believe me?'

Grace thought about it. She actually did believe him. She'd seen how conniving Celine could be. The woman was desperate. But did she trust him? That was the bigger question. She wasn't going to let him off the hook that easily. Celine had obviously thought that she'd still be welcome in Will's bed. Something or someone must have given her that idea.

'I'm thinking about it.'

Will sighed. 'Just now I repeated what I said to her that morning, that I didn't see a future with her, and that she had to stop giving people the impression we were still together.'

No wonder the woman had been on the verge of tears. Grace started to feel some sympathy for her. Only a little, because of the way Celine had behaved. But to have had Will in the palm of one's hand and then to have lost him would be tough to get over. It was almost better not to get involved in the first place.

'I see. Poor woman. Having anything to do with you is obviously dangerous.'

'It doesn't have to be.'

He was giving her that look again. But she needed time to think. For once, she wasn't going to rush in all guns blazing and make a decision that she'd up end regretting. This might be the most important decision she had to make for the rest of her life. Grace plastered on a jolly smile.

'I'm hungry. What do you fancy for lunch? There's some spinach pie and salad left over from yesterday.'

Will's employers had arranged for homemade meals to be delivered from the grandma's cooking place in town fresh each day, so that she didn't have to worry about cooking as well, which was a relief.

'Yeah, sounds fine.'

Grace could hear the disappointment in his voice.

By the weekend Will was strong enough to make it downstairs and onto the terrace in the afternoons, leaning on her arm. He still spent every morning in bed, but Grace felt confident enough now to leave him and go for long swims. The temperature was still in the late twenties during the day, and it only dropped by a few degrees at night. She was barely out of a bikini and a sarong unless they had visitors.

Those she was monitoring very carefully. Angeliki and Nick were welcome any time, because she could see how much Will enjoyed their company, and luckily Celine hadn't dared show her face again.

Grace had had her own visitors, when Charlie, Sarah and Buster had turned up one morning, once they realised where she was staying. Charlie had taken over her lessons and filled her in on Irene's progress, plus that of Stelios and his parents. He was also surprised at how far Nick had come on in such a short space of time. Having a girlfriend who was fluent in

English was obviously the key to unlocking the businessman's potential.

The three of them spent ages playing with Karen, throwing little balls for her and pulling her onto their laps for long strokes. Grace had been worried that Buster would be jealous and go for the kitten, but he was as gentle as a lamb.

Grace was sad to see them leave, as she might not see them again for quite some time. She only had a week left on the island, and a decision about the next step was looming fast. These lazy days with Will would come to an end before she knew it. She hoped he'd be well enough to cope on his own if she went back to England, or with a little help, as long as that help wasn't coming from Celine.

Not that it would be any of her business who was looking after him if she decided to leave. They'd kept things light ever since the Frenchwoman's visit, but Grace wasn't getting much rest these days. Being across the corridor from Will wasn't exactly conducive to a good night's sleep. She'd been awake most of last night.

A snooze on the terrace in the afternoon heat would do them both good. Before she closed her eyes, Grace noticed that Will was already well away.

The sound of a car on the road above pulled her out of a dream in which a dark-haired man had gathered her up in his arms and was about to kiss her.

Grace reached for the robe she kept hanging up behind the table and went to investigate. A sleek black BMW had stopped, and she was surprised to see Elena, and a well-dressed man she didn't recognise, get out of the car.

She shook her sleeping beauty awake.

'Will!'

'What?'

'Someone's coming down the path. It's my boss and a man I don't know.'

She grabbed the T-shirt that she kept nearby for Will.

'Here. Put this on.'

Will pulled it over his head and Grace helped to arrange it around his torso, resisting the urge to stroke the soft hairs on his stomach.

The couple was getting closer. Their faces were now in full view. Will leant forward.

'Ah, it's my boss too.'

'I knew they knew each other, but why have they come together?'

'I think we're about to find out.'

Grace vacated her seat, and indicated for the man, who introduced himself as Panos, to take it. He'd obviously got something important to say to Will. She and Elena could sit inside.

Elena was already at the kitchen door. Grace looked from her to Panos.

'Can I get you both a coffee?'

Elena shook her head.

'No, we've just had coffee, thank you. I'd like to talk to you, in private. Can we go inside?'

'Sure.'

Grace left Will and his boss on the terrace and pulled out a chair for Elena at Will's blue dining table.

Elena stumbled on her words for a moment.

'Grace … you have been so kind to me. I never really

thanked you properly for what you did. I didn't want Panos to hear our conversation, as he has no idea what went on.'

Grace nodded. She'd always suspected there was a nice woman hidden somewhere under the layers of convention and money.

'It's nothing, honestly.'

Elena put her hand on her arm.

'No, you were brave. You took a risk and told me the truth. Not many people would have done that and put their own position in danger.'

Grace looked down at Elena's loose white linen dress embroidered with tiny daisies. The baby bump was definitely visible. Elena stroked her stomach before speaking again.

'The baby is kicking all the time now. We're so excited about what's to come. And we have you to thank for pushing us into facing up to our problems.'

Grace tried to bat the compliment away with her hand, but Elena locked eyes with her.

'I love Giannis, for better or worse, and if you love someone, you must be prepared to take risks.'

Elena stared out at the terrace for a moment.

'Don't let true love slip through your fingers. It's a rare and precious thing.'

Grace wasn't quite sure what this all had to do with her.

'Panos is out there with a proposal for Will. He is extremely grateful to him for putting his life on the line. And Giannis and I are grateful to you, Grace, for putting our lives back on track. If you decide you want to stay on the island and make a life here...' Elena looked back at the terrace again. 'We would be happy to offer you a full-time or indeed part-time job and sponsor your visa.'

Grace didn't know what to say.

'And before you start to think it's just out of gratitude…' Elena smiled. 'It's really not. We've had the best feedback for you that we've had for a teacher for many years. Your students love you, and they've all been asking us if there's any way you can stay on. At the end of the day, it's purely business.'

Elena shot her a big wink. It was nice to be appreciated. But it was too soon to think that far ahead. She still had one lifechanging decision that she could only make on her own.

'Thank you for the offer, Elena.'

The smiling woman rose to leave.

'You don't have to decide now. If you need to sort some things out, after Christmas would work as well. Just let me know when you're ready.'

Grace got up to say goodbye to her guest, as Will waved Panos off too. They flopped back down in their seats and watched the couple walk down the path and drive off. Will spoke first.

'Well, that was a bit of a shock. Panos has basically brought forward my retirement to now, on a full pension, as a thank you for what I did that night.'

Grace watched his face carefully.

'I'm free, Grace. To do what I want, whatever that is.'

Will lay back in his chair.

'I've always fancied buying a camper van and travelling round the rest of Europe.'

'That sounds fun.'

Grace didn't let on that she'd already done it. Travelling

with Will would be a totally different experience anyway ... if she agreed to go with him.

Will put his hand on hers.

'Do you mean that?'

Grace's phone alarm went off before she could say anything more.

'Oh, drat. It's the reminder that my daughter Lottie's gender reveal party is about to start. I'd better get the computer set up.'

She hadn't yet had a chance to let the girls know she'd moved into Will's place. It had been nearly a week now, but it needed some explaining and it never seemed to be the right time. The plan had been to position herself against a blank white wall for the gender reveal, and pretend she was in her room at the language school. But she had so little time, it would have to be Will's dining table and hope for the best. After the reveal, the three of them had agreed to stay on the call and chat. She needed Will out of the way for that.

His hand was still on hers.

'I'm waiting for an answer.'

Grace leapt up.

'Well, you'll have to wait a bit longer. Why don't you have a shower now, and I'll be up later to check you're OK.'

Will's slow smile was something she couldn't look at for long.

'Promise?'

'Yes, I promise.'

Grace helped him halfway up the stairs and checked that he'd got into his room. They'd moved Karen up with her basket, and she could hear Will murmuring endearments to the kitten. She raced back and pressed on the link. There was her daughter, flanked by friends and Brad's family. So far away. Brad had his arms round Lottie's middle, and a big iced cake was centre stage in front of them. She hadn't missed any of it, thank goodness.

Lottie was poised with a huge knife, which made Grace look away for a second. Knives weren't her favourite thing at the moment.

There was a countdown going on.

'Five, four, three, two, one!'

Those watching around the table screamed their heads off as Lottie plunged the knife into the cake. Grace had to admit it was a bit more exciting than being told the sex of your baby at a scan. But still not as exciting as waiting for the baby to be born first.

Lottie and Brad pulled out the first slice of cake. Grace could clearly see the blue sponge inside. Lottie held it up in the air.

'It's a boy! We're having a boy!'

Grace had a little tear as the couple danced around together and hugged everyone present. She looked up to the sky and blew a kiss.

'Now we know, Phil. It's a boy, a little grandson.'

'Mum? Mum, are you there? And Flo?'

The screen had switched to a three-person call.

'Yes, darling, I'm here.'

'Me too, sis.'

Lottie's face was wreathed in smiles.

'Did you see? It's a boy! I'm having a boy. Dad would have

loved to have had one of those in the house to stop us ganging up on him, wouldn't he?'

'He would, sweetheart.'

Grace was able to talk much more normally about Phil now without being overwhelmed by the gut-wrenching grief she'd felt in the first couple of years following his death. Greece had certainly helped with that.

After some more baby talk, Grace noticed Flo's eyes narrowing.

'Where are you, Mum? That doesn't look like your room.'

'It's a long story, sweetheart. I'm helping out a friend who's unwell.'

At that moment, Will appeared behind her on the stairs, with just a towel wrapped round his waist. Oh, great. She hadn't realised that the angle she'd chosen allowed watchers to see that far.

Lottie let out a low whistle.

'And who .... is that?'

'That's the friend I was telling you about.'

Flo was chiming in now.

'Some friend. You were giving us the impression it was a little old lady... And you've gone red.'

'Yes, Mum, you've obviously got plenty to tell us.'

Grace put on her best schoolteacher voice.

'Lottie, you need to get back to your guests. I will explain everything to both of you tomorrow, I swear. I'll set up another call for the three of us, but for now I have to go. I love you both very much.'

Go, Mum were the words still echoing in Grace's ears as she switched off the computer. She could hear Will moving around upstairs.

'Grace? Are you coming up? I'm still waiting…'

'Just give me a couple of minutes. There's something I've got to do first.'

'Do you want any help?'

'No, thanks. It's something I need to do on my own.'

It had been seeing the girls that had helped her slot in the last piece of the jigsaw.

Chapter Thirty

Grace ran to search the kitchen drawers before putting a piece of paper, a pen, a tealight and a box of matches into her bag.

It was thankfully quiet on the beach. The tourist season was coming to an end and people were leaving the island to go back to their full-time homes. Grace drew a single heart on the piece of paper and folded it into the shape of a boat, the way she'd done for generations of pupils over the years. She lit the tealight with a shaking hand and placed it in the centre of the boat. It wasn't exactly a Viking long ship, but it would do.

The warm sea caressed her body as she waded out up to her thighs. She took a moment to scan the horizon before she placed the little boat on the surface of the water and pushed it on its way, its fragile light burning bright.

Grace followed its progress through the waves with an aching heart.

'Goodbye, my darling. I'll never forget you as long as I live.'

Her voice caught in her throat, but she forced herself to continue. She hadn't been able to speak at Phil's funeral, it would have undone her, but she could speak now.

'You gave me two wonderful daughters, and a life full of love and laughter every single day we were together. You'll always be a part of my life, and you will live on in our girls and our unborn grandson. I'm so sad you'll never meet him, but you'll always be a part of him.'

Grace blinked away the tears that blurred her vision.

'But it's finally time to move on, like you always told me I should. I'm sure you don't want the details, but honestly, you'd like him. He's a good man, and I know that I can be happy with him, like I was happy with you.'

Grace watched as the tide took the boat further and further away, the tiny flame of the tealight dancing in the breeze until it disappeared from sight. She touched her fingertips to her lips and let the kiss float free.

'Godspeed my love, until we meet again.'

Grace's arms and legs were heavy as lead as she walked back up the beach. She shivered in the heat of the afternoon. But the sight of Will standing waiting on the terrace made her heart lift.

He opened his arms wide.

'Come here, you. I was watching from the balcony… You've been to say goodbye to him, haven't you?'

Grace nodded. She couldn't keep anything from this man. She flew into his arms and laid her head on his chest. She could feel his heart pumping away madly as he stroked her hair. Gently he pushed her out of his embrace.

'Let's go back upstairs and talk. It's time.'

Grace nodded and followed him, all the way to their favourite chairs on the balcony.

Once they were seated, Grace went to speak, but Will leant over and put his finger on her lips.

'Let me go first, please.'

Grace turned to face him.

'I need to say it out loud. I love you, Grace. I love you like I've never loved any woman. I've realised I can't live without you. And it's not just because you've been bringing me breakfast in bed every morning.'

Grace swallowed back more tears.

'But seriously, I knew I'd have to wait until you were ready. That there was something stopping you from acknowledging that you – I hoped – felt the same. When I realised that night on the beach that you hadn't finished grieving for your husband, it all fell into place. I tried to give you some distance, to stay away from you, but I failed miserably.'

Grace looked down at her hands.

'You drive me crazy, Grace, in both senses of the word. You're impetuous and you always think you know best. Although I have to admit that you usually do.'

Grace raised her head again and smiled.

'You're also the bravest, smartest, funniest and sexiest woman I know – have ever known, I should say. I've not been big on commitment in the past, but I'm offering you the rest of my life to do with whatever you want. Yours, and only yours, now and for ever.'

It was all she'd wanted to hear him say, and more, but she still had to make one hundred per cent sure that he meant it.

Grace reached for his hand and looked him directly in the eye.

'I have to ask you this one last thing. I'll be a grandmother soon; it's a boy, by the way…'

Will's face registered bewilderment.

'Er … congratulations.'

'Thanks. Look, you've only just turned sixty…'

'And? Where is this going?'

'You could easily be with someone younger.'

'So could you!'

'Yes, but my childbearing days are well and truly over. Are you absolutely sure you don't want to have any more children?'

Will's laugh echoed across the balcony, but the effort turned into a painful-sounding cough, and he clutched his side.

'Bloody hell, Grace. Only you could hear my heartfelt declaration of love and then ask supplementary questions. I already have a much-loved son. There's no way I want any more kids. Do you really think I'm fantasising about dealing with teenagers in my seventies? I can assure you, hand on heart, that that bit of my life's done and dusted. And when it comes to other women … how many times do I have to say it? I don't want another woman as long as I live. You're more than enough for a lifetime. You … are it for me.'

His speech brought on a prolonged bout of coughing that had Grace rushing to his side.

'Let me help you back into bed.'

Will attempted to smile through the pain.

'Well, if you're offering.'

Grace got Will settled and passed him a glass of water, which stopped the cough. He still seemed uncomfortable though. She'd let him recover a bit before she spoke her truth. She didn't want to make things worse. As she went to fluff his pillow, her left breast in her bikini top grazed his face for a moment.

'For God's sake, Grace.'

Will's voice was almost hoarse.

'How much of this do you think I can take? Cover up or get in here.'

Will flung back the sheet, and Grace was faced with the reason why the man was so uncomfortable. She climbed in beside him, and his mouth came down on hers with a hunger that matched her own. She pulled away a moment.

'I don't want to hurt you.'

'We'll be careful.'

Grace pulled on the ties at the sides of her bikini bottoms and the fabric fell away. She climbed astride his body with one fluid movement and kept eye contact with him all the way as she helped him slide into her. His brown eyes had almost turned black.

It had been no fluke the first time on the beach, which was good to know, but it didn't alter her decision. At last, they peeled apart, and lay back against the pillows to get their breath back.

Grace put her hand on his chest to check his heartrate.

'Are you OK? I wouldn't call that careful exactly.'

'Bloody fantastic though.'

'Agreed.'

Will leant up on one elbow.

'Grace? I've poured my heart out to you. And as wonderful as it is, it's not just sex I'm after. It's a whole life together. Am I on my own here? Or do you just want to use me as a sex toy?'

Grace put her head on one side.

'It's a serious consideration.'

Will frowned and pursed his lips.

'I've never seen a man pout before.'

But it was finally time for her to speak. She mustn't keep him hanging any longer, however much fun it was. Grace rolled towards him, so they were almost nose to nose, and looked into the face that had become so precious to her.

'You're not on your own.'

She kissed his lips.

'I love you too, Will Lancing. With my whole heart. I'm in it for however long we both have left on this earth. It feels like a miracle that we've found each other. You're it for me too.'

His smile at her answer lit up his whole face.

It didn't matter where they ended up living, whether they stayed in Greece, travelled to Australia to see the baby born or toured Europe in a camper van, as long as they were together.

She knew Will would agree that they'd never have been right for each other years ago. They'd both had other lives and known other loves. But she knew deep in her heart that they were right for each other now. Those previous lives and loves had shaped the people they were today and were never to be forgotten. There was still plenty to discover about each other, and they'd enjoy every moment of doing so. It had taken her all her time in Greece to realise that for her, home wasn't a location; it was a person. And that person was Will.

He bent to kiss her again, and just his touch on her skin was enough to light the flame inside her again. His body made it obvious that it did the same for him. She stared into his darkening eyes.

'Are you sure you're well enough?'

He pulled her underneath him with one stroke.

'Absolutely sure, my love.'

Acknowledgments

Firstly, I want to say a big thank you to anyone who is reading this book. It's my first, and I hope you enjoy it.

Huge thanks go to my agent, the wise and kind Broo Doherty, who kept the faith; to Charlotte Ledger, Publisher at One More Chapter, for taking a chance on me; and to Helen Williams, my editor, for her clear instructions and enthusiastic support.

It's been a long road to get to this point, and I also want to show appreciation for my fellow students on the Creative Writing MA at St Mary's University, Twickenham, plus tutors Jonathan Gibbs and Russell Schechter, for their input on my writing. Thanks goes especially to those who still meet regularly to chat about all things book over many drinks. So, here's to Sarah Kirwan, Sarah Nelson, Clare Rees, Joel Bradley, Robbie Westacott, Ezra Harker Shaw, Adam Sharp, and Molly Gartland.

My beta readers, David Young, Louise Gannon, Yasmin Pasha, Elke Tullett, Pat Chappell, Hazel Easterbrook, and Jane Goodwill, have all given extremely helpful comments along the way, most of which I've agreed with!

And to other friends and family who have also shown their support in various ways, from the TV Girls and the School

Mums Posse to my brother and sister, Paul Smith and Helen Chandler, and my friend Elina Vovou for her tips on Greek language schools – Cheers! Or, as the book was inspired by my love of Greece, *Yamas*!

ONE MORE CHAPTER

YOUR NUMBER ONE STOP

FOR PAGETURNING BOOKS

The author and One More Chapter would like to thank everyone who contributed to the publication of this story...

Analytics
James Brackin
Abigail Fryer

Audio
Fionnuala Barrett
Ciara Briggs

Contracts
Laura Amos
Laura Evans

Design
Lucy Bennett
Fiona Greenway
Liane Payne
Dean Russell

Digital Sales
Laura Daley
Lydia Grainge
Hannah Lismore

eCommerce
Laura Carpenter
Madeline ODonovan
Charlotte Stevens
Christina Storey
Jo Surman
Rachel Ward

Editorial
Janet Marie Adkins
Kara Daniel
Charlotte Ledger
Laura McCallen
Ajebowale Roberts
Jennie Rothwell
Tony Russell
Helen Williams

Harper360
Jennifer Dee
Emily Gerbner
Ariana Juarez
Jean Marie Kelly
emma sullivan
Sophia Wilhelm

International Sales
Peter Borcsok
Ruth Burrow
Colleen Simpson
Ben Wright

Inventory
Sarah Callaghan
Kirsty Norman

Marketing & Publicity
Chloe Cummings
Grace Edwards
Emma Petfield

Operations
Melissa Okusanya
Hannah Stamp

Production
Denis Manson
Simon Moore
Francesca Tuzzeo

Rights
Helena Font Brillas
Ashton Mucha
Zoe Shine
Aisling Smyth
Lucy Vanderbilt

Trade Marketing
Ben Hurd
Eleanor Slater

The HarperCollins Distribution Team

The HarperCollins Finance & Royalties Team

The HarperCollins Legal Team

The HarperCollins Technology Team

UK Sales
Isabel Coburn
Jay Cochrane
Sabina Lewis
Holly Martin
Harriet Williams
Leah Woods

And every other essential link in the chain from delivery drivers to booksellers to librarians and beyond!

ONE MORE CHAPTER

YOUR NUMBER ONE STOP

FOR PAGETURNING BOOKS

One More Chapter is an
award-winning global
division of HarperCollins.

Subscribe to our newsletter to get our
latest eBook deals and stay up to date
with all our new releases!

signup.harpercollins.co.uk/
join/signup-omc

Meet the team at
www.onemorechapter.com

Follow us!

𝕏 @OneMoreChapter_

f @onemorechapterhc

📷 @onemorechapterhc

♪ @onemorechapterhc

Do you write unputdownable fiction?
We love to hear from new voices.
Find out how to submit your novel at
www.onemorechapter.com/submissions